Isolation

Books by Mary Anna Evans

The Faye Longchamp Mysteries
Artifacts
Relics
Effigies
Findings
Floodgates
Strangers
Plunder
Rituals

Isolation

A Faye Longchamp Mystery

Mary Anna Evans

Poisoned Pen Press

Poisoned Pen Press
6962 E. First Ave., Ste. 103
Scottsdale, AZ 85251
www.poisonedpenpress.com
info@poisonedpenpress.com

Printed in the United States of America

For little Oliver

Acknowledgments

I'd like to thank all the people who helped make *Isolation* happen.

Tony Ain, Amanda Evans, Michael Garmon, Erin Garmon, and Rachel Broughten read it in manuscript and provided their customary astute observations. Faye's adventures wouldn't be the same without the thoughtful attention of those near and dear to me.

Nadia Lombardero, Kelly Bergdoll, and Jerry Steinberg were my consulting environmental scientists. Attentive readers will see that Nadia and Jerry have namesake environmental scientists in *Isolation*. Very attentive readers will recall that Kelly had a namesake environmental scientist in *Artifacts*. I am deeply grateful for their generosity in sharing their expertise. They are responsible for the passages in which I got things right, and they are innocent of wrongdoing on any occasions when I did not.

As always, I am grateful for the wonderful people at Poisoned Pen Press. My agent, Anne Hawkins, and my editor, Barbara Peters, have been my partners in bringing Faye to life for a very long time now. My publicist, Maryglenn McCombs, does a masterful job at getting the attention of people who will enjoy Faye's stories.

And, of course, I am grateful for you, my readers.

**Excerpt from the oral history of Cally Stanton,
Recorded in 1935 and preserved
as part of the WPA Slave Narratives**

Secrets hold power. My mama told me so, more than ninety years back. The power of secrets holds true for everybody, I expect, but it holds a lot more true for people who ain't got power of their own.

Think about a young girl, born a slave. Try to imagine that she has any power over her Missus at all. You can't, can you?

Now, think about a young girl, almost a woman, who has been tending her Missus since she was big enough to carry a chamber pot. Maybe before that. Maybe she's been tending her Missus since she was old enough to carry a bottle of bourbon. Maybe she's spent her short life listening to the things her Missus says when she's been into the bourbon since noontime.

A young girl like that knows how much her Missus pines for her home up north. She knows how much her Missus wishes the Master remembered where her bedchamber was. She knows the thing that even the Missus can't know, because she can't think it when she's sober. Only after several goodly portions of bourbon can her Missus listen to herself say, "He married me for my money. Now it's his, and all I've got for company is you, Cally."

So, yeah, you could say that I stepped out of my cradle knowing how to keep a secret. And I stepped into womanhood knowing how to use it to my advantage.

Maybe you're thinking that I'm heartless with my secrets, using them for my gain and for the ruin of others. No, that ain't so. Sometimes there is only one gift a body can give another person. Sometimes that gift is silence.

Chapter One

Fish know which docks are owned by people who are generous with their table scraps. In the evenings, they gather around wooden posts that vibrate with the footsteps of a human carrying food. They wait, knowing that potato peels and pork chop bones will soon rain from the sky. They race to skim the surface for floating bread crumbs. They dive, nibbling at each half-eaten hot dog as it sinks. When a restaurant, even a shabby dive where hungry people clean their plates, throws its detritus off one particular dock every night, fish for miles around know all about it.

On this night, the fish wait below a dock that has always offered a nightly feast. Tonight, they feel the vibrations of familiar feet. The food falls into the water, as always, and the sound of a stainless steel spoon scraping the bottom of a stainless steel pot passes from the air above to the water below. Everything is as it has been, until a sharp noise jabs into the water hard enough for the fish to hear it. The spoon falls.

The spoon is large, designed for a commercial kitchen, so it hits the water with a smack that can be heard both above and below the surface. A scream falls into the fishes' underworld along with the spoon.

A big pot, with food scraps still clinging to its inner surface, hits the water an instant later. Only creatures with the agility of the waiting fish could scatter quickly enough to avoid being hit.

After another heartbeat, something else falls among them, something bigger and softer. Soon there are two somethings, both with arms and legs and feet and hands, one that gurgles and another that leaves when the gurgling stops.

The thing that stays behind is a human body. As it settles in the water, tiny minnows nestle in the long hair that floats around it like seaweed. Catfish explore its ten long fingers with their tentacled mouths. None of them associate its two bare feet with the sprightly vibrations that had always signaled a rain of food.

Before long, predators appear, drawn by the smell of blood.

Chapter Two

Joe Wolf Mantooth was worried about his wife.

Faye was neglecting their business. She was neglecting her health. He wanted to say she was neglecting her children, but it would kill her to think he believed such a thing, so he spent a lot of time telling that part of himself to be quiet. He also wanted to say she was neglecting him, but it would kill him to believe it, so he spent the rest of his time telling that other part of himself to be quiet. Or to shrivel up and die. Because if he ever lost Faye, that's what Joe intended to do. Shrivel up and die.

The children seemed oblivious to the changes in their mother. Michael, at two, saw nothing strange about her leaving the house every morning with her archaeological tools. She had always done that.

Amande was away from home, doing an immersion course in Spanish at a camp situated so high in the Appalachians that she'd asked for heavy sweaters long before Halloween. Faye had been too distracted to put them in the mail. Joe had shopped for them, boxed them up, and sent them off. Faye seemed to have forgotten that her daughter had ever said, "I'm cold."

Amande was perceptive for seventeen. If she hadn't noticed that Joe had been doing all the talking for the last month, she would notice soon. Lately, when faced with a call from her daughter, Faye murmured a few distracted words before pretending that Michael needed a diaper change. If Faye didn't come up with another excuse to get off the phone, Amande might soon call 911 and ask the paramedics to go check out her brother's chronic diarrhea.

Though Joe did speak to Amande when she called, surely she had noticed by now that he said exactly nothing. What was he going to say?

The closest thing to the truth was "Your mother's heart fell into a deep hole when she miscarried your baby sister, and I'm starting to worry that we may never see it again," but Joe was keeping his silence. Faye had forbidden him to tell Amande that there wasn't going to be a baby sister.

Was this rational? Did Faye think that her daughter was never going to fly home to Florida, bubbling with excitement over her Appalachian adventure and the coming baby?

If she did, it was yet more evidence supporting Joe's fear that Faye's mind wasn't right these days. Every morning brought fresh proof of that not-rightness as she walked away from him…to do what? As best he could tell, she was carefully excavating random sites all over their island. If she'd found anything worth the effort, he sure didn't know about it.

In the meantime, Joe sat in the house, face-to-face with a serious problem. This problem was almost as tall and broad as Joe. His hair had once been as dark. His skin was the same red-brown, only deeper. This was a problem Joe had been trying to outrun since he was eighteen years old.

His father.

"Try this spot."

Faye Longchamp-Mantooth believed in intuition. It had always guided her work as an archaeologist. After she'd gathered facts about a site's history, inspected the contours of the land, and scoured old photographs, she always checked her gut response before excavating. Her gut was often right. It was only recently, however, that her gut had begun speaking out loud and in English. Lately, her gut had been urging her to skip the boring research and go straight for the digging.

"Have you ever excavated here before?" its voice asked.

Faye's answer was no.

"Then try this spot."

Every day, Joyeuse Island sported more shallow pits that had yielded nothing. Of course, they had yielded nothing. Faye had failed to do her homework. But going to the library or sitting at her computer would require her to be still and think. Thinking was painful these days, so she skipped it.

"Okay," she said, not pleased to see that she'd begun answering the voice out loud, "I'll give it a shot. But I don't think there's anything here."

Her hand was remarkably steady for the hand of a woman who'd been hearing voices for a month. She used it to guide her trowel, removing a thin layer of soil.

She would have known this old trowel in the dark. Her fingers had rubbed the finish off its wooden handle in a pattern that could match no hand but hers. Since God hadn't seen fit to let her grow the pointy metal hand she needed for her work, she'd chosen this one tool to mold into a part of herself.

Faye was working in sandy soil as familiar as the trowel. It was her own. She'd been uncovering the secrets of Joyeuse Island since she was old enough to walk, and she would never come to the end of them. As she grew older, she saw the need to mete out her time wisely, but she rebelled against it. The past would keep most of its secrets, and this made her angry.

Faye didn't know where to dig, because she didn't know what she was trying to find. It would help if the voice ever offered a less hazy rationale for ordering her out of the house. All it said was "You can find the truth. Don't let this island keep its secrets from you."

Her frenetic busyness was an antidote for the times the voice tiptoed into ground that shook beneath her feet. It crept into dangerous territory and then beckoned her to follow. It asked her to believe that she was to blame for the baby's death, for the mute suffering in Joe's eyes, for every tear Michael shed.

This was craziness. Two-year-olds cried several times a day. Men who had lost babies suffered. And there was rarely any blame to be handed out in the wake of a miscarriage, even late miscarriages that carry away a child who has been bumping around in her mother's womb long enough for mother and daughter to get to know one another.

Still, the voice said Faye was to blame, so she believed it. And it told her that it was possible to dig up peace, so she dug.

Chapter Three

Joe had promised himself, time and again, that he would call his father, then he had let another year roll on. After he'd left home at eighteen, he'd thought, "When I get settled somewhere, I'll let him know where I am." But he'd wandered for years, working odd jobs and sleeping wherever he could pitch a tent.

He'd lingered so long in North Carolina, learning to flintknap from Old Man Kingsley, that he'd thought, "It's time. I need to call my dad and let him know I settled down." Then Old Man Kingsley died, which is what people with nicknames like "Old Man" tend to do, and Joe had taken to wandering again.

If Faye had kicked him off the island like she should have— why had someone with her brains let a vagrant camp on her island, anyway?—he would be wandering still. Instead, he'd acquired a wife who had never met her father-in-law, fathered a son who had never met his grandfather, and adopted a daughter who also hadn't met her new grandfather.

When they'd found out Faye was pregnant again, Joe had thought, "It's time," and he'd invited his father to spend Thanksgiving with them on Joyeuse Island and stay to meet his new granddaughter. Then he'd waited too long after the miscarriage to call him and ask, "Could you come another time?" So now Joe was stuck on an island with a wife who wouldn't talk to him, a father he didn't like, and a two-year-old. Happy holidays.

Sylvester "Sly" Mantooth didn't ask his son why his daughter-in-law left the house every morning. He didn't do much, really.

Joe couldn't put his finger on the reason his father annoyed him so. The man just sat, coffee cup in hand, and talked the live-long day. He talked to Joe. He talked to Michael. He talked to himself, when Joe and Michael left the room and forced him to do that. He didn't say anything much, but he talked a lot.

Faye didn't seem to notice. Every afternoon, she came home empty-handed and avoided Amande's daily calls. She silently ate the supper Joe had cooked, letting Sly's endless words swirl around her. At dusk, she gave Joe and Michael distracted kisses before nodding at Sly, showering, and falling into the bed where she spent a lot of time not sleeping.

Joe had to do something. He didn't know what it was, but he had to do it. If this situation rocked along until Amande got off that airplane, lugging a huge teddy bear for the baby-that-wasn't, he wasn't sure his family would survive intact.

If Joe didn't know something was very wrong with Faye, he would have been angry. Okay, he was angry. But he would get over it.

Since Faye had stopped her obsessive monitoring of their finances—the normal Faye could pinch a penny in two and spend it twice, so what was up with that?—she hadn't noticed that Joe had been spending more money than he should at Liz's Bar and Grill. For the two weeks since Sly Mantooth's arrival, Joe had loaded his father and his son into the john boat every morning, as soon as Faye was out of sight, and he had pointed it toward the marina that their friend Liz owned and called home.

On every one of those mornings, he had savored the fact that the noise of the boat motor silenced his father by making conversation impossible. Once ashore, there were the very welcome, time-killing activities of carefully securing the boat and fueling it, before leading father and son into the grill. Inside, Liz's crooked grin and her peerless fried eggs made another sliver of the morning easier to bear.

The state of their budget said that Joe ought to stay home and fry his family's eggs himself. Except Joe didn't really know the state of their budget, since Faye had stopped balancing the checkbook. Playing short order cook would have saved him a few bucks, but his stomach roiled at the thought of sitting at the breakfast table with his absent-eyed wife, his toddler son, and the father who had never actually told him how long he'd been out of prison. Or why he'd been there in the first place.

Faye was doing her share to save on groceries. Every morning, she tucked a single banana in her work bag as she trudged across the island to do whatever it was she did these days. And every morning, before she'd even disappeared into the distance, Joe said, "Ready for some biscuits? Then get in the boat!" in the happy voice of a man looking forward to quality time with his father and son.

This morning, as always, Sly had answered, "Damn straight!" and Michael had run in circles yelling, "Bikkits! Bikkits!"

Joe always enjoyed that one moment of feeling like the family hero. It was totally worth thirty bucks for three breakfasts and a big tip. More than thirty bucks, actually, when he factored in enough fuel to get there. Still. Totally worth it. Also, Liz needed the money more than they did, if such a thing could be possible.

Twenty minutes after starting his boat's wonderfully loud motor, they arrived at the marina that housed Liz's Bar and Grill for the fourteenth time since his dad had stepped off the plane. The place had been seedy when Wally had owned it—actually, calling it seedy would have been generous—but Liz had poured her heart into giving the place a homey ambiance.

Joe understood how she felt. He'd grown up in ramshackle houses that were held together by duct tape and landlords' promises. Faye's plantation house on Joyeuse Island wasn't the home of his dreams. It was a home beyond his dreams. Joe felt like somebody had crawled inside his head to see the biggest and finest house he could imagine, then they had searched the world until they found something bigger and finer than that.

Faye loved the old house. It was her home. But, still, when she looked at it, she saw ancient plumbing and wall plaster that she would never finish patching.

Joe looked at it and thought, "I can't believe this is really ours."

Every square foot of Liz's business—the marina, the convenience store, the bar and grill, the dock, the grassy yard with its benches and picnic tables—showed the hand of a woman with only a little money but a lot of pride. She'd peeled up the sticky linoleum Wally had installed in the restaurant and store, and she'd put a multicolored epoxy coat on the concrete beneath. That floor was always as clean as her mop could make it. She'd painted the dark paneling a happy yellow, and Joe was damned if Liz didn't learn how to run a borrowed sewing machine so she could make curtains for the place.

She'd mowed the grass herself, from the back wall of the kitchen to the seawall where her dock stretched out into the Gulf. Joe didn't know how she'd scraped together the money to re-gravel the parking lot, but she'd managed it.

Liz Colton herself hadn't weathered the years since her son Chip's death nearly so well as her business had. Too much bourbon had added a little more grit to the plain-spoken redhead's voice. She waited too long to touch up her roots these days, and the white stripe through the middle of her long and bushy orange locks was not a good look for her. She was surly to most of her customers, except Faye and Joe, and Liz was in a business that depended on her good humor. People didn't want their fishing trips spoiled by a woman who called them stupid for buying the wrong bait. They'd begun buying their bait elsewhere, and also their ice and their gear, not to mention the fried flounder dinners that Liz had served them on those days when the fish weren't biting.

It didn't make sense to Joe that Liz was still nice to him and Faye. They'd watched her son die after he'd come damn close to killing them both, so Liz had to feel a jolt every time she saw them. Joe was pretty sure Liz only tolerated them because Michael's toddler grins made tiny moments of her life easier to bear. So she sucked it up and said nice things to Michael's parents, but she couldn't bring herself to say nice things to anybody else.

Every day, while Liz was cooing "Who's the cutest little black-haired boy in Micco County?" in her gravelly baritone, Joe was calculating just how much he could overtip without hearing her tell him to go to hell. And, for the last two weeks, every time he'd parked himself on one of Liz's barstools—which was every single freaking day—he was also wondering what in the hell he was supposed to say to his father.

He should probably have led with, "So, Dad, how long have you been out of prison? And what, exactly, did you do to get sent there?"

Instead, he had bought the man breakfast every day, thus funding Sly's improbable flirtation with Liz.

"How's my favorite redheaded bombshell today?" Sly would ask in a booming voice that filled the shabby grill. Every day. He asked this every day and Joe wanted to fall through the floor every day.

"She's ready to serve you up something hot and steamy and just the way you like it" was Liz's invariable response. Every day, Joe wondered if it were possible to fall through a floor twice.

Yes, Sly and Liz were about the same age. And, yes, they both possessed the cagey brains and crude senses of humor that marked them as survivors of a lot of hard years. Nevertheless, a woman with Liz's street smarts should have looked at Sly and seen trouble on two legs. And a man with his father's long and tough history should have looked at Liz and seen heartbreak in the flesh.

In the movies, they would have found happiness and healing in each others' arms. In real life? Joe had once witnessed two bears fighting for territory. The air had been full of blood, rage, and flying fur. He would expect pretty much the same results from any attempt at a romance between Liz and Sly.

Nevertheless, Joe continued to put Sly in his john boat and take him to these early morning trysts because he couldn't think of any better way to pass the morning. In one more week, Thanksgiving would come and go, then Sly would go home to Oklahoma. Not that Joe knew for certain that the man possessed a return plane ticket.

Joe eased the boat alongside the dock. Once it was secured, he set Michael down to see which way he ran. When he was lucky, Michael ran away from the restaurant door, insisting on delaying breakfast long enough to watch fish and turtles gather at the end of the dock. Liz had been throwing her kitchen scraps in that spot for years, and the fish knew where free food fell from the sky.

Joe was big on time killers these days, and this one was actually pleasant. The sun glinted off the water and the fishes' scales, and his blood pressure always settled down when he spent a little time listening to the creaking and sighing sound of seafaring crafts safely moored.

Michael hurried toward the spot where the fish waited for him. He burbled happily while Joe produced a slice of bread from the leather bag that always hung from his waist, full of necessities like stone tools and food. Sly, who didn't move like a man in his late fifties, dropped to his knees beside the boy and told him about all the fish, just like he did every morning.

"See them minnows, all different shiny colors? Purty, ain't they?" Flailing his hand at a few bigger fish floating among the multitude of minnows, he said, "Them's pompano."

Yes, they were. They had been pompano every single day for two weeks now and they always would be, but Michael didn't mind hearing about them again.

"And over there?" The big hand flailed at a silver flash further away from the dock, gliding underwater like a bird. Only its wingtips broke the water. "Stingray."

Right again. Sly Mantooth knew a stingray when he saw it. Soon enough, Michael would, too. In the meantime, all three of them watched its flat, undulating body pass by.

Joe was irritated with his father's constant chatter, no doubt. It had been his understanding that ex-cons weren't talkative, not when the wrong word might put them in life-or-death trouble with their fellow prisoners, but maybe prison didn't mark everyone in the same way. If anything, Sly was chattier now than he'd ever been when Joe was a child. Leave it to his dad to do everything backwards.

Still, Joe watched his father with a flicker of interest. Looking at Sly lean easily over the side of the dock and riffle the silty water with a relaxed hand, Joe thought that maybe there was some hope that he himself wouldn't move like an old man before his time, either.

As always, the fish rose from the darkness, fluttering their pectoral fins and piercing the surface of the water with their gaping mouths, and Michael talked to them as if they were familiar playmates. Joe supposed that they were. Bending his head toward the bag hanging from his belt, he reached a hand in to fetch some bread before Michael started to whine for it, so he missed the moment when Sly flung himself headfirst off the dock.

Michael had left the dock, too, intent on following his grandfather into the water, but Joe reached out a long arm and plucked the boy from midair. Caught off-balance, he nearly toppled over the edge himself. When he gained his footing, Joe found himself on the dock's edge staring down at Liz. Ten feet from the dock, she floated below the murky water's surface with her arms outstretched through circling schools of minnows, catfish, and pompano. Her hair, iron gray and faded red, snaked through the water as if reaching out for air.

Joe was as much a man of action as Sly and he needed to be in the water. He needed to be doing everything in his power to save Liz. He looked reflexively for Faye, so that he could hand their child to her and dive in, but she wasn't there. Sly, burdened by nothing to stop him from yielding to the impulse of the moment, had already wrapped both arms around Liz and yanked her to the surface. He was shaking her, slapping her, doing anything to rouse her, but she hung slack in his arms.

It was no accident that Joe was a strong swimmer. His father had made time to teach him very few things, but Sly had ensured that Joe could handle himself in the water because he himself swam with the power of a killer whale. Joe's father turned Liz on her back, wrapped one big arm around her chest, and struck out for land.

Joe paused only to dial 911, then sprinted up the dock while carrying a struggling child and barking information at the emergency dispatcher. Sly was already dragging Liz onto the muddy shoreline before Joe got there. It was littered with soda cans and candy wrappers that had held snacks sold by Liz herself.

Sly checked her airway and started CPR. Joe wondered if they taught emergency resuscitation in prison these days.

Chapter Four

Faye was using her phone to take a picture of her latest pointless excavation. She'd dug down to groundwater, which wasn't very deep on Joyeuse Island, and she'd uncovered exactly nothing. Taking a picture of the wet hole seemed like a waste of electrons and pixels, but she was trying to at least go through the motions of working like a professional archaeologist. As she aimed the phone at the ground, it rang.

Joe's number was displayed on the screen and she heard his voice as soon as she put the phone to her ear.

"Something bad happened to Liz."

"Tell me."

"We found her floating off her dock. Shot in the back. Drowned, too, maybe, if she wasn't dead when she went in the water. We tried—Dad tried—to save her. The paramedics say she's been dead for hours. They've already taken her body away. Dad's talking to the sheriff now."

Faye dropped to a crouch and put her palm on the ground to steady herself. "Liz? Oh, God. Liz? Who would have shot Liz? There's something wrong with a world where things like this happen."

Joe said something that was probably "Yeah," but she heard him choke on the word.

She tried to think of something else to say, but she couldn't. She just murmured "Okay," when he said, "Michael's fine. I had some snacks for him and the new sheriff is letting him play with his badge. I think we'll be home by lunch."

Faye tried to say good-bye, but she choked on that, too, so they both hung up.

Joe could tell that the new sheriff wasn't quite sure what to make of his father. Sly was weeping as if he'd lost a wife, while answering the sheriff's questions by confirming that he'd only known Liz two weeks. Liz had been nothing to Sly but a nice lady who'd cooked eggs for him about fourteen times, so Sheriff Rainey must have been confused by Sly's tears. Joe elected not to try to explain his father to Rainey, who had held office for a couple of years now, but whom Joe still considered "new" because he wasn't Sheriff Mike.

Sly was getting louder by the minute. "So young. She was too young to die. It's not right. It's just not right!"

"I know it's hard," the new sheriff was saying, "but I need you to answer my questions. It's the only way I'm going to find out why your friend is dead."

As the law officer spoke, he was making eye contact with Joe, communicating one silent word: *Help?*

Joe wasn't surprised by his father's behavior. The man had never had a governor on his emotions, and he'd been as quick to rage when Joe was a boy as he was to grief now. The rage hadn't shown itself since he and his father became reacquainted. Yet. Joe's memories made him wary.

Looking at Sly was like staring into a distorted mirror. His father's shoulders and biceps, so like his own, were impressive for a man pushing sixty. Like Joe, he had the black mane of a Creek warrior. His hair was still as thick as Joe's, though he kept it cut to jaw length and it was streaked with white. Age had thickened his waist, but there was no paunch to his belly. His tears were streaking down skin coarsened by age but not yet wrinkled.

Joe could have given the sheriff a very good idea of why his father was overreacting to Liz's death, if he had trusted himself to speak. His dead mother had worn her red hair long.

◇◇◇

Sheriff Ken Rainey studied the weeping man for a good long minute. He would give Sly Mantooth credit for honesty. He had been upfront about his time in an Oklahoma prison. Rainey had asked a desk-bound deputy to run Sly's history while he interviewed him.

As it turned out, the elder Mantooth's criminal record wasn't a long one, but his one offense had taken him straight to the pen. Truck drivers who decide to sell their transportation services to the highest not-legal bidder tend to be quick casualties in the War on Drugs.

Sheriff Rainey had no love for the people who sold and transported the mind-twisting substances that had ruined and then ended his brother's life, but he was fair. Men like Sly, who had lived several decades without a single instance of violence blotting their criminal records, rarely hauled off and killed somebody late in life. He wouldn't say it never happened, but murdering thugs were not usually born at the tender age of fifty-eight.

He nodded at the other witness to Liz's murder scene, the taller and younger man who was silently helping his little son throw rocks in the water. Joe Wolf Mantooth gave every indication of having known the dead woman well. If Sly Mantooth did not look like a murderer, then Joe looked like a Vatican-certified saint. Either of them was physically capable of throwing a mortally wounded woman into the water to drown, but Sheriff Rainey didn't think either of them had done it. He had seen a tear leak out of the corner of the younger Mantooth's eye as he watched his son, and he suspected that this man wept a lot less easily than his father did.

Rainey had questioned them both. He would be keeping tabs on them, but it was time to let the Mantooth men, all three of them, go home.

◇◇◇

Joe was ready to load his father and Michael into his john boat and head for Joyeuse Island. It was time to make one last phone call before cranking the motor. When Faye answered, he said, "We're heading home."

The cell phone's reception was predictably terrible, but Joe could hear Faye clear her throat before she answered him. He knew she'd been crying for Liz. No, probably not. She was probably trying so hard not to cry that her throat had closed up on her. Joe thought Faye could use a good cry, but he didn't think she was ever going to let herself have it.

She said only, "Be safe."

He said he would and hung up.

Joe balanced Michael on his hip while he stepped off the dock. Sly followed, settling himself in the john boat just as easily as Joe had. The older man was still wiping the back of his hand across his eyes now and then, and Joe had gotten over being irritated with his father over his public display of emotion. Liz's death *was* sad. She deserved some tears.

Faye had checked in by phone more than once since Joe had called her with the news, but she should have been here with him. Joe saw Faye's absence at Liz's death scene as a clear sign of the depth of her distress. The real Faye would have been in her skiff, headed for shore, before Joe had finished telling her what had happened.

Why did her absence upset him so? What, really, would her presence here have accomplished?

Nothing. Michael was oblivious to what he'd seen. Faye couldn't have quelled Sly's inappropriate grief. Joe himself would suffer over the loss of Liz, but he would do it later, in private, and Faye would be there. He didn't need Faye with him now, but he wanted her. He wanted his wife back, the wife who cared about everything. She cared too much sometimes, and it made her do stupid things for love, but that was so much better than the vague words of grief he'd heard coming out of the phone this morning.

"Oh, poor Liz," she had said. "I can't believe it."

She'd gone no further or deeper than that, and Joe thought he knew why. Acknowledging the hole Liz left in their lives would rip open another hole that hadn't begun to heal. Faye couldn't let herself think too much about the daughter they'd lost.

◇◇◇

Faye picked up her trowel and tried to concentrate on her work, as if she were naïve enough to think that this would make her stop thinking about Liz. She stood on the far west end of Joyeuse Island, in a place where an outward curve in the coastline exposed her to sea breezes from two directions. A big live oak rose in front of her, but it was too far away to offer shade. Otherwise, she was surrounded by scattered small trees—saplings, really—and shrubby undergrowth that didn't cover the ground. Sandy soil dotted with weeds sloped to the waterline behind her. Technically, it was a beach, but it didn't look like much. Everything around her was November-drab. Her surroundings looked about as cheerful as she felt.

She scraped a thin layer of soil from the bottom of the unit where she'd been excavating. Then she thrust the point of her trowel into the soil again, midway up the unit's wall, trying to square up the corner. A pungent odor struck her. Immediately, a thin stream of clear liquid started running down the wall.

Using the side of her trowel to try to find the source of the leak, she uncovered just enough old and corroded metal to see that it came from a container that was gently curved, like a tank or a drum. The odor grew as the liquid continued running down the wall and puddling into the bottom of the excavation. Its chemical edge said, "Danger."

The fumes continued to rise and she started imagining fires and explosions. Should she call 911? An environmental response team?

She backed away from the edge. Her miscarriage had been so recent that she still cradled a protective hand on her belly when she felt threatened. She did it now, as if there were still a baby inside who could be damaged if she breathed in something toxic. The part of her that had forgotten that she lost the baby was warning her not to breathe the fumes. And the part of her that blamed herself for the baby's death wanted her to breathe deeply and take her punishment.

Chapter Five

If his phone hadn't been lying face-up on the seat beside him, Joe would have missed Faye's next call. The motor's noise drowned both the phone's sound and its vibration, but he saw its face light up.

It was Faye. Joe knew before he answered that Faye had reached her limit. There had been a tautness to her mouth for a month, but this morning every line of her face said that she'd reached her tipping point. And then they'd lost Liz. All day, his phone had been in his hand more than it had been in his pocket. When he'd boarded the boat, he'd risked losing it to water damage by laying it on the seat next to his thigh. If his wife called him, he wanted to know.

Their dock was in sight, so he cut the motor and used the boat's own momentum to ease it into place. Faye's voice was higher-pitched than normal and it was loud in the suddenness of the motor's silence.

"Joe?"

Joe tucked Michael under one arm and left his father alone to secure the boat himself.

With both feet already pounding the dock, he said, "I'm coming, Faye. Tell me where you are."

"I'm on the far west side of the island, under that big oak tree standing all by itself next to the water. Something's not right, Joe. I'm not sure what it is, but something's not right."

◇◇◇

Joe had been wrong. Faye hadn't broken. In fact, she looked more like herself than she'd looked since...well, in more than a month.

She had met them halfway, saying, "You need to carry Michael. It's not safe to let him run loose around here."

Now she was crouched by an open excavation, trowel in one rubber-gloved hand and phone in the other, studying the problem at hand. The focused expression. The pursed lips. The curious squint that should have put wrinkles into the golden-brown skin around her eyes, but somehow hadn't managed it yet. The impatient shake of the straight black bangs that she was always too busy to get cut. This woman was the person he'd known for more than ten years.

Well, she was almost his familiar Faye. An occasional fidget in her thin shoulders said that all was still not well, but an unanswered question was a tonic for Faye. Now she had one.

Waving the phone, she said, "I checked the Internet. It told me I should call the emergency responders, so I did."

Balancing Michael on his knee, Joe squatted beside her. He might have asked, "What's the emergency?" but his nose and eyes were already giving him the answer.

Faye leaned her head in the direction of the dark wet spot spreading slowly down the side of the pit and across its bottom. "Diesel?"

"Smells more like kerosene to me."

She pointed her trowel at a dark area about midway up the far corner of the excavation. "See that spot? I was working on the corner of the unit, trying to square it up, and the point of my trowel grazed something hard. I felt something give a little, then release. Right away, something wet started bubbling out of the wall. I smelled something strong—kerosene, I guess—as soon as it happened."

"What did the Internet say we should do?"

"I looked up legal reporting requirements for petroleum spills. Diesel, kerosene...they're both petroleum, and so's everything else that smells like that. The emergency response website said that spills bigger than twenty-five gallons have to be reported."

"That ain't anywhere near twenty-five gallons," Joe said, assessing the shallow puddle of glistening liquid at the bottom of the excavation.

"No," his wife said. "Not yet. But it's still coming. Who knows where it's coming from or how to stop it or how bad it's going to get?"

Joe studied the darkened soil. "Going by how fast it's spreading from that one little spot, I'd say you poked a hole in a tank or a drum or something. Can't tell if that buried tank's more than twenty-five gallons without uncovering it. Couldn't we have tried that before calling in the environmental people?"

Faye held up a hand, sheathed in a protective glove. "That's why I've got these on. I was all set to dig up the tank myself, because we'd really rather not have emergency responders come out here. The website says that property owners can get saddled with paying for disposal of abandoned waste, even if they weren't the ones who dumped it. I thought maybe if I tried to uncover the problem, it might turn out to be just a leaky five-gallon bucket and we could legally keep this to ourselves."

"But you called the emergency people instead of doing the digging yourself?"

She waved the phone again, pointing it at something behind Joe's back. "Unfortunately, this phone tells me that, in our case, it doesn't matter how big the spill is. If the state's waters are involved, we have to call."

Joe looked where she pointed. An iridescent oil slick spread itself over the water behind him. It hadn't been there when he arrived.

Michael squirmed in Joe's hands as his parents watched the water's surface twinkle with each wave. Joe couldn't believe this was happening.

Joyeuse Island had miraculously escaped contamination by the Deepwater Horizon spill. Not even one tar ball had washed ashore. Now, after they'd dodged that bullet, an environmental cleanup crew was going to descend on their island? For what? For maybe a quart of liquid kerosene soaked into a small spot of soil? For an oil slick so tenuous that he expected it to be gone by dark? And did he hear Faye saying that there was a good chance they'd have to pay for whatever the cleanup ended up costing? This sounded like writing a blank check to a government agency that had absolutely no motivation to keep down costs.

"It's the law," Faye said, and he wanted to remind her that there had been times when she'd been a little casual with the law, and this might have been the time to remember how that was done. Then she said, "And we don't know how bad it's going to get. Better to call in the professionals now than to find ourselves sitting in a puddle of petroleum goo."

"You made the right decision."

This was true, and Joe was glad to be able to say so. It proved that Faye's logic circuits hadn't completely failed. He was looking at a problem that could cost them a small fortune, but that problem had brought him a feeble indication that his hyper-rational wife hadn't completely slipped away into her grief. He watched the spot of kerosene-stained soil grow bigger by the minute and reminded himself that some things were harder to lose than money.

◇◇◇

Joe stood in the shade and watched his home being overrun by environmental protection people. His father was enjoying this too much. Sly had been on the dock all afternoon, chatting up serious-faced scientists who obviously weren't interested in telling him every last detail about their jobs.

Joe didn't want to talk to those specialists, not at all. He wanted to lurk and observe, because he was a hunter and that was how hunters behaved when faced with potential adversaries.

Joe didn't like to think of environmentalists as potential adversaries. He shared their goals. Joe figured that he and Faye left a lighter footprint on the world than most. Their house was totally off the grid. They got their electricity from the sun, and their hot water, too. They'd rehabbed Joyeuse's old wooden rainwater cisterns, so they drank and bathed in what came out of the sky, just like the people who built those cisterns in the 1800s. Joe shot, netted, and grew most of what they ate.

Joe was pretty sure he cared about the earth just as much as the environmental protection people headed for the west end of Joyeuse Island, so they'd ordinarily be his friends. Today, they looked to him like an invading army.

Joe had met the scientists at Joyeuse Island's only dock, but he'd stayed there just long enough to meet the man in charge, Gerry Steinberg, and to say hello to the sheriff. Steinberg, a not-tall man with graying hair and hazel eyes, had said that he worked for the county environmental agency, but that he was also a sworn deputy working as a detective for the Micco County Sheriff's Department. He'd explained that this dual arrangement streamlined the investigation of accidents like this one, as well as the enforcement of environmental crimes.

Faye had said, "It's always good when two arms of the government can work together."

Joe had thought, "Yeah, because maybe it will save us some time and money," but he didn't say anything.

Faye had asked if they should call the investigator "Deputy Steinberg" and he'd said, "Oh, no. Just call me Gerry."

This made Joe worry that Gerry was trying to be all folksy, so that they wouldn't notice when he ran up an environmental cleanup bill so big that it would have restored the Everglades to the pristine condition it had enjoyed before the Army Corps of Engineers got hold of it. Joe had noticed that the government was not totally consistent in its approach to environmental preservation. He had also noticed that anything the government touched became immediately expensive.

Gerry was already asking Faye questions as they left Joe and headed for the place where the spill was still happening in slow motion. The sheriff walking beside him hadn't said much. It was at least a ten-minute walk from Joyeuse Island's sole dock to the west end of the island, and the two were soon out of sight. Joe occupied himself by seeing just how high he could push

Michael's tire swing without making him squeal in fear. Pretty high, as it turned out.

As he pushed the swing, he considered the size of the crew that had come to check out his little kerosene spill. He saw a need for Gerry, the site manager. He saw a need for Nadia, the chemist who would be using her boat-based lab to test samples of the stinking mess Faye had uncovered. He saw a need for the safety specialist, since somebody had to decide whether the tank (or drum or whatever) Faye had uncovered was going to explode. He maybe saw a need for the nameless helper following Gerry around.

He saw no need, however, for the sheriff himself to show up for this little tiny fuel spill. Something wasn't as it seemed, but Gerry and the sheriff were keeping their mouths shut.

While Faye led the sheriff and Gerry Steinberg across the island, Nadia had stayed behind on the work boat that served as a floating analytical laboratory. Joe had been watching her for half an hour. From his position behind Michael's swing, Joe could see her packing equipment into one of the coolers stacked on its deck. She periodically went into the cabin to fetch more technical-looking stuff. He could see a reason for every motion she made. This was not a woman who wasted time.

Sly's mouth had been moving since Joe walked away, so the petite scientist with the Spanish accent had been listening to his folksy come-ons for quite a while.

Sly had led with "Don't pretty ladies like you get tired of standing in a chemistry lab all day? Don't the smell ever get to you?"

Nadia had said only, "I like the way my lab smells."

He'd followed up with "Can I help you load up any of that stuff? It looks too heavy for a little thing like you."

She'd said nothing, just locked eyes with him as she hefted one fully loaded cooler to waist height and lowered it on top of another.

"Can I come on that boat and get you to explain that lab to me? I like the ladies, but I like smart ladies the most."

"No, you can't come on the boat. Not unless your safety training is up to OSHA standards."

Ouch. Shot down again. Sly didn't even look flustered. Men like Joe's father who flirted constantly must see it as like buying a lottery ticket. If you hit the jackpot, great. If not, fork over another dollar and buy another chance to win.

Nadia looked about Faye's age, early forties, so Sly wasn't quite old enough to be her father, but he was pretty close. Nadia's body language said she wanted to push him off the dock and then go wash her ears out with soap.

Holding up a hand to stop the flow of Sly's words, she took a phone call. Then she pulled something white and shiny out of a bag and put it on. It was a protective jumpsuit, probably disposable, and it covered her from neck to wrists and ankles. Despite the fact that she was putting it on over her clothes, she was going through the motions of getting dressed and Sly was taking an unseemly interest in watching her do that. Joe wanted to go wash his eyes out with soap.

Draping the strap of her equipment bag across her body from shoulder to hip, Nadia hoisted a small cooler. Sly reached out a hand to help her carry it, but Nadia didn't acknowledge him. Her long dirty-blond ponytail switched from side to side as she set off walking without looking back. Sly dogged her steps like a man who couldn't tell when he wasn't wanted.

It might be November, but the air blowing off the Gulf was still damp and sticky. Joe thought Nadia might soon be wishing she'd waited till she got where she was going before putting on a waterproof jumpsuit that would hold in every drop of sweat, but she seemed like a smart lady. She wouldn't make that mistake twice.

Faye squatted beside Gerry as they watched Nadia sample the contaminated soil at the bottom of Faye's archaeological excavation. Nadia's trowel wasn't shaped like Faye's. It looked more like a garden trowel, designed for scooping soil samples into a jar, rather than scraping the thin layers of archaeological work. Still, there was some overlap in their field technique. Nadia treated each gob of scooped soil with the same care Faye used to brush grains of dust away from something mysterious and long-buried.

Faye could see by the way Nadia handled the trowel and sample jar that they were clean and that they needed to stay clean. Nothing could go into the jar but that gob of soil. After Nadia hauled it back to the work boat, her portable laboratory was going to reveal every single chemical in that soil. Watching the chemist handle the samples with care, Faye felt confident that any god-awful contamination Nadia found would be honestly hers. She could own that god-awful contaminant, whatever it was.

Faye was also confident that, if Nadia's patience were to be tried much further, she would shove Joe's talkative and lecherous father off the lip of the excavation and into the stinking puddle of kerosene at its bottom. Presuming it was kerosene.

Maybe it was kerosene and only kerosene. Faye hoped so. Maybe kerosene would be cheaper to clean up than some Love Canal-like PCBs or dioxins or whatever. Faye really didn't know.

Gerry was saying, "My emergency response crew can get this thing stopped. Whatever is leaking—a drum, a tank, whatever—they have the know-how to uncover it, contain it, and get it out of here before your problem gets any worse. To be honest, if they don't uncover more than what we're looking at, you should be fine."

But what if they *did* uncover more noxious stuff? Faye pictured dozens of rusty drums buried under the soil in front of her, leaking God knew what. Imagining the cost of cleaning all that up made her feel faint.

"Were you listening, Faye? I said everything is probably going to be fine."

"What will this emergency response contractor's crew do?"

"They'll use shovels and hand tools to uncover the vessel that's leaking, but gently, so that they don't bust it wide open in the process. Then they'll check out the stained soils visually to get an idea of how big your problem is. We call those saturated soils a 'point source.' As long as the point source is in place, the contamination will keep spreading. The groundwater's really shallow here, so if the kerosene reaches it, it will leach out of the soil into the water, given a chance. And since we're right here on the Gulf, it's almost certain to spread into surface water. There's no place else for it to go. That contaminated soil needs to be taken out of here sooner rather than later."

The darkened soil where Nadia was sampling looked still more sinister.

"And how will the contractor do that?"

"I'm thinking a small backhoe will do it. They'll load the saturated soil into drums and haul it to an incinerator. They'll also check the groundwater to make sure it's clean, and they'll retest to make sure they didn't leave any contaminated soil behind. If there aren't any soil or groundwater contaminants at levels that exceed cleanup standards, then you'll be good to go."

A backhoe. Groundwater testing. Drums. An incinerator. Personnel to load the soil in the drums. A boat big enough to carry all that. And a return visit from Nadia and her expensive-looking laboratory boat. Faye was beginning to wonder whether Joe should start whittling some wooden toys for the kids. They weren't going to be able to afford to buy them much for Christmas.

Chapter Six

Faye stood a safe distance from the excavation where Gerry and Nadia were directing two technicians swaddled in safety gear. The technicians were digging soil away from a buried cylindrical vessel made of tin. It had a volume of maybe five gallons, which should have been a good thing. Five gallons just wasn't much kerosene. Arguing against that optimistic viewpoint were the words Gerry had uttered when its curving side came into view.

"What in the hell?"

When the man in charge of a project that Faye was probably funding, a project with no budget that Faye knew about, looked and sounded perplexed, Faye could feel her bank account dwindle.

The thing that made the archaeologist in Faye stand up and take notice, though, was not the rising price tag of her environmental cleanup. It was the obvious age of the container that had been holding the kerosene. Except for the hole in its side that she had punched with the sharp point of her trowel, it was in excellent condition for something so old. Faye would wager that this thing dated to the 1930s or before. If so, it had waited here underground, filled with kerosene, since Cally Stanton, Faye's great-great-grandmother, had been the mistress of Joyeuse Island.

Faye owned the house and island that Cally had held onto through Reconstruction and into the Great Depression, but she had almost no physical connections to the ancestor she idolized. She had one photograph of her. She had a copy of the memoirs that Cally had dictated to federal workers collecting the oral histories of former slaves like her. She had dug up some random bric-a-brac that might or might not have belonged to Cally. And now she had a leaking kerosene tank that Cally perhaps had buried or abandoned in this completely illogical spot. Only an archaeologist would consider this bad-smelling object exciting.

Faye and Joe had both showered and gotten ready for bed. They had sent the day's sweat down the drain, along with rainwater from their cisterns, some sandy grains of dirt, and some petroleum fumes. Faye tried not to think that Joe had showered away a few drops of seawater and blood that had rolled off Liz's body and clung to Joe's during those frenzied moments when he helped his father try to revive her.

Faye crawled under the bedclothes, still shivering because their solar-heated water tank had been emptied of hot water by her father-in-law's long shower and there wouldn't be any more until the sun shone.

"Somebody shot Liz in the back before she went in the water? Oh, Joe. That's awful."

It wasn't fair that Joe had been one of the ones to find their friend dead. He was such a gentle soul.

"The bullet went in between her shoulder blades," he said. "Came out through her breastbone. She didn't crawl down to the end of the dock in that kind of shape. If she'd managed it somehow, she'd have left some blood behind, and I didn't see a drop anywhere that wasn't close to the spot where she must've been standing when she got hit."

"It would've been late, after she closed up the grill."

"Moon was full."

Yes, it had been. Faye remembered it streaming through their bedroom window, just as it was doing now. When Liz died, she had been lying awake in this bed with Joe sleeping beside her.

Faye had been lying awake a lot lately. She had watched the moon grow every night for the past two weeks. Right now, it was behind a raincloud, but it was out there and it would emerge again. When it did, there would be less and less light for the next two weeks until the moon was gone.

That's what the moon did, waxed and waned. Right after the darkest night, the knife-edge slice of the new moon showed itself at sunset and the whole cycle started again. Faye was ready for the light to come back into her life. More than ready. She was ready to stop being caught up short by the echo of a baby's cry. These days, the inside of her head was a terrible place to be.

A fire roared in a two-hundred-year-old fireplace that had been built to warm this room when it was Joyeuse's plantation office. Now it was their bedroom. Michael's room was next to theirs, and the bricked backside of this fireplace warmed his little room on those rare nights when a Florida house got cold. Amande's room was on the other side of the hall and it held the other ground floor fireplace. Sly was sleeping in there while she was gone. He'd move into the smaller room next to hers when she came home. If this cool snap hadn't passed by then, he'd have to let himself be warmed by the backside of Amande's fireplace.

Faye took an extra blanket from the foot of the bed and spread it over Joe and herself. "Why do you think somebody did that to Liz?"

"The window in the kitchen door was broken. I was looking through it while the sheriff and the deputy stood next to the cash register and talked. They talked a long time."

"You think they were saying maybe a thief shot Liz?"

"The cash drawer was open and it didn't look like there was any money in it, so it makes sense that there might have been a thief. I also saw a little bit of water on the concrete outside the kitchen door and another damp spot just inside the door, so I showed them to the sheriff. They weren't footprints, really, nothing that would point to one particular person. Just some wetness to the cracks in the tiles and the concrete. A person who'd been in the water with Liz, holding her head under till she drowned, would have left wet spots in just those places if they went inside afterward."

Faye hoped the new sheriff appreciated Joe and his tracking skills as much as Mike McKenzie had, back when he was sheriff.

"What did the sheriff say? Did he think Liz was killed by somebody who came to rob her?"

"Maybe. I didn't tell him what to think, and he didn't so much ask me what I thought. He just kept asking me questions about what I saw. Really seemed to want to hear if anything seemed different or unusual."

"That's what sheriffs are supposed to want to hear. What did you tell him?"

"I told him that Liz closed up the grill at the same time every night and then she usually had a drink or three. Then she went out there to feed the fish every night, right before going to bed. If somebody had been watching her, getting ready to rob her, then that somebody picked the right time to find Liz alone. But if the killer had been watching her for long—for any time at all, really—it would've been obvious that she lived upstairs and that waiting another thirty minutes would've put her in her bed asleep. Passed out drunk, probably, like she's been nearly every night since Chip passed. There wasn't no reason to kill Liz to get her money."

Faye knew how little Liz charged for a plate of eggs and grits. "There couldn't have been enough money in that drawer to make it worth killing somebody, anyway."

Joe shook his head. "No. I don't think so, either, and I told the sheriff that. Maybe if it was somebody too strung out on crack to wait thirty minutes to get their hands on some more. But for a normal person and for most criminals? There ain't no reason Liz had to die for somebody to get into that cash register."

Faye pictured the grill and the marina and the dock, trying to imagine what she'd take if she were a thief. "None of the boats were missing? And nobody took anything off the boats?"

"Not that I could see. I guess somebody could come check on their boat and find something missing tomorrow, but there wasn't a sign that any of 'em was tampered with."

"The storage lockers? The tool shed? Tommy's maintenance shop?"

"Everything looked fine to me."

Liz was dead and nothing Faye could do would change it. She might not be feeling like herself, but she could do simple math. Everybody for miles around knew that Liz's business was struggling. There were other cash registers in the county that could have been emptied. Maybe Liz was the unlucky victim because hers was less heavily guarded, but if that was the motive for choosing her, why didn't her killer just wait for her to go to bed?

It was certainly possible that Liz was the random victim of a criminal too stupid to do the math that said there was no payback in her murder, but Faye had never been comfortable with illogic. Tonight, though, she had no choice but to let illogic lie.

She wanted to see justice done for Liz, but she couldn't even summon the energy to continue this conversation. She gave Joe's arm a good-night pat and pulled the blanket to her chin. She had no faith that she would sleep tonight, but she needed to close her eyes and try. Sleep crept up on her in fragments these days, and sometimes she thought that those fragments were the only thing between her and a breakdown.

A few moments later, she felt Joe get up, arrange the covers carefully over her, and walk out into the chilly night. It was raining, so he wouldn't be going far. She pictured him standing under the front porch, listening to rain hit the leaves of trees he couldn't see.

He would certainly be lighting a cigarette. If she knew her husband, he was doing this on purpose, because she always yelled at him when she smelled tobacco on his breath. And she knew he wanted her to yell at him. Or cry. Or something. She wished she had the energy.

Chapter Seven

The morning of the day they buried Liz was awful. Joe had stirred up some eggs to scramble, stared for a long minute down into the yellow glop in the bowl, and then just walked away.

Faye, who did actually know how to cook but who stayed out of Joe's kitchen because she wanted to stay married, offered to cook the eggs so they wouldn't go to waste. All she got out of Joe was "Go ahead. Just don't cook any grits, or—"

He swallowed and she could hear the words he wasn't saying. *Or I'll start thinking about Liz and her grits and I won't be able to stop.*

He tried again. "Just don't cook grits. I won't eat them." Then he stomped outside and sat under the tree where he always sat to chip stone. She could tell that he was knocking two rocks together, but she couldn't see that he was focused enough on what he was doing to make anything more useful than the stone chips that were flying everywhere. The ground around that tree was covered with flakes of chert that would still be there when Joe was dead.

The morning stretched out. Faye burned the eggs and had to throw them out. Michael threw a tantrum because he wanted some grits. Sly drained his tenth cup of coffee and said, "You folks must have an ax around here somewhere," as if this observation somehow pertained to the conversation nobody was having.

"In the shed under the back porch."

She had hardly said it when Sly was gone.

Ten minutes later, Joe was at the sink, rinsing blood off the hand he'd just nicked with a half-finished stone knife. When Joe couldn't handle his sharp toys, Faye's whole world was askew.

"What was my dad planning to do with that ax?"

"I don't know. Chop something?"

A moment later, they heard the ring of an ax striking wood, again and again. Faye decided that Sly and Joe weren't far wrong to think working with their hands might beat back grief. She got out a bowl and her grandmother's hand mixer, with its narrow 1940s beaters and the crank on its side that made those beaters go round. It was time for her to decide what she was going to cook for the mourners at Liz's wake.

Faye loved funeral food well enough to spend the morning after a long night making a mess in the kitchen. She had baked a hummingbird cake to add to the feast that would follow Liz's memorial service. She hated eulogies and the scent of carnations and the heavy footsteps of people who were carrying sadness, but she loved the custom of gathering the mourners afterward for a communal meal.

Everyone had their funeral food specialties and she knew that people would be looking for her hummingbird cake. Liz's mourners were Faye's friends and neighbors, so she had known what to expect when they gathered at Emma Douglass' house. Here were the familiar heavy casseroles, brightened by the butter and salt in their cracker-crumb crusts. Beside them were improbable combinations of fruit, nuts, and cottage cheese molded into Jell-O salads. Faye's offering was not the only tender-crumbed cake baked from scratch. Faye wished she were hungry enough to eat some of the feast.

Emma Everett had tried, mounding food on a paper plate and putting it on the table in front of Faye with a thwack. "Eat something. You look like a runway model, and I don't mean that as a compliment."

Emma's marble kitchen counters were not nearly as laden with funeral food as they had been after her husband Douglass had died. Douglass had been a prominent businessman, active in the Optimist Club. He'd been chairman of the deacons at his church. He'd lived in Micco County from birth to grave. The whole county had turned out for his funeral, and everybody had brought enough food to feed their families, and also the families of people who maybe didn't know how to throw a casserole in the oven or (and this would always be unspoken) the people who couldn't afford the ingredients to cook for a crowd.

Liz hadn't had Douglass' lifelong connection to the community, but she had lived in Micco County for fifteen or twenty years. Nobody at the funeral was quite sure how long they'd known her. Liz had appeared at the stove of Wally's Bar and Grill in mid-life, and no one knew a thing about her past. Her status as the single mother of a son who was teenaged when she arrived proved that she'd had a life before Micco County, but she had never talked about it. She'd never mentioned a family. No relatives had shown up at the funeral, just a few dozen people saying, "I didn't know her well, but I'm so sad to hear that she's gone."

There had been no publicly acknowledged lovers to prove that Chip's father wasn't the last man in Liz's life. Faye had always suspected that Liz and Wally had been more to each other than an employer and the short-order cook who kept his business afloat when he was too drunk to do it himself.

Faye would never forget the day Wally died. She had caught him as he fell and his blood had covered her, pooled around her, dripped from her hands. She had sat with Wally, red-stained, looking for someone to explain to her what was happening, and she had found herself looking at Liz.

Liz had given her no answers, but for that moment the woman had worn no shield to cover her naked heartbreak. She had loved Wally. Faye had no doubt of it. And Wally had given his life to save Faye, so she too had loved him, in her way. He should have been here for Liz today, instead of lying cold and dead in the ground. But then, Liz should have been here, too.

Without Wally and Chip, the list of guests at Liz's funeral was bound to feel scant and incomplete. A few longtime customers had come to the service, but more of them had shown up beforehand at Emma's house with a Jell-O salad, murmuring their regrets that they weren't going to be able to make it to the funeral.

Faye felt rather sorry for Sheriff Ken Rainey and his deputy Gerry Steinberg. She guessed they needed to be at the funeral as part of their investigation, in case Liz's murderer showed up and confessed. Or, more likely, they needed to be at the funeral in case one of the guests said something they wanted to overhear. It was too bad that there was no way for the sheriff and his deputy to blend into the thin crowd. They felt awkward and it showed.

After the funeral, they had stopped by Emma's house for a few minutes, then excused themselves. Faye took this to mean that she and her closest friends had told Rainey and Steinberg all that they wanted to hear, for now.

Most of Liz's real mourners now sat with Emma in her living room, relaxing in the deep upholstery of her leather furniture. Faye. Joe. Sly, who was mingling with his son's longtime friends as if they hadn't always known him as Joe's mysteriously absent father. Mike McKenzie, who had been retired for years, but who would always be Sheriff Mike to his friends. Sheriff Mike's wife, Dr. Magda Stockard-McKenzie, who was Faye's archaeological mentor and best friend. Their late-in-life daughter Rachel McKenzie, who was barely older than Michael but who was enough of her mother's daughter to be giving Michael sage supervision in the piling up and knocking down of multi-colored wooden blocks. The look on little Michael's face, who would never understand why Liz wasn't around to call him the cutest little black-haired boy in Micco County, was enough to make Faye cry, but she held strong.

Faye watched Rachel bend down and say to Michael, with the exaggerated patience of an adult instructing a student driver, "I already told you! You can't stack anything on top of that pointy block. It'll all fall down."

Joe, listening, elbowed Sheriff Mike. "Wonder where she got that attitude from?"

Faye saw that Joe got Sheriff Mike's elbow in his own ribs.

"He better get used to it," the sheriff said. "Our wives have already decided that my daughter is marrying your son. I don't give Michael very good odds, not if he goes up against Faye, Magda, and Rachel. He might as well knuckle under and marry my baby girl. There's worse things than that could happen to a young man."

Faye thought of what had happened to Chip and remembered when he'd been a clumsy teenager, hardly more than a little boy. Her heart ached like a broken tooth.

Too sad to talk, she just kept people-watching as Magda walked across the room and flopped her stocky body down on the couch between Joe and Mike. She was smirking like a woman happy to deal out some insults of her own. When she made this move, Emma and Sly were left to make one-on-one conversation. Faye would have thought that the rough-around-the-edges ex-con trucker wouldn't have had a thing to say to the widow of the richest man in Micco County.

Faye would have been wrong.

Judging by the way Sly's mouth stayed close to Emma's ear and the way she ducked her head and laughed, Faye thought he was probably telling her jokes unsuitable for the widow of the chairman of the deacons at the Blessed Assurance AME Church. Or maybe not so unsuitable. Emma looked like she was having a good time.

Faye tried to picture the long-ago Douglass who had wooed Emma. He had been the son of a sharecropper before he parlayed his charisma and brilliant mind into big money. When Emma had met him as a teenager, Douglass would have been in his twenties. He would have been rough around the edges, and he would have had the same testosterone-laden charm as Sly Mantooth and his son Joe.

Sly leaned in to deliver a probably bawdy punch line, gently brushing Emma's shoulder with his own. Emma leaned further in, laughing, and swatted at his muscled forearm. Faye's first thought was that Sly had Joe's devilish grin, then she realized that she needed to turn that around. Joe had Sly's devilish grin.

Faye wanted to be glad that Emma was getting a chance to enjoy a little man-woman chemistry. She didn't think anybody ever got too old to want that. But she would feel untrue to Douglass' memory if she didn't worry about the thought of Emma with a man whose history included time in the penitentiary.

It had been a long time since Faye laughed, but laughter bubbled around her. Six adults and two children brought so much life to this lovely room where Emma usually sat alone. This was as it should be. Funerals should be celebrations of life. The actual service had been a drab affair, officiated in a drab nondenominational way by a drab man who had never met Liz. The attendees who were not in this room had scattered immediately after he said "Amen."

If the funeral had been held here, with only these people in attendance, Liz would have lost only a few half-hearted mourners and she would have had a better memorial. Less religious, maybe, but more personal. These good people had come together now to remember her, and that was something, but Faye thought warmhearted Liz had deserved more.

More respect in death.

More happiness in life.

Just more.

◇◇◇

Joe had cornered Sheriff Mike. He knew this wasn't good funeral behavior, but he wanted to talk about Liz's death with a lawman who wasn't keeping his mouth shut because he was working the case. Besides, Sheriff Mike clearly had opinions and he wanted to share them. He looked happy to be cornered.

The retired sheriff cleared his throat. "I don't like to second-guess Sheriff Rainey's methods. He's a good man, and a smart one, too."

Sheriff Mike might indeed think the new sheriff was a good man and a smart one. Joe agreed. But he knew that Sheriff Mike was itching to second-guess Rainey's methods anyway. He just needed to take a little time to be polite first.

"So you think he's right to be questioning a bunch of kids?" Joe asked. "That's what everybody's saying. He's rounding up teenagers with records, asking them a few questions, and letting them go."

"Well, when the presumption is that a person got killed during a robbery gone wrong, then yeah. You look for juvenile delinquents, and you look for repeat offenders who have been committing crimes since they *were* juvenile delinquents. Ain't nothing wrong with that, unless you're not keeping an eye out for an unexpected motive, something besides a regular, everyday robbery. Besides, we don't know that Rainey's only talking to kids. Just because the only names you've heard from the rumor mill belong to kids, that don't mean he's not talking to anybody else. Rainey don't answer to you nor to me, except when it comes time for us to vote."

Joe saw Faye looking their direction. She was sitting next to Magda, but she wasn't talking.

"So, as a man who used to be sheriff and isn't anymore, what do you really think?'

"I think I don't have a clue what happened to Liz. Yeah, I'd be talking to the delinquents if I was in his shoes, but I keep picturing Liz at the end of that dock, looking out into the Gulf. There's a lot that goes on out there. A lot of people are out there doing things they don't want anybody to see. If I was him, I'd be wondering what Liz could've seen that she wished she could unsee."

Joe saw Magda say something to Faye. Neither of them laughed after she said it and that felt wrong. Funeral or not, when Faye and Magda got together, the room was full of woman-laughs. That's the way Liz would have wanted it. She had her own raucous woman-laugh, and Joe was going to miss it.

The sheriff was watching them, too. His face said he didn't think things were quite right, either. "You gotta remember, Joe, that Liz owned that marina. Her and the bank owned it, anyway. Boats come in and out of there all the damn time. Anything could be on those boats. Anybody could be on those boats. And it's not just that Liz could've seen something she shouldn't. She could've been *doing* something she shouldn't. You know she was always hard up for money. It could have been as simple as somebody paying her to look the other way. Then maybe she stopped looking the other way. Or maybe she wanted a bigger cut. These things happen and Sheriff Rainey knows it. He'd be a fool if he's just talking to delinquent kids, and he's no fool."

Faye and Magda were talking, but Magda wasn't as soft-spoken as Joe's wife. He could hear her plainly as she said, "What has that crazy dude Oscar been saying lately?"

Faye launched into an inaudible tirade that involved more words than he'd heard her say in the past four weeks, combined. She and Magda beckoned to Emma, who joined them on the couch. The three of them put their heads together as Emma, with her own quiet voice, began to wave her hands and speak inaudibly.

His wife and her two best friends were an impressive sight—tiny Faye with her sleek black hair and quicksilver motions, broad-faced and blunt-spoken Magda, and the very patrician Emma with her crown of tight black-and-grey curls. They looked like a posse having a final meeting before going out for vengeance.

Joe wished he knew what they were planning. More to the point, he couldn't believe that he didn't *already* know what they were planning. Joe knew no one by the name of Oscar.

Joe had lived on an island with Faye for a decade. They worked together. They slept together. They did everything together. Their social life largely consisted of the people in this room.

Joe was a homebody who only left Joyeuse Island when it was absolutely necessary but, in recent weeks, even Joe'd had more interaction with the outside world than Faye. So who was Oscar and why was Magda calling him crazy and why did Faye's shadowed eyes grow even darker at the mention of his name?

Sly was back in the woods with his ax as soon as they got home from the funeral. When it got dark, he came inside looking for a lantern. At bedtime, Joe and Faye could see its distant glow from the window near the foot of their bed, and they could hear the rhythmic blows of his ax.

"You think he's planning to do that all night?" Even as she asked the question, Faye wasn't sure she cared about the answer. She doubted she'd be sleeping much, and she liked the sound of Sly's ax hitting fresh wood. It would be okay with her if he kept swinging the ax all night long.

"I don't think that lantern's battery will go all night. I don't know what Dad's thinking. He's gonna need a lot of trips with a wheelbarrow to bring the firewood he's splitting back here to the house. We got trees way closer to the house than that. He's just making work for himself."

Faye had a notion that Sly was working far away so that the noise wouldn't bother them. She also had a notion that he didn't mind making work for himself because work made him feel better. He wasn't dim-witted enough to think that this was an efficient way to chop wood for heating the house.

The lantern's battery lasted late into the night. After the ax was silent and the lantern went dark, Sly built a campfire and just sat there a while. Faye knew he did this because she could see a soft reddish glow on the undersides of tree branches deep into the distance.

Joe must have seen the glow, too. After a time, he went outside, his big feet padding softly on the floor. It was his habit to commemorate the dead with a time of fireside meditation. She knew that he liked to mark the occasion by burning purifying herbs. He could probably find those herbs in the dark by their fragrance, gathering them along the path that took him to Sly and his fire.

It was a long time before the two men came back in the house. A single footfall and the slight creaking of an old door were the only things Faye heard as Sly passed. Joe moved with his usual utter silence. He merely eased into the bed beside her, his long black hair smelling like warm sage and smoke.

Faye knew all these things because she wasn't sleeping and had no hope that she might.

Chapter Eight

The morning sunshine looked weak and watery, even for November, but the air was tolerably warm. Faye was glad for its warmth and she was glad to let the heavy wooden front door of Joyeuse shut behind her. Again, she was headed out for a day of unpaid work on her own island. The stout door cut off the sound of Joe's "Good-bye," and Michael's "Mommy!" as it closed behind her.

She knew it hurt Joe when she disappeared for the day, but it would hurt him more if she sat around the house, gloomy and silent, and she just didn't have anything to say. It didn't help that they had already made plans to convert her office into a nursery when she miscarried. When she sat in that room, all she could see was the delicate shade of pink that they'd intended to paint the walls.

This morning, unlike recent mornings, she had a coherent plan for her day. It was not to earn money, which was too bad since Amande wanted a guitar for Christmas. Today's plan was to keep more money from flowing out the door and into the hands of environmental cleanup contractors. Faye was heading across the island to watch every move that Gerry and Nadia and their environmental technicians made.

She had gotten the impression that none of the scientist-types thought that this was any huge environmental tragedy. She had heard Gerry use words like "limited in extent" and "accelerated cleanup schedule." Since time equaled money, "accelerated" sounded a lot cheaper than "long and drawn-out."

Faye's plan for keeping an eye on Gerry's crew wasn't too detailed. Mostly, she was going to watch as Nadia sampled and tested soil and water. She was also going to hope that Nadia's test results told Gerry not to dig up and expensively incinerate too much of Joyeuse's dirt.

Gerry knew she was going to do these things, but he didn't know everything Faye planned to do today. He had no idea that Faye would be asking him some questions he might not want to answer.

◇◇◇

Tommy had been watching while Gerry Steinberg stood beside the marina's boat ramp, supervising as a boatful of expensive equipment was lowered slowly into the Gulf of Mexico. Tommy's boat maintenance shop sat in full view of the boat ramp, but it was an unobtrusive shed that looked like it had sat through one too many hurricanes. He had pulled a stool up to his workbench so he could peer out a tiny window fogged by time and grease.

The rumor mill said that all this equipment, plus the environmental personnel who'd be running it, was being launched in the direction of Joyeuse Island. This would put Detective Steinberg and his friends out of Tommy's sight all day long, all of them, and he'd be out of theirs. It seemed like a good day to take his personal boat far out into the Gulf, so far that nobody would see what he threw overboard. He had a feeling that the law was onto him, and he had some business that needed finishing.

Tommy had customers waiting for him to get their boats working again, and they would be pissed if he didn't work today. Too bad. Most of them would be about as anxious to talk to the cops as he was, and the cops had been highly visible at the marina ever since Liz died, so they should understand his position. They had no other choice, not if they wanted their boats back. They might grouse, but they trusted Tommy to get the job done eventually.

Why, exactly, did they trust him? Tommy couldn't figure it out. He would absolutely steal a Little Leaguer's favorite catcher's mitt if he could sell it for a good price without getting caught, but he seemed to have an honest face. His customers left boats worth tens of thousands of dollars at his maintenance shop without even asking for a receipt saying, "I, Tommy Barnett, took this big and expensive thing to work on, but I promise to give it back."

His other customers? The ones who hired him to do shadier work than making boat motors hum? For some reason, they instinctively trusted that he would get their work done for them, and they believed that he would always keep their secrets.

Tommy knew that his face wasn't honest at all, because it covered a mind that didn't much care about the difference between right and wrong. If the day came when it was better for Tommy to disappear than it was for him to stay in Micco County and run his businesses, then he would go. And he would go in the finest boat that was currently in his care, despite the fact that its owner trusted him implicitly.

Boats leave no tracks, and Tommy knew a place where the boat buyers didn't ask questions. It was a place where he could get enough money out of a fancy stolen boat to start over. He didn't want to start over, but if he had to do it, he could.

Joe washed bits of egg off the breakfast dishes, doing his best not to think about why he'd cooked them himself instead of paying Liz to do it. Faye had dressed and left the house in less time than the eggs had taken to scramble. He'd tried to make her eat, but she'd waved a granola bar at him as she walked out the door. Joe wasn't sure how long it was supposed to take a seven-months-pregnant woman to get her figure back, but Faye had done it. And more. She was too thin.

As Joe scrubbed a skillet clean, he was wondering whether he could get off the island without Faye finding out. He had a couple of good reasons to talk to Emma about things Faye didn't need to hear

Sly's thick Oklahoma accent rumbled out of the next room and it made him sound almost grandfatherly. "Hey, kid, let's get out your train track. If we run it up this chair and down the side of that one, we can have a hell of a crash. I mean heck."

Joe knew Michael well enough to know that he could happily build and destroy train tracks for the full two hours it would take Joe to boat to shore, talk to Emma, and get home. If Sly picked up the pieces every time Michael knocked down the whole setup—and Joe thought Sly might actually enjoy doing that while he drank yet more coffee—they'd both be fine.

Okay, maybe "fine" was optimistic. They'd be fine enough. There was no reason to drag them along, and he'd be back that much sooner if he went alone.

Ordinarily, he would have texted Faye before he went ashore. Maybe she needed him to pick up some laundry detergent. Well, she should have thought about that when she started ignoring his texts.

Joe stuck his head in the family room and said, "Dad, can you play trains with Michael for a couple of hours? I've got some stuff I need to do in town."

Sly nodded.

Joe plunked a couple of juice boxes and a box of really healthy unsweetened cereal on the table at Sly's elbow, and said, "If he gets hungry."

Sly nodded again.

Joe was gone before his dad could ask him to bring back a few more pounds of coffee.

Faye looked Gerry over and decided that this was not a man who needed her to hem and haw. If she had something to say, she could go ahead and spit it out.

"Saw you at Liz's funeral yesterday. It was really good of you to come."

Gerry looked up from a lab report that contained a full page of numbers, spaced in a regular grid. "Hmm? I thought it was the least I could do."

"How did you know Liz? Were you a regular customer at

the grill? I never saw you there, but it's not like I was there all day, every day."

"I ate there a few times. She never said much to me beyond 'Do you want butter on your grits?' but I liked her."

His lab report became fascinating. Faye wasn't in the mood to leave him alone.

"You said you lived in Tallahassee. You come down to the marina to fish? You got another boat besides that big government barge tied to my dock?"

Gerry's swarthy face could have been tanned by Saturdays spent on the water, but Faye didn't think he was a fisherman. He looked like a man with naturally olive-toned skin who spent his Saturdays reading Dostoyevsky. He also looked like a man who was too smart to try making island-dwelling Faye believe he liked to fish.

He asked a question that proved he was smart enough to derail Faye's line of questioning completely.

"Is this the first time you've found buried contaminants on your island? You had any problems with people dumping out here in the past?"

Faye had panicky visions of bulldozers scraping the surface off her entire island, looking for illegal dumping. "No! Think about it, Gerry. I called for an emergency response for this," she gestured at the small hole with its small volume of contaminated soil. "You and I both know that it was a borderline situation. Joe and I could have covered it up and forgotten about it. We wanted to do the right thing. So we did. Why would you think we'd ever have ignored people dumping anything out here?"

"Yes, you did do the right thing. I wasn't accusing you. It's just that this is not the first cleanup we've had to do out in these islands, and it's certainly not the worst. You win the trophy for the smallest dump site in Micco County. Ten gallons of kerosene isn't going to get you put on the Superfund list."

So there wasn't a spot on the Superfund list for her? Praise God for small miracles.

"And you also win the trophy for the oldest contamination

problem I've ever seen. Did you have a chance to look at the mount on that kerosene tank?"

She had. It had been a metal frame constructed so that the tank could be mounted on pivots. Someone filling a small kerosene can for household use could tip the tank forward with a single hand, letting the fuel pour easily out of a spigot. It was a clever design, built for an earlier age. It had been a long time since most people needed a daily supply of kerosene to run their households.

"So this isn't the first cleanup you've done around here? Is it common for people to dump nasty chemicals on any convenient island?"

Now she had Gerry's attention.

"On islands?" he asked. "Oh, yeah. If they think they can get away with it, people will put nasty chemicals anywhere. It's really easy to pitch them overboard, right into the Gulf, but sometimes they find a nice secluded place to bury it. Secluded and beautiful, just like this."

He made a sweeping motion with his hand that encompassed the island, the Gulf, and maybe even the sky. "Sometimes, the stuff wouldn't have even cost all that much to dispose of properly. It's just too much trouble to find out where to take it. Or maybe they're afraid that paying for disposal will cost more than it really does. And then there are those people who don't want to do things the right way, no matter what, because they don't like the government telling them what to do. Micco County's got enough undeveloped land to attract idiots like that. Those people are the reason the sheriff's department partnered with the state environmental department to create my job."

"It's nice when the government's right hand is willing to work with its left hand. And it's rare."

"No joke."

He lowered his eyes to the lab report in his hand, as if to signal that he really needed to get back to work. Faye couldn't believe Gerry really thought he'd successfully deflected her from asking questions about Liz.

"So you've done enough environmental enforcement around here to make Liz's acquaintance, maybe eat some meals at her marina?"

She heard herself say the word "marina," and all the conversational threads clicked into a coherent whole. Gerry looked like a man who realized she'd put two and two together, but who really didn't want her to ask him whether he agreed that they equaled four.

Too bad. She wasn't finished with him. "Dumping in the islands requires a boat. People who use boats have to either get them in the water or keep them in the water. If I had your job, I'd keep my eye on any public boat ramps—and there aren't any for miles around, but you already know that, don't you?—and on private marinas like Liz's that charge people to use their ramps and boat slips. There's only one marina for miles around and Liz owned it. That's why you've eaten more than a few meals she cooked. Isn't it?"

Gerry shrugged like a teenager who couldn't be bothered to answer his parents' questions.

"And it's why you were at her funeral yesterday. I get it that the sheriff had to be there as part of the investigation, but you're not an ordinary detective. You've got this dual-job-thingie with the environmental department, and he's got other people to work his murder cases. There's a connection between your environmental work and her murder, isn't there? If your illegal dumpers used the marina, they knew Liz. Maybe they rented a boat slip from her." She got no response from the detective, not even an adolescent shrug.

Faye had spent enough time at the marina to be able to hold an image of the whole thing in her mind, picturing it and all the people who frequented it. She pictured the marina's maintenance shed, located near the slips Liz had rented to people wealthy enough to pay rent so that their boats would have a place to stay. The shop was rented out to a man named Tommy Barnett who worked on balky boats when he worked at all.

Her mind also turned to Wilma, the woman who paid Liz for the right to sell fuel to the marina's customers. Neither Tommy nor Wilma seemed to make much money, but they were never without customers and they didn't seem to work all that hard. The very definition of a "captive market" would be "a person sitting at Liz's dock in a boat that won't go."

"You talked to Tommy and Wilma yet? About the murder? Or about whatever environmental case was sending you to Liz's place?"

Gerry was studying the papers in his hand hard, like a man who was trying not to listen.

"When you think about it," Faye said, "any boat that's not a sailboat is a useless bucket without a working motor and fuel. When it comes to fuel, Wilma's the only game for miles around. As for motors, putting metal in salt water is just stupid, but that's what we do. When a motor quits—and sooner or later, it *will* quit—Tommy's the only game for miles around. Anybody that uses this marina is going to cross paths with Tommy or Wilma sooner or later. Guaranteed."

Gerry gave the lab reports an impatient twitch, as if he longed to swat her away like a fly. "I get your point. Tommy and Wilma see all and they know all."

"Well, they did, until Liz died and her marina stopped being open for business."

Gerry finally met her eyes. "Do you think either of them realized—"

Nadia, breathless, interrupted him with a single deadly word. "Arsenic."

Faye's head swiveled in Nadia's direction and Gerry's did the same. Notorious poisons have a way of attracting attention.

Gerry tucked the reports he'd been reading under one arm and reached for the new ones in Nadia's hands. "Arsenic? Just arsenic and nothing else?"

"I see volatiles, but they belong at a petroleum site. Other than the usual suspects, I only see arsenic, but why would I be getting hits for arsenic? And there's something else weird. The arsenic contamination isn't in the same pattern as the petroleum.

It's spread over a wider area and it's not centered on the kerosene hot spot around the old tank. What the hell?"

Faye wasn't sure how sick she should feel about the discovery of a famous poison on her property.

He asked Faye, "Did anybody ever run cattle out here?"

"Only small-scale, for their own use for meat and milk. Never at a commercial level. And it was a long time ago."

He looked around the spot where they stood, so close to the shore and on soil so sandy that it was almost a beach. "This doesn't look like a place where anybody ever grew crops."

"Not to my knowledge," Faye said. Then her honest mouth betrayed her and she said, "The whole island has been rebuilt by hurricanes several times, though. It's possible that, at some point, this was a spot where somebody might have tried to grow something. But if they did, I don't know about it."

Nadia and Gerry huddled over the lab sheets. He mumbled something apparently intended for Faye, since Nadia would already know it. "In the old days, arsenic was a key ingredient in agricultural chemicals."

Oh, dear God. Most of the island had been used for agriculture in "the old days." These people really *were* going to scrape off the entire surface of Joyeuse Island, then charge her for the cost of incinerating the dirt.

Chapter Nine

Joe sat in Emma's kitchen, which was tastefully decorated in serene shades of blue and yellow. Her lovely face, too, was serene. The window over her sink looked out on the Gulf of Mexico. A breath of wind stirred its waters, spreading ripples of turquoise all the way to the horizon. Emma was one of those people who could make you feel good by being herself, yet here Joe sat, intending to bring up two subjects that would make Emma feel bad. He felt like a clueless oaf.

Speaking of clueless oafs, she opened the conversation with a question about the most clueless oaf of all. "So how's your dad?"

Was she asking because she cared about Joe and his fractious relationship with Sly? Or was she asking because Joe's dad had been obviously and publicly hitting on this very dignified woman? His father liked women and women liked him, but Emma wasn't just any woman. Joe imagined that the goddess of trees would look like Emma, tall and straight-backed, with skin the color of seasoned mahogany. Sly Mantooth looked like a long-haul trucker with a history of forgetting to come home when his wife needed him.

"My dad is the same dose of bad news that he's always been. Why do you even let him talk to you?"

"I like your dad. He's going to take me fishing this afternoon."

Joe did not know this, despite the fact that Sly could only keep this date with Emma if he had the use of Joe's john boat.

"Young man, if I could handle Douglass Everett all those years, I can certainly handle your father. He's smooth, but he ain't that smooth. If he wants to get me out of this house and show me a good time, I will let him do it and I will smile the whole while. I am bored. I am lonely. And if you're going to start telling me what to do, you're going to feel the rough side of my tongue."

Joe said the only thing that a man raised by his mother could say to a lady who had said her piece. He said, "Yes, ma'am."

Emma had started their conversation by bringing up one of his two difficult topics—his father—then demolishing his arguments against Emma spending time with Sly before Joe even got a chance to put them into play. Joe's father might not be all that smooth, but Emma was.

Joe caved. He left the subject of his father and moved on to his second conversational topic.

"Who is Oscar, why was my wife talking about him yesterday, and how come you know about him and I don't?"

Faye watched Nadia use a trowel to scoop dirt into a jar with her customary precision. The dirt, enclosed by the hyper-clean jar, was destined for Nadia's floating laboratory.

This time, Nadia was sampling for arsenic and arsenic only. She had already found the limits of the kerosene contamination. The spot of fuel-tainted soil was only a few feet across, and it penetrated only a few inches into the soil. In other words, the tank had not been sitting there leaking for years and years. Faye was the one who had poked a hole in it, so she was solely responsible for any kerosene contamination that she had caused. Fortunately, there didn't seem to be a lot of it, and it didn't seem to have reached the groundwater.

The arsenic, however, showed a different pattern. The levels were high enough to be worrisome. There was no identifiable source. And the contamination was more widespread. Even non-chemist Faye could tell that these were bad things.

Gerry had made Faye's problem visible by sticking red surveyor's flags into the spots where Nadia had collected contaminated samples that tested positive for arsenic. While waiting for the next batch of lab results, he'd gone back to studying his site map. This meant that he didn't notice that Faye was studying him. And those damnable red flags.

There seemed to be no end to them. Nadia had sampled an area the size of…hmm….how big was it? Faye judged that it was the size of a two-car garage. And the arsenic levels had refused to drop to zero as the sampling locations kept creeping outward. This couldn't be good.

The current set of samples was being collected far, far away from those red flags, so far away that they were almost guaranteed to be clean. Gerry called them "background samples" and they were going to tell him the natural state of Faye's dirt. It was possible for arsenic to be naturally present in soil. In other words, it was possible that Gerry's red flags marked nothing that God hadn't put on Joyeuse Island on the day of creation. To test that theory, Gerry had asked Faye to help Nadia find the best spots to collect background samples.

Some of them had come from the front and back lawns of Joyeuse's great house, where no crops were ever grown and, thus, no nasty old-style agricultural products had ever left any arsenic behind. Now Nadia was collecting a sample under the big oak tree that dominated the landscape on this end of the island. It looked to be more than two hundred years old, so if anybody had ever farmed the spot where it stood, they'd done it long ago. She also planned to collect a bit of the very sandy soil near the high water line. Other than those spots, there was no place on the island where Faye could swear that no one had ever tried to grow a crop or pasture a cow.

Faye didn't like the idea that her entire island might have been covered with a fine dusting of arsenic by Mother Nature herself, but her pocketbook hoped that this was true. The state of Florida would be hard-pressed to make her clean up a bunch of arsenic, if she could prove it was a natural part of her island.

This put Faye in the strange position of hoping that Nadia's background samples simply reeked of poison.

Too antsy to wait for the lab results, she decided to walk a circle around the contaminated area, for no better reason than to take yet another look at her problem. An open, shrubby area, dotted by small trees, lay inland from the excavation. Blackberry vines, briars, and shrubby weeds filled the spaces between the trees, so Faye was grateful for her boots and long pants. As she shuffled through the spiny undergrowth, one of those boots struck a piece of wood about the size of her thigh. It looked familiar.

Faye squatted to get a closer look. It wasn't a downed tree branch, nor any other kind of wood that could have gotten there naturally. Though it was weathered and splintery, she could tell that it had been hewn into shape by humans. It took her a second to remember why it looked familiar. When she was a kid, she'd walked this whole island with her grandmother many times, and she remembered a clearing that had once been scattered with several chunks of wood like this one.

She looked around and saw that the trees around her were easily less than thirty years old. She was pretty sure she was standing in the clearing she remembered from childhood.

Faye studied the piece of wood. It had the curved outline of a hollowed-out tree. What had her grandmother said about the broken pieces of wood strewn about the clearing? She'd said that they had once been part of a feed trough. Faye pictured a long, crudely hollowed log holding feed for livestock. The chunk on the ground in front of her looked like a broken piece of a feed trough like that.

Leaving the wood on the ground and circling it in an organized search pattern yielded nothing. The other pieces of the trough had not survived the tropical storms of the years since Faye's grandmother had died. She squatted again to study the weathered wood, pulling out her cell phone to take a picture of it in context with its surroundings. The archaeologist in her wanted to know how old it was.

She reached for the wood, thought again, then donned the rubber gloves in her pocket. If there was arsenic in her soil, there could be poison anywhere. She picked up the wood chunk, and marked the spot with a heavy rock. The wood felt heavy, solid, substantial. Carefully cradling it in both hands, she headed for Nadia and Gerry.

"Nadia, can you test this thing for arsenic?"

"It would take a different extraction technique, but yeah. I could test pretty much anything for arsenic, with enough time and the right equipment."

Gerry looked at Faye like she had suggested looking for arsenic in a turnip. "Why would we spend the money to do that? I only run lab tests when I've got a good reason. That's what they pay me for—to make an efficient testing plan. Otherwise, a robot could do this job. Taking unnecessary samples is like going fishing, just to see what you can find. And it's a waste of time and money."

Faye made a mental note that Gerry got a teeny bit defensive when somebody wanted to change his work plan.

"A long time ago, my grandmother showed me a wooden vat over there. I mean, she showed me what was left of it. Just pieces, really." She pointed at the woods. "She thought maybe it had been a watering trough for horses and cattle, but she didn't remember it ever being used."

Gerry started walking in that direction, but Faye held up a hand. "It's not there anymore. I think this is all that's left."

"A wooden trough from—what? The late 1800s? Early 1900s, maybe? A trough that never held anything but water and horse spit? Why should we test that?"

"I told you that my grandmother didn't remember seeing it used. What if it wasn't for water? You said that cattle farmers used arsenic as a pesticide. Could they maybe have used the trough to dip small animals in flea and tick repellent? Piglets? Maybe even calves or foals?"

Gerry stopped being defensive and nodded his head. He silently pointed at the wood. Nadia took it from Faye's hands, asking him, "You want me to take sample of this, do an extraction, and test it for arsenic?"

"While you're at it, you might as well send it to Tallahassee and tell them to look for pesticides, too. Hell, I don't know. Maybe they kept other stuff in there. Have them do a full screen for inorganics and organics, including herbicides."

A hot, hard knot formed in the pit of Faye's stomach. What had she been thinking? She'd been so intent on puzzling out the reason for the arsenic, she hadn't thought through the consequences of more testing. What if Nadia found something else noxious?

She had gotten no further with her worrying when Gerry's phone rang. He'd hardly said hello when he started running for the shoreline like a man who couldn't care less about Faye's arsenic and kerosene problem. As he ran, he used the hand that wasn't holding the cell phone to fumble with the binoculars around his neck. Being nosy at heart, Faye grabbed her own binoculars and followed him.

Gerry was still yelling into his cell phone when she caught up with him. "—got him? He's still on the water? You got witnesses? Yeah. I can get between him and the marina, if I go right now. Before I do that, tell me you've got the evidence and that you're sending me plenty of backup. We have to get this right." He pointed the binoculars at a black dot on the horizon. "You're sure?"

Gerry must have gotten the answer he wanted, because he wheeled around and ran up the path that led to his boat. He must have sensed that Faye was coming after him, because he turned, pointed a single finger at her, and said, "No." Then he poked the finger toward the ground at her feet and said, "You stay here. This is official business."

Faye would have considered his orders fair enough, if he hadn't delivered them to her like she was a well-trained dog. Maybe Gerry was heading off on official business that had nothing to do with Faye, her property, and her livelihood, but maybe he wasn't. She trained her own binoculars in the direction of that spot on the horizon, twiddled with the focus, and stood there an extra few seconds to be sure she understood what she was seeing.

She knew that boat.

It belonged to Tommy Barnett, the boat mechanic. If Gerry's job was to track down chemicals that had been illegally dumped in the Gulf and on its islands, he would have to be interested in Tommy's boat business. Tommy probably never did a job that didn't generate used oil or solvents or paint, and all that waste had to go somewhere.

Faye paused a moment to judge her level of personal interest in what happened to Tommy. The man wasn't old enough to have buried the kerosene tank on her island. Probably nobody alive was that old. The arsenic? Maybe, but she couldn't think of any boat maintenance chemicals that could have caused her arsenic problem. Maybe paint? She was going to guess no.

Even if Tommy had dumped a trainload of pollutants—and, given Gerry's level of interest, perhaps he had—Faye didn't think he was the cause of her problem, because the tank was just too old.

But this didn't mean she had no personal interest in his fate. If Gerry was after Tommy for environmental crimes, it seemed likely that he'd used the marina as a base for committing them. Could this be why environmental specialist Gerry was working Liz's murder case? Could Tommy's crimes be the reason Liz was killed?

Liz had been Faye's friend. Therefore, Faye had a personal interest in anything that might be related to her murder. Gerry and the person on the other end of his phone call were, even now, trying to catch Tommy while he was still on the water. Maybe Gerry was within his authority to tell Faye to stay away from a rendezvous that might turn dangerous. But was he within his rights to tell her to sit and stay like a naughty cocker spaniel?

Oh, hell no.

Faye knew of no reason that she, as an ordinary citizen with civil rights, couldn't get in her skiff, which was sitting a stone's throw away in waters that belonged to the State of Florida and not to Detective Gerry Steinberg. She saw no reason that she couldn't take it to the marina, getting a very decent head start on Gerry, whose boat was docked a ten-minute walk from where they stood. She could get even further ahead of him before he reached shore, since he would presumably be stopping to arrest Tommy on the way.

Liz would not be at the marina to sell her a piece of pie to eat while she waited, but there was a perfectly nice wooden bench under a shade tree. And there was nothing to keep her from sitting on it until she saw Gerry and his fellow officers bring Tommy to shore.

Chapter Ten

Joe looked more than a little like his father. Emma knew that Joe wished this were not so, but it was, and there was nothing he could do about it. She wished there were a tactful way to ask Joe to describe his mother, or even to ask him to show her a picture of the woman she now knew as Patricia, because Sly had mentioned her by name.

She knew Sly had mentioned Patricia by accident. Emma sensed that he rarely spoke of his dead wife. She rested in a vault inside him that he rarely opened, and he'd kept her name locked in his mouth all these years. When he'd heard himself say, "Patricia," the man's flirtatious patter had sputtered, just for a second, then resumed. Emma wondered why he had opened his mouth for her. What had she done to make him look into that vault?

They'd been talking about Joe and she'd said one of those things a father likes to hear. Something like, "You raised a good son. You'd think he believed there wasn't a grocery store in all of Micco County, if you looked at all the fish and venison he brings me. I keep telling him that I am well able to buy groceries, but the man behaves like he can't hear me. He keeps on filling my freezer."

When Sly had heard himself say, "It was Patricia what taught—" he'd flinched and lost the thread of his thought. His hank of glossy hair had swung in reaction to the reflexive head-bob that filled a silence so brief that she'd almost missed it. Then Sly had picked the thread back up and finished his thought.

"Joe's mama taught him to fish. Can't take credit for that. I like to fish, too, but I was doing long hauls back then, and they don't leave a lotta time for fishing. I was on a real long one when she decided Joe had got big enough not to stab his own thumb with a hook. By the time I got home, he knew near as much as she did, which was a lot. But I did teach him how to handle a bow."

It was a quick conversational skip from this moment of paternal pride to Emma's admission that she hadn't gone fishing since Douglass died. An even quicker shift led to Sly's offer to remedy that situation. Now she was looking forward to being on the Gulf late that afternoon, bundled up against the weak chill of Florida in November. She'd packed some snacks—venison jerky, dried plums, shelled pecans. Come to think of it, Joe had stocked her pantry with all those things, just in case there was an apocalypse that took all the world's groceries but miraculously left Emma whole and able to defend herself.

She wanted to ask Sly whether he'd taught his son to make jerky, but she didn't. She wasn't willing to watch the man swallow hard if the answer forced him to say, "Patricia taught him to do that," or, more likely, "Joe's mama taught him how."

During that momentary silence when Sly hid his grief behind a bobbing head, Emma had time to wonder what Patricia had looked like. Joe's eyes were green and Sly's were black, or nearly so. Sly's hair was black, too, and Emma had seen the sun bring out hidden rusty tones in Joe's hair. Joe's skin tone, which she ordinarily saw as a strong and deep bronze, looked several shades lighter when he stood next to his father. It was possible that Sly was a hundred percent Creek, but Joe obviously was not.

In her mind, Emma folded Joe and Sly into a vision of the absent Patricia. She had been a real live woman—Emma could almost feel her presence—but her image was mutable. Patricia's hair had been blonde or maybe red. Her eyes were green, but perhaps they were blue. Her skin could have been as fair as Snow White's. Joe's limbs were longer and leaner than his father's, so perhaps his mother had been a willowy thing.

Unless she could get one of the Mantooth men to talk about Patricia, there was no way to know anything about her. Why did Emma care, anyway? Maybe for the same reason that she was happy whenever a conversation turned to Douglass. It seemed ungrateful to forget the dead, never looking back.

Joe sat waiting for her to speak. He looked about as stern as it was possible for a tenderhearted man to look, and he wanted her to tell him about Oscar. She would have preferred to divert the conversation to his mother, but that would have been cruel. So…Oscar. What could she say about Oscar without betraying Faye's trust?

Joe repeated himself. "Who is Oscar? And why don't I know about him?"

Emma began with a truthful, but careful, response. "Faye is my friend."

Joe rolled those green eyes that didn't look like Sly's. "I know that."

"I don't rat out my friends."

Oh, crap. Now he looked like she'd slapped him. If she let the conversation die immediately after refusing to betray Faye's trust, then Joe would be free to imagine what Emma might be helping his wife hide.

Infidelity? Gambling debts? A drug habit?

All the obvious things people hid from their spouses sounded ludicrous when applied to Faye, but Joe's imagination was going to use them for a jumping point into madness. By the time he got home, he would have decided that Faye was hip-deep in international espionage, which actually seemed to fit her personality better than run-of-the-mill vices.

Emma was no rat, but she had to do something.

"Don't you need to stop by the museum?"

Joe was already imagining infidelity and gambling debts. There was no room in his head to think about her not-shocking Museum of American Slavery.

She touched him on the arm. "You know I spend my afternoons at the museum. Why don't you stop by today?" She did her best to add weight to her voice, hoping that he would understand that there were things to be learned at the museum that she couldn't say out loud. She repeated herself. "You should come today. This afternoon."

Joe never stopped by the museum, except to see Emma, and he was seeing her now. His eyes said that he was wondering why she wanted him to come to this place he'd seen so many times before. Ever polite, he couldn't turn down her invitation, but he clearly didn't understand why she'd made it. Faye was lucky to have married a man who was so without guile.

"Go find yourself some lunch, Joe. Kill a little time. Then come see me at the museum about two."

"And you'll answer my question then?"

"No. Because Faye will still be my friend at two o'clock this afternoon."

Seriously. How dense could a man be?

"But if you come to my museum at two, you may get your question answered anyway."

Emma wondered if Joe would be able to get the answer to his question quickly enough to get himself and his john boat home by four. If he didn't, there was no way that Sly was going to be able to pilot that boat back to shore in time to take her fishing. And she didn't want to miss that fishing trip. It had been a long time since she'd been alone in close quarters with a good-looking man.

Chapter Eleven

On the surface, the Museum of American Slavery looked almost exactly like it had when it was a rich man's hobby, but Joe knew that things had changed. After Douglass passed on, Emma'd had no place else to focus her loving attention, so she'd lavished it on his museum. Faye had helped her add interactive displays for children. Together, they'd trained volunteers to help kids learn to use scrub boards and hand-cranked cotton gins, and the museum patrons loved the hands-on activities. Joe wasn't sure that these historical games fully illustrated the concept of "It wasn't fun to be a slave," but he was glad Emma's museum was busy.

She opened her office door when he knocked. When he saw that she had visitors, an older man and a woman about his age, he tried to excuse himself, but Emma looked at him with an expression that he used to see on his wife's face, before Faye got so sad. It said, "Would you stop being so clueless?"

Her mouth just said, "It's good to see you, Joe. Come in and sit down." So he did as he was told.

Emma turned to her guests and said, "Joe Wolf Mantooth, I'd like you to meet Delia Scarsdale and Oscar Croft. They're visiting from Ohio." She leaned a little bit on the word "Oscar," and gave Joe a look that said, "Still feeling clueless?"

Joe shook both their hands. Emma clearly wanted him to say something, so he went with the first thing that came to mind. "What brings you folks to Florida?"

While waiting for their answer, he checked their hands, hoping to see wedding rings. No luck.

He trusted Faye. Besides, if he ever lost her, he hoped it wouldn't be to a creaky old dude like this one. But could it be that Faye and her friends were upset with Oscar because he'd been hitting on her?

"Oscar's interested in history—a real scholar, actually—and I'm helping him out. I'm his personal tour guide while he researches his family history." Delia said this with a sparkly smile, like a TV newscaster.

"Don't be silly. You're the scholar." Oscar's veined hand cupped her elbow, just for a second. "Delia here has a PhD in American history and she's a certified genealogist. 'Tour guide' doesn't even begin to describe what she does for clients like me. She interviewed me, learned about my family and my interests, and planned this research trip for me. There's no better way to see this country than to hire Delia as a tour guide, not if you're interested in history."

Joe was still trying to read Delia and Oscar. Emma clearly thought he was going to be able to figure out why Faye was bothered about Oscar. She also clearly didn't intend to help him. He couldn't think of any brilliant questions to ask, so he responded to Oscar's statement about what a brilliant tour guide Delia was.

"I have my own historian to show me the countryside. Well, my wife's an archaeologist, not a historian, but there isn't a spot of ground around here that she can't spend an hour talking about. She knows all the families that lived here and all the battles that happened here. Faye's as smart as they come."

"Your wife's an archaeologist?" Oscar said. "I'm an idiot. I heard Emma say your last name was Mantooth, but I didn't put two and two together. Is your wife Dr. Faye Longchamp-Mantooth?"

"Yes. You know her?"

"We met her once, briefly," Delia offered.

"Emma introduced us," Oscar said. "I had more questions for her than she could have answered in one conversation. Faye took some notes and said that she'd get back with me about the answers, but it's been weeks. I suppose she's been busy with a dig?"

Joe thought of the hodge-podge of pointless holes that Faye had been digging for weeks and said only, "Yes," because it was true. Technically, a pointless hole was a "dig." He also thought that Oscar must have a lot of money if he was paying this historian to spend weeks touring him around Florida.

"Delia is the genealogist, not me. She's helped me trace my family back for generations. But there's a question neither of us could ever answer. We both thought that coming here might get me that answer."

Joe gave Emma an uncertain glance, but he couldn't read her face. He asked Delia the only obvious question. "What's the answer you're looking for? Is there an old family mystery?"

"Yes!" Oscar's eyes lit up under his bushy gray eyebrows. "One of my ancestors went missing right here in Micco County, just after the Civil War."

"Are you thinking Faye can find him?" Joe pictured the holes all over Joyeuse Island. Surely Faye wasn't looking for a man who'd been dead for more than a century.

"Not *him*. Not his body. I'm sure it's gone to dust, although that doesn't mean we won't check every old cemetery in the county while we're here. But I'd give anything for some clue of what happened to my great-great-grandfather. His name was Elias Croft. We know he was sent to Louisiana early on, spending most of the war there. We know for certain that he survived the war, because he sent his medals home for safekeeping and Delia dug up the dates the government gave them to him. That was a pretty bit of detective work she did. She also found his name in a newspaper article about the soldiers occupying Micco County after the war, which was a nice confirmation of stories that came down through the family. We'd always thought he was in Florida at the end of the war, and that he stayed here during Reconstruction. Thanks to Delia, we know for sure."

Delia ducked her head and smiled, peeking up at him through thick lashes. "All you need to know is where to look."

"Well, you did. But that's all we know. There's no record of his death or of his discharge from the Army. When I was a kid, my grandfather had some letters he sent home from Florida, but they went missing after Grandpa went into a nursing home, years ago. I never actually read them, but Grandpa said that he seemed to be doing fine until his letters stopped coming."

"*Stopped*," Delia added, snapping her fingers with their candy-pink nails.

"Grandpa also said that one last letter came, years later, not written by his hand, but by the woman who tended him in his last sickness. She said that Great-great-grandfather Elias had died and that he had asked her to send his sword to his wife in Ohio. As the story goes, his wife burned the letter as soon as she had read it, laid the sword across her husband's pillow, then crawled in bed beside it. Before long, the tuberculosis she'd had for years finally took her, although some say she died of heartbreak. I have the sword, so I know this part was true."

No, Joe thought, *all you know is that you've got a sword.* He said, "So what do you think happened to him?"

"Grandpa told me about some other letters that came during the years after my great-great-grandfather went silent, but before his sword came home. The other letters came from a woman who lived near here in Panacea, who was very upset because Great-great-grandfather Elias was living in sin. She said that he was trying to hide his sin, but she'd seen it. He was living with a woman in an unholy state and he couldn't have done anything about their unholiness, even if he'd wanted to and even if he'd been free to marry, because the woman wasn't white. She said his wife needed to come down here and fetch him home. I never saw those letters, because my grandmother would have never let a little boy read about something sinful."

Joe thought this sounded like a Civil War soap opera. "Did she come? Did she try to fetch him home?"

"By that time, the tuberculosis had her housebound. My grandmother said everybody always said that Elias' wife hung on for all the years after his letters stopped coming, hoping for another one that said what had happened to him. The letters from the busybody in Panacea tortured her, because she was hoping for news when she opened them and she got slander instead. But still she hung on, because those letters told her he was alive."

"Until the sword?" Joe imagined getting a letter from a stranger, telling him Faye was dead and giving him one last thing to remember her by. "She hung on until she got the letter and the sword? Did they come from the busybody in Panacea?"

"No," Oscar said, "though the busybody did do a lot of mailing, all letters telling horrible tales. Or maybe there was more than one busybody writing letters, because they changed in tone over the years. Later letters said that Elias wasn't living in sin. He was being held captive. There were a lot of stories floating around in those days about Union soldiers and the women the Confederate soldiers left behind. I know you've heard some of them."

"There's a house in Mississippi that's supposed to be haunted by the daughter of its owner," Emma said. "They say a Yankee soldier seduced her and she jumped off the balcony when he went away and never came back."

"The legends went both ways. Sometimes it was the Northern soldier who was mistreated," Delia said. "*Gone with the Wind* is our most famous Civil War story, and what does Scarlett do about halfway through the movie? She shoots a Yankee soldier dead. Yes, he's stealing her mother's treasures and he is probably planning to rape her, but that just highlights the conflict. Bad things happen in war, and sometimes civilians are involved. We want to know if Elias Croft was held against his will, perhaps even murdered."

Joe thought the whole thing sounded far-fetched. "So you don't know who the Panacea busybody was? And I bet you don't know anything about the woman who sent home the sword, either."

"Oh, but we do!" Delia looked like someone so delighted by a piece of nasty gossip that she couldn't contain herself.

Delia put her hands on her knees and leaned forward as if she were telling ghost stories around a campfire. She held her silence until she was sure the other three were all listening. Only then did she speak.

"Oscar's grandfather said her name too many times for him to ever forget it, but that's all we have at the moment. I can't seem to track her down, and I've tried. I've found no birth or death records. I've tried all the possible ways to spell her name. I've found a few people in surrounding counties with her surname, or one like it, and some of them were women, but none of them were born at the right time. None of them could possibly be the woman who sent Elias' great-great-grandfather's sword home."

'Then all you got is a story," Joe said.

"I have more than that," Delia said in a voice that reminded him of Faye's in its determination. "I did my doctoral work in a library, sifting through old papers, and I know what you can find when you don't give up. I have more than a story. I have a real woman's name. I know she lived in Micco County, just after the Civil War. That's enough to find her."

"It better be an unusual name," Joe said, "if you're hoping to find one lone woman after all these years."

"It's unusual enough. Somebody around here knows something about Cally Stanton and I'm going to find out what it is."

Chapter Twelve

"So now do you understand what Faye's looking for? Joe?"

He had been looking through Emma, or maybe he'd just been looking at the artifacts lining the museum walls, neatly arranged and cataloged by Faye. He'd been thinking about Faye ever since Oscar Croft and Delia Scarsdale had left the museum, and he'd been thinking about Faye's great-great-grandmother, Cally Stanton, too.

"My wife is looking for something a hundred and fifty years old that probably doesn't exist. It's killing her to think that her great-great-grandmother is being accused of keeping that man against his will. Maybe even murdering him. She wants to prove that it's not true. But what could Faye possibly find to prove that Oscar Croft is wrong?"

"You're talking about this like you think she's looking for a thing. Things are nothing. Faye's looking for an idea. She wants to clear Cally's name. I tried to tell her that somebody made up Oscar's story a long time ago, because it was fun to imagine a man trapped on an island with a crazy woman. I'm sure it was a lot more fun than imagining somebody you loved getting killed in a war or dying slowly of a natural disease. It's just a fairy story they're telling. I told her that. I told her to let it go, but she can't. She's not herself these days, Joe. You know that."

"How did Oscar's family get Cally's name? Stanton ain't such a common name and Micco County ain't such a big place."

Emma didn't look like a woman who wanted to conjure up ghosts and make up sordid stories about them. "Maybe the man met Cally. Maybe he wrote home about her. Maybe he said he had reason to visit her on her island. That doesn't mean that she locked him up on Joyeuse Island for years and years."

"You don't think it could be true?"

"I wasn't there in eighteen-sixty-whatever, so I could be wrong, but no. I don't think it's true. Probably nobody but Oscar, and maybe Faye, thinks it's true. It sounds like the plot of a Clint Eastwood movie I saw before you were born. Maybe Oscar's family got its crazy notions from that very movie and they confused them with the real story about a man who went to war and never came home. Faye should just let Oscar chase his make-believe moonbeams and get on with her life, but you and I both know she's got good reason not to be in her right mind at the moment."

Joe checked his phone. If he didn't get home soon, he was going to be so busted, but Delia and Oscar had taken forever to leave and he wanted to finish this talk with Emma.

"Did these people really tell Faye that her great-great-grandmother kidnapped a Yankee soldier and kept him prisoner until he died? Then, after he was good and dead, she gloried in what she'd done so much that she mailed his sword home to his dying wife?"

"They didn't know Cally Stanton was her great-great-grand-mother—still don't—but yeah. That's what they told her. I still maintain that saying it doesn't mean it's true." Emma handed him a cup of coffee and an oatmeal cookie. "It's my fault she met them in the first place. They came here looking for information on Joyeuse Island, so I introduced them to Faye. I didn't know they would fill her head full of crazy talk."

An oatmeal cookie seemed too heartwarming and homey for this conversation, but Joe didn't turn it down.

"You're sure they don't know that Cally is one of Faye's ancestors?"

"Not that I can tell. How could they? Cally's daughter, Faye's great-grandmother Courtney, was illegitimate, so the family connection almost certainly doesn't show up in the records. That means there's no marriage certificate for Cally and her husband. Probably no birth certificate for Courtney. The Stanton name disappears after that, because Courtney took her husband's name, Wells, when she married. Faye says that even their marriage certificate doesn't show up in the official record. There is no paper trail to tie Cally to Faye. None. Besides, Oscar doesn't seem interested in Cally's descendants, so we don't even know if he's looked."

"Delia would look," Joe said.

Emma nodded to acknowledge the truth in his statement.

Joe thought better when he was chewing, so he took a bite of the oatmeal cookie. "Oscar just wants the truth about happened to his great-great-grandfather."

"Exactly," Emma said in a voice that was about twenty decibels louder than her usual ladylike tone. "And there's nothing wrong with that! Genealogy is fascinating. It's just too bad Oscar is obsessed with a story that sounds like something out of Grimms' Fairy Tales. By the time he finished telling me about his great-great-grandfather being lured to an island, trapped in a cabin in the woods, tortured for years, and murdered, I was expecting him to tell me that Cally was also the wicked witch from 'Hansel and Gretel.'"

"Faye's been reading Cally's stories since before we got married. Longer than that. She's been studying Cally's oral history for as long as I've known her. Faye's great-great-grandmother is as real to her as you and me. She worships Cally Stanton."

Emma let her bone china cup clank into its saucer. "Of course Faye worships that woman! Cally Stanton survived slavery, rape, a hurricane, a war, Reconstruction, Jim Crow, and most of the Depression. And when she wasn't doing all that, she raised a daughter all by herself. There is no room in Faye's image of Cally for murder. For evil."

In Joe's imagination, Cally had always looked like Faye, except she was wearing the faded cotton dress of a woman born a slave.

"How do you know that Faye's not wrong?" he said. "Maybe Cally did do what this man said she did."

"He hasn't got a shred of proof, other than some old stories. All Faye's got is Cally's old stories, too, but I think they hold more weight because somebody wrote them down for her and we still have them. They've survived in her own words and Oscar's ancestor's story hasn't. Cally's memoirs never come out and say, "No, I didn't mistreat Elias Croft, and I didn't kill him, either," but her words don't sound like they came from the mind of a psychopath. Faye's showed me some of that oral history. I admire Cally a whole lot."

"Me, too. I don't like to think that we were wrong about her." The rest of the cookie disappeared into his mouth. "A year ago, my wife would've told Oscar to shove his made-up stories into his suitcase and take himself home."

Emma studied the squint lines at the corner of Joe's eyes. Some of them were new. Living mostly outdoors gave a man wrinkles before his time, but these didn't look like weather wrinkles. They looked like worry wrinkles.

She slid another oatmeal cookie across the table in his direction, as if she thought that comfort food might tamp that worry down a bit. "A year ago, your wife hadn't lost a baby. She wasn't clinically depressed. She wasn't swimming in all those hormones, the ones that were supposed to make her fall in love with a baby that's never coming. Haven't you figured out the last part of this story yet? Where was Faye when she lost the baby?"

His dark face grew still. "She was here with you."

"She started bleeding as soon as Oscar finished telling her his noxious stories and left. I took her to the hospital and you came running. We both know what happened after that." She took his hand. Her fingers were cool. "It wasn't anybody's fault, Joe. You know the doctor said that the baby had been dead for days. But Faye doesn't listen. She's got it in her head that she's carrying Cally's guilt around. She thinks losing that baby was her punishment. No, it doesn't make sense, but it explains why she's so obsessed with digging up proof of Cally's innocence. She calls me night and day, asking if Oscar's said anything else she needs to know. Joe, why don't you take that woman to a doctor and get her some antidepressants?"

"I did. She won't take them. I can't cram them down her throat. And I can't check her into a hospital when she's not sick enough to need it."

"It wouldn't take much to make her that sick. There are days when I think that burning the breakfast toast might be enough to put her over the edge."

Shit. Joe had been hoping that he'd been overreacting. He'd been praying that bystanders who didn't have to live with this weird new Faye were thinking she'd snap out of it any minute now.

"You talk like somebody who thinks she still eats breakfast."

"I see the bones sticking out of her little wrists. I know how much she doesn't eat."

Joe had learned archaeology on the job with Faye. He knew that an archaeologist without a work plan was just a dummy with a shovel, digging worthless holes. "She goes out every day and digs holes to nowhere. What does she think she's going to find, going out there every day and digging willy-nilly?" he asked. "Elias Croft's body? How would she know it was him? Unless she can prove how he died and she can show that it wasn't murder, how's she going to prove that Cally didn't kill him?"

"You think she's hoping to find his skeleton holding a miraculously preserved note that says 'Cally Stanton is a kind and generous woman who did not torture me to death,' in perfect 19th-century penmanship?" Emma took Joe by both his calloused hands and made him lift his gaze from his toes. "Only a woman in Faye's state of mind would think that digging random holes would help this situation. I think she's just digging holes because she can't rest with Elias Croft's death on her mind, and she doesn't know what else to do."

"My wife is hoping for a miracle?"

"Pretty much."

◇◇◇

Faye settled herself on a bench with an excellent view of the Gulf of Mexico, easing her heavy satchel off the shoulder that ached all the time. If anybody were to pilot a boat into this marina that had belonged to Liz, Faye would be their witness. So would the two people sitting over across the parking lot in the car marked "Micco County Sheriff's Office." She figured they were waiting for Gerry to arrest Tommy Barnett and deliver him to them.

She missed Liz in weird little ways. It was unthinkable that she was within shouting distance of the grill without a Coca-Cola in her hand, but there was a padlock on the door that should have taken her to a cooler full of Cokes. Faye had learned to hustle through that door and buy one as soon as she set foot on Liz's dock. If she didn't, Liz would soon show up, shove a can in her hand, and disappear back into the kitchen. If Faye made the mistake of waiting that long, trying to pay for it inevitably resulted in profanity. If, however, Faye managed to get inside, grab a Coke, and show up at the cash register with her money in hand, Liz would usually let her pay.

Was this logical? Was friendship ever logical?

Sitting on this bench without doing the Coke dance with Liz made Faye feel empty. Worse than empty.

Even the boat slips were empty. Faye missed the slapping sound of waves on the fiberglass hulls of pleasure boats. The marina had emptied overnight, as people acted on their fears that their boats might be impounded by the police, although if they hadn't been impounded already, Faye reckoned they weren't going to be. More likely, they might be seized by the bank that held Liz's business loans.

The few remaining boats were in the slips Liz rented to Tommy for boats belonging to his clients. Despite being shiny and well-maintained, Faye knew they were just broken toys, so it made her sad to look at them

Her own oyster skiff was the only functional boat in sight, except for the dark spots on the distant water. Faye's binoculars identified these spots as the law enforcement vessels that were poised to nab Tommy.

Gerry seemed to think the sketchy boat mechanic was dumping chemicals in the Gulf. Was he?

Faye stood and walked toward Tommy's shop. It, too, was padlocked, although the padlock didn't look as final as the one on the restaurant that was keeping Liz's old customers out. Tommy's padlock looked like it was opened and locked again on most days. The metal around its keyhole was scratched and polished bright by its daily encounter with a key. The old door sported an oil stain behind the spot where the lock hung, and the stain measured at least a foot across. It was a remnant of an owner with greasy hands. Tommy had probably turned the padlock's key not long before, just before he got into the boat that Gerry and his fellow law enforcers were now chasing.

Faye walked around behind the maintenance shop to get a better view and she saw that every owner of a functional boat hadn't skedaddled. A familiar john boat had been dragged onto the sandy shore and Faye realized that she hadn't seen Joe's car in its usual spot in the back of the parking lot. Liz had always let him keep it there for free, right next to Faye's. If he'd brought Michael and his dad ashore without even the feeble entertainment that Liz and her restaurant had offered, he must really be bored.

The sound of boat motors reached her ears. Even before she looked out into the Gulf, she had a fair idea of the boats she'd see. Certainly, she'd see Tommy piloting his crappy-looking boat that was faster than it looked. And, equally certainly, she'd see Gerry's official boat streaking across the water in Tommy's direction, accompanied by the backup he'd requested.

She fiddled with the focus on her binoculars and she saw that she wasn't wrong. Tommy, Gerry, and the boats carrying Gerry's backup were all heading her way.

The boats' motors were straining, the sound rising in volume and intensity. Tommy and his pursuers had picked up speed. Squinting into the distance, she saw four dots converging on a single dot that didn't have a chance. She guessed that Tommy had minutes of freedom left to him, but no more.

◇◇◇

"Dr. Longchamp-Mantooth, if you don't get in your boat and go, I'll arrest you, too."

Faye had quite enjoyed watching the boat chase that had ended with Tommy being escorted into the backseat of a marked car. Gerry looked like he hadn't enjoyed being part of the chase nearly as much as Faye had enjoyed watching it.

"You'll arrest me for what?" she asked.

"Obstructing justice."

Faye looked around. "Your suspect is being arrested way over there. I'm sitting on a bench way over here. I'm not obstructing anything. And I'm sitting here peacefully, I might add, so don't threaten to arrest me for disturbing the peace." She crossed her arms across her chest. "I heard what you said before you rushed out to arrest Tommy. You think he's dumping chemicals... somewhere. Probably out in the Gulf. I want to know whether you think he's the reason you and your people are digging up my land. Has Tommy been dumping on my island? Tell me that much and I'll go away."

"I don't have to tell you anything. But think about it, Faye. Where would Tommy have gotten that antique kerosene tank?"

She watched as the marked car carrying Tommy eased out of the parking lot and onto the narrow, two-lane highway skirting the shore. "Farmers around these parts don't waste much," she said. "If one of them had a tank that could last a hundred years, then the tank wouldn't get dumped. It would get used. Having no money makes you creative that way. But maybe somebody thought that tank might start leaking any day and they decided that they wanted to get rid of it before it turned into a problem. Maybe Tommy got paid to get rid of it."

"Didn't look like it to me. Looked like the dirt on top of that kerosene tank had been there a long time, but I'm not an archaeologist. Maybe I was wrong."

She shook her head. "No, I don't think you're wrong. I think the dirt did look like it hadn't been disturbed in a long time, so long that we might as well call the tank mine. But I don't know where the arsenic came from. I've looked up all the most common uses for arsenic and I'm stumped. I've got a list that starts with 'old agricultural chemicals' and goes through 'outdated cures for leprosy' and ends with 'pressure-treated lumber.' I don't think Tommy has been handling any of those things."

Gerry gave a short shake of his head, probably because he was too pissed off at her to say, "I don't think so, either," out loud.

Since he didn't seem inclined to help her figure out her problem, Faye kept talking. "If Tommy is dumping waste illegally, I figure it's something common like waste oil and paint thinner and old solvents. Those things don't have arsenic in them, so he probably didn't give me my arsenic problem. But if I'm wrong about that, will you tell me? If it turns out that Tommy poisoned my island, I want him to feel the consequences. And I want to know that he felt them."

"I suppose if somebody slipped into my backyard and poured herbicide on my vegetable garden, I'd feel pretty harsh toward the polluter, myself. My final report on your fuel spill will cover all the possible sources of your pollutants, and it will be in the public record. If Tommy did this, you'll know it."

"There used to be a bunch of leaky drums stored out back of Tommy's shed."

Gerry's head jerked involuntarily toward the concrete pad behind the shed. "When? I've never seen anything back there."

"I'm sure you've been watching Tommy for a long time. Maybe months. Maybe a year?"

Gerry declined to give her a time range.

"Well, I've been using this marina as a jumping-off point to get to my island for way more than a year. I've had my own boat slip since Wally owned the place. My grandmother used this boat ramp since before I was born. I can't tell you exactly when they were there, but I'm sure I remember drums on that pad. They were rusty and they stank. They wouldn't have stunk if they weren't leaking. And if they were leaking something like water or vegetable oil, they still wouldn't have stunk."

"Please tell me you have pictures."

"I have pictures of my son fishing over there. I took them last year." She pointed to the secluded shoreline where Joe's john boat was beached. "And I have pictures of my other boat, the *Gopher*, after Joe and I finished restoring her, sitting in a slip right next to Tommy's shed. That was maybe three years ago, before I started keeping the *Gopher* at home. If the drums were there when either of those pictures was taken, they'll be in the background. If you need me to go back further, I can dig around on my computer. And if you need me to go way back, I have my grandmother's picture albums."

Again, the slight nod of a man who accepted information when it was offered, but didn't give it easily.

"I'll look at those photos with the best magnifying glass I've got, looking for a drum labeled 'Arsenic' but, Gerry, you know a lot more about these things than I do. You know what products have arsenic in them and you know what color drums they're sold in and you know what their company logos look like. If I bring you those photos and they tell you where my arsenic is coming from, will you tell me?"

"Yes. You'll know it as soon as I do."

Faye knew this was a bold and forthright statement for a man who used information for currency. She felt victory, but she could be as noncommittal as he was, so she said only, "That's good to know."

The feeling of victory ebbed when she saw her husband pull his car into the parking lot and step out of it alone. Faye's fragile grasp on rationality might have held if he'd walked right over to her and said something like "I just came ashore to pick up a jug of milk." Except there was no milk in his hand, no bread, no eggs. Still, if Joe had been a better liar or even a better poker player, she might have been even-tempered enough to ask him nicely where he'd been and listen to his answer before she flew off the handle.

But Joe was no liar. When his eyes met hers, she saw that he had wanted this odd trip ashore, which had been important enough to leave Michael and Sly behind, to be a secret. She and Joe didn't have secrets. She didn't know what he had been doing, but she could see on his face that it had been a betrayal.

If she'd given Joe a chance to answer her silent accusation, she knew he would have said, "We never had secrets before, but we do now. You've been keeping secrets from me for weeks," and he would have been right.

Faye gave him no such chance. She excused herself and left Gerry staring at her back. The motor of her oyster skiff was roaring to life within seconds. The marina's no-wake zone was theoretical in the absence of other boats to be jostled around by the powerful waves she left behind her, so she violated it. She knew that Joe was looking at her back, too, as she goosed the throttle as high as it would go.

◇◇◇

"Shit."

Joe didn't curse often. This particular curse word was prompted by the sight of Faye standing between him and his boat. It was followed by "Oh, holy shit," when she looked him dead in the eyes before hustling straight to her skiff.

He hurried to his own boat, but not because he thought he had any prayer of catching up with her so he could talk some reason. Faye had a head start, she was practically born in a boat, and she had nerves of steel. She would be getting to Joyeuse Island first, no question about it. If Joe were a betting man, he'd bet that she would disappear into its woods and not reappear until bedtime. If she didn't show up at bedtime, he didn't know what he was going to do.

Chapter Thirteen

Faye's feet hit her dock and she started running for the woods. She didn't even go indoors to set down the satchel she always carried because it was more practical than a purse. Her home was at her back and she kept going, heading for…somewhere. The contamination site? A random spot where she intended to dig yet another pointless hole? Who the hell knew?

She only knew that she couldn't look at Joe, not right now. She saw that look on his face, morning and night. It said, "Talk to me. Hold me. I lost a baby, too." This afternoon, it had also said, "I'm going to fix things between us, whether you like it or not."

Faye wasn't ready to be fixed.

When Joe neared the island, he saw that Faye's oyster skiff was bumping hard against the dock with each passing wave, because she had done a terrible job of tying it up. This one thing, a lurching boat, spoke as clearly to Joe as anything Faye could have said. His wife was struggling, trying to keep her face above water, and that was all she could do. She couldn't even spare the emotional energy to take care of her boat.

Her trail headed into the woods. Footprints, scuffed leaves, disturbed pine straw, broken twigs. He could track her. She knew he could track her. But should he do it or should he leave her alone?

He wasn't finished securing his boat and Faye's when his father walked up, holding Michael by the hand.

"I'll take that john boat off your hands, Son, if you don't mind."

"Emma told me you were taking her fishing, so I reckon you're gonna need a boat. Help yourself."

Sly carried a canvas bag and a tackle box. Joe would guess the bag held two peanut butter sandwiches and two beers. When he was a kid, his bottle had held root beer, but Emma was of age. She could drink and make decisions for herself, even bad decisions like dating his father. Joe handed over the boat and received his son in exchange.

Sly paused at the head of the dock, looking down at Faye's dainty tracks running away from the house, her family, everything. Joe knew his father was as good a tracker as he was, so he, too, could write the story of Faye's trail by the shape of the prints she left behind.

"Going after her, Son?"

"Don't know. Would you?"

His father stepped down into the boat, bending to stow his gear. His face was hidden for a moment, then he stood up and pushed thick black hair out of his eyes. "Why the hell you asking me what to do? Did I make your mama happy?"

As he stooped over his work again, a few mumbled words escaped from behind the curtain of his hair. "Make a lot more sense to do the opposite of what I would've did."

The roar of a starting motor silenced everything else. Sly Mantooth headed for his rendezvous with Emma without a backward glance.

Joe looked down at his own son. Was he going to take him along on a search for his mother? It wasn't like he could sneak up on her while Michael was singing "Pop Goes the Weasel" at the top of his lungs.

Without Michael, Joe was fully capable of moving silently under the trees until he found his wife, but if she really didn't want him with her, he didn't want to be there. Arguing against that was his father's advice to do the opposite of what he would have done. Joe's clearest memory of his parents' marriage, and of his own childhood, was his father's absence. By that logic, he should go to Faye.

In the end, he decided to take Michael back in the house and feed him some supper. His father wouldn't be out late, because it was a first date and Emma was a lady. She would send him home. If Faye hadn't come home by the time Sly got back, Joe would go looking for her then. He didn't feel good about this decision that wasn't a decision, but he was going to have to live with it.

Sheriff Rainey studied the lowlife across the table from him. Law enforcement in Micco County had taken a strange fork in the road lately. Rainey knew he didn't understand the science required to bust Tommy Barnett for his environmental crimes. That's why he needed Gerry Steinberg. But Steinberg had no experience dealing with this kind of lowlife. Tommy Barnett wasn't Steinberg's typical perpetrator. Rainey imagined that a typical adversary for Steinberg would be the CEO of a chemical company that had violated its hazardous waste storage permit.

Tommy Barnett had been caught redhanded, throwing paint cans and five-gallon buckets of mystery sludge overboard in broad daylight. He had been behaving like the typical adversary of the sheriff of a rural county, which was to say that he'd been acting like a drunken idiot who might possibly have recently murdered a nice lady. This was why Steinberg needed a cagey lawman like Sheriff Ken Rainey.

Barnett had been surrounded by Steinberg and his men, but he had kept acting like a man bent on believing that all the laws of probability might fall in his favor this time. He really seemed to have been hoping to hit the criminal's lottery. First, he'd thrown everything in his boat over the side. Why did he think this was a good idea? Deputy Steinberg had been getting video and there had been a half-dozen witnesses in those boats chasing Tommy Barnett.

Because Barnett had behaved like a drunken idiot, Rainey now needed to send down some divers to fetch the evidence. And also to make sure the evidence didn't leak anything noxious into the Gulf of Mexico, which was already suffering enough. Tommy should have known that this move was only going to make the sheriff mad.

Then the fool had taken off for shore as fast as his piece-of-junk boat would take him. Granted, the thing would fly. Boat engine maintenance was Tommy's legitimate business and, judging by the speed of his attempted escape, he was actually pretty good at it. But what did he hope to accomplish? Even if he had made it to shore ahead of the four law-enforcement boats that had pinned him so efficiently that he would have had to ram one to get away, what did he plan to do? Get in his car and drive to Mexico? Surely he knew that Steinberg had stationed officers on the single highway that served the marina.

Stupid. And provably so. But was he stupid enough to kill the landlady who lived and worked thirty feet from his mechanic's shop? Rainey didn't know, so he thought it was time to find out.

"What did Liz think about your hazardous waste dumping habits? Did she use your services? Did she ask you to pay her to keep quiet about it?"

"What did she have that needed dumping? Leftovers off her customers' plates?"

"Lots of people paint. Lots of people change their oil. Maybe there was some asbestos in the kitchen."

Tommy's face was fleshy and sunburnt. Even the flesh of his eyelids looked tan and thick. Wrinkles networked his forehead. Broken blood vessels showed through the skin of his nose. This was the face of a man who lived outside, worked outside, played outside. It was also the face of a man whose liver was working hard to keep up with years of abuse. Alcohol, probably. Or maybe he had breathed in enough chemical waste to overstress his liver.

"Would you have killed her if she found out what you were up to?"

"I gave you my alibi the day after she died, the first time you came sniffing around. Lolita told you where I was the night Liz died."

"I don't find it hard to believe that you visit hookers, Tommy. What other woman would have you? But you cannot make me believe that you pay them by personal check."

"Just one. She knows me. When I don't have cash, she takes a check. I don't hardly ever have cash."

"You're telling me that her johns are willing to give her a piece of paper with their names signed on it."

The eyelids looked heavier, like they were narrowing due to their own weight. "I don't know about the others. I just know about her and me and the way we do things."

Rainey wouldn't have believed it if he hadn't seen the check, written and dated on the morning after Liz's death. It neatly tied up the loose ends of Lolita-the-hooker's story that Tommy had been with her all night. It didn't prove anything, but when accompanied by an unbroken line of cancelled checks that said Tommy had paid Lolita the same fee every Saturday morning for time out of mind, it added some heft to the man's alibi. She could still be lying but, for Lolita, it would be like a lie told by a guilty man's wife, not like a lie told by a woman who was being paid to hide the truth. Good luck with getting Lolita to change her story.

There was no way that college boy Gerry Steinberg was going to be able to deal with these people. It looked like Rainey and Steinberg were going to be bound together tight until they disentangled Tommy Barnett and his dumping from the murder of Liz Colton.

Rainey nodded at Tommy, not politely. Then he told him he could go, but not to even think about leaving town.

Sly had stopped fishing when Emma said, "We're going to sink this boat if we keep pulling fish out of the water. We should leave a few of them where they are. For next time."

If a bear could laugh, it would sound like Sly Mantooth, and Emma liked bears. She listened as he gave her his growly laugh and said, "I thought you were going to outfish me, until I started letting you bait my hook. That's when I started hauling 'em in. Don't laugh! You saw it. I think they like the way your pretty hands smell."

He reached for her hands and she let him, trying not to be nervous about whether they smelled like fish scales.

"I'm having a real good time, but the sun's getting low. I should get you home," he said, turning one hand over and stroking a single finger across its palm. "Can we do this again?"

"Absolutely. Next time, I'll have the makings for coleslaw and hushpuppies in my kitchen. If you'll gut the fish, I'll fry them."

"I'm sold." He let go of her hand long enough to secure their rods and close the tackle box. Then, deliberately, as if he'd been thinking hard and waiting for the time, he touched her again. This time, his hand was on her neck and his thumb was taking a slow path down her jawbone. The kiss was firm and slow, but there was only one.

He pulled away, grinned at the setting sun, and bellowed "We're losing daylight!" over the roar of a boat motor that was just getting started. As the john boat wheeled around toward shore, it kicked up a crystalline spray of sea water. It had been years since Emma had laughed for no reason at all.

Then they flew past Liz's marina on their way to Emma's private dock and her laugh caught in her throat. She remembered that Sly had been the one who found Liz and she wondered how it felt for him to pass the spot where she died. She looked up at him, but he mistook her glance. With a grin calculated to charm, he reached out a hand and squeezed her gently on the knee.

Sly was gone. There had been just one more kiss and Emma was the one who had stolen it.

She opened the refrigerator. She felt thirsty, despite the thermos of lemonade that Sly had very hospitably provided. The sandwich he'd brought her was also long gone. Being on the water made her thirstier and it also made her hungrier, so she poked around until she found the makings of a ham-and-cheese sandwich. She'd eaten half of it before she remembered to look at her phone.

Flicking on the ringer, she saw a message from an unfamiliar number. She tapped on the notification and Oscar Croft's voice spoke.

"I'm sorry to have missed you, Emma, and I apologize for the spur-of-the-moment invitation, but there's a show at a dinner theater in Tallahassee that I thought you might enjoy. If you get this message before five, I think we could still make it, so give me a call and let me know if you're interested. I've been wanting a chance to get to know you better."

Well, this was a first. She'd met Douglass when he was an ambitious twenty-five-year-old who knew what he wanted. He had wanted to be the most successful contractor for miles around, and he had wanted sixteen-year-old Emma Fairbanks bad enough to wait until her daddy couldn't stop her from marrying him. Emma wondered what Sly would think if he knew that he was only the second man who had ever kissed her.

And now there was another man asking for the pleasure of her company. Oscar didn't have Sly Mantooth's looks, but it wasn't fair to compare the two. Sly had at least a ten-year advantage on seventy-ish Oscar. Emma didn't care so much that he was older. Douglass had been about Oscar's age, and she would have taken Douglass right then, on the kitchen floor, if she could have had him back for the evening. She just wasn't sure Oscar was for her.

Testosterone had hung in the air around Douglass, just as it did around Sly. A manly aura can't be faked, and Oscar didn't have it. But he was confident and worldly, and she was pretty sure he was smart enough to provide interesting dinner table conversation.

She must not be all that vain, because Oscar's invitation surprised her. She wouldn't have thought she was his type. She hadn't been able to pinpoint his relationship with Delia, who was certainly young enough to be his daughter. Maybe his granddaughter, if he'd started early.

Delia was solicitous of Oscar, but maybe she was showing respect for his age. And, well-mannered though he might try to be, Oscar couldn't hide his appreciation of her perky blonde looks. Emma hadn't been sure, but she'd thought they might be a May-December couple until the day she saw him flirting shamelessly with Liz, right in front of Delia. After that, she'd mentally filed Oscar and Delia under the category of "Flirtatious, but Just Friends."

She doubted there had been time for Oscar to ask Liz out before she died, if that had been the goal of his flirting. Liz would have enjoyed the dinner theater, and Emma would have happily lent her a dress for the occasion, since Liz had certainly not owned one. She and Liz had been friends and Emma missed her, but they couldn't have been more different. She would never have thought that a man who had been attracted to Liz—or to Delia, for that matter—would see anything in her.

Every bit of Delia was calculated to attract attention, from her glossy hair to her pedicured and sandaled feet. If Emma mentally subtracted thirty years of hard living from her memory of Liz, she got a fiery-headed bombshell. Liz wouldn't have had Delia's polish, nor her PhD, but she would have had the same unapologetic sex appeal. Being in the same room as Liz's bawdy repartee had always made Emma want to loosen up and live a little.

Emma, by contrast, wore her hair natural and was letting it gray at its own speed. Her clothes flowed free in places where women like Liz and Delia would have worn them tight. She thought of herself as sedate, conservative, even matronly, but maybe there was still a possibility of romance for her, after all.

She checked her watch. Oscar's five o'clock deadline had come and gone while she was on the water, but she would call him when she finished her sandwich. There was no sense in looking too anxious. Emma wondered what Douglass would think if he knew that she was learning to juggle men at this late date.

Chapter Fourteen

Faye's brain was fogged when she reached the far side of the island and she was tired all over, so tired that she wished she could sit down in the weeds and stay there. There were times lately when she believed she was sad for no reason and that there was no beginning or end to it. Then she would remember the baby and remembered the beginning of it. When she remembered that there would never be another baby, she believed the sorrow would never end.

She wasn't sure how to find her way through the sadness, but right now she was sure that she needed to find the overgrown spot on her island that had once been a clearing. She remembered that her grandmother had told her something about those chunks of wood, something that Gerry and Nadia should know as they waited for the results of the arsenic testing, but she couldn't remember what it was. Faye needed to find the place and sit there until her mind was still, until she could trust her memory.

What had her grandmother said about the wood? Faye remembered that she'd said it had once been part of an old trough or tub, but that the trough had been cracked and broken to pieces for as long as she remembered. When was her grandmother born? Around 1930. So the trough dated to the early twentieth century or before. Maybe it was as old as the buried kerosene tank.

Something else was brushing against Faye's memory, but her mind had felt like a frail thing since the miscarriage. She walked straight to the spot where she'd found the wood and crouched there. Closing her eyes helped her call up her grandmother's face. Without her eyes to distract her, she was free to focus on memory alone. She could hear the waves and the feel of the wind's breath on her cheek.

The waves and the wind hadn't changed in the twenty-five years since she'd lost her grandmother. They hadn't changed in thirty years. Three hundred. It took no effort to believe that her grandmother was there again, right there beside her. Faye missed her so. She could hear her grandmother's quiet whisper over the noises of the water and air. "Mama said that this was where The Monster Man lived. This very spot."

Now that she was a mother, Faye marveled at her grand-mother's ability to tell her this scary story so matter-of-factly that young Faye hadn't been left with a paralyzing fear of monster men. Faye's grandmother hadn't believed in any monster men, but *her* mother Courtney Stanton Wells had believed wholeheartedly, and Courtney's fears had somehow gotten connected in Faye's grandmother's mind with a battered and broken wooden trough.

Faye's grandmother had said that Courtney was scared to death of The Monster Man. She'd tried to make her daughter believe in him, but Faye had known her no-nonsense grandmother. Good luck with any effort to make her believe in anything beyond the here and now. This had not endeared her to the minister who had spent a great deal of his career trying to save her soul.

Faye's grandmother had said that Courtney never went to this end of the island, not even when she was old. Courtney had put a lot of effort into convincing her daughter to fear this place the way she did. Therefore, after Courtney passed, Faye's grandmother had liked to go there now and then, just to tempt fate and to vex her mother's ghost. Not that she had believed in ghosts.

"Mama said his cabin was over thataway when she was a little girl." Faye's grandmother's hand had shaken when she pointed her finger, not from fright but from age and ill health. "She said if she went up in the top part of the big house, she could see his lantern glowing at night. One time, she saw that light spill out the door when he opened it up and come outside. She said that if she woulda tried to sneak through the woods and get a look at him, her mama would have switched her legs good. Mama wouldn't never have done anything her mama told her not to do, because she was always a good little girl, but I would have. Just to prove he wasn't real. Or if he was real, I would've wanted to prove that he wasn't really no monster."

So Cally had believed in him, too. She'd believed in him well enough to take a switch to her daughter Courtney to keep her out of these woods.

Oscar Croft believed that Cally herself was a monster. He thought she'd imprisoned a man and, eventually, killed him. And he thought she was cold-blooded enough to write his wife when she was done and tell her he was dead.

If she were holding a man prisoner on the far end of her island, would Faye threaten to take a switch to Michael, if it were the only way to keep him from finding out? It was a pointless question, because Faye could never make herself believe she could hold someone prisoner. If she couldn't imagine that, then she certainly couldn't imagine beating the curiosity out of her own child.

Faye reached into her satchel and pulled out photocopies of the sheaf of pages she'd found in her two-hundred-year-old house. They had been hidden in a book even older than the house. When the oral historians from the Federal Writers' Project had come to ask Faye's great-great-grandmother Cally Stanton for her memories of being a slave, Cally had given them a lot more than tales of the time before emancipation. She seemed to have given them every memory she had. Parts of her oral history read more like the transcript of a session on an analyst's couch than straight-ahead autobiography.

Faye had pored over these pages. She had thought often of publishing them, but she'd always shied away from showing this private thing to the world. Perhaps it was silly of her. Cally had told the stories to someone who intended to publish them but never got around to it, but Faye didn't think a woman who lived her whole life on an island that rarely even got mail could have conceived of the digital age and its absence of privacy.

On these pages, Cally had left behind a real and gritty look at what it was like to be enslaved, but she'd also left herself here. Anger, love, regret, pride, an occasional bit of spite—Faye felt like she knew Cally. She felt like some parts of her *were* Cally. Nothing could sway Faye toward Oscar's belief that Cally had killed his ancestor Elias Croft...nothing but the fact that she was pretty sure that Cally herself had mentioned the name Croft, maybe more than once.

Faye had been carrying these pages around for weeks. She'd been afraid to read them, afraid they might tell her that she was descended from someone who did something purely evil. If she let her mind slip down that path, she was only steps from believing she had inherited the same taint from Cally or, before her, from Andrew Whitehall, the slaveowner who had raped Cally's mother. And if it were true that evil could be handed down in that way, then maybe it was her fault, after all, that the baby had died.

Joe wouldn't let her voice that fear, but he couldn't stop her from feeling it. Liz's death seemed to carry the grisly proof of it. So did Chip's and Wally's. And Douglass...oh, how could she even stand to think that his death might be her fault? Maybe everything she touched was doomed to go to dust before its time.

Faye knew that she shouldn't be alone these days. Without Joe or Magda or Emma nearby, it was too easy to listen to the doubts that whispered to her when no one else could hear. It was unwise to re-read Cally's diary, looking for evil, without mooring herself to her friends and their stability. Unwise or not, here she was doing it.

Leaning back against a tree, Faye thumbed through the familiar pages. She turned to the end, because she remembered that Cally had closed her memoirs with the story of the day Yankee soldiers came to Joyeuse Island. Cally's common-law husband, Courtney Stanton, had just died, and she had named their baby girl after him. How odd to think that Oscar's great-great-grandfather might have been there that day, alive and looking at young Cally and her new baby.

Excerpt from the oral history of Cally Stanton, recorded by the Federal Writer's Project, 1935

I always laugh when I remember the day the Yankees came to liberate the slaves on Joyeuse. They were naturally more gape-jawed when they found us already free.

Mister Courtney always said I was a charming liar. Well, I did him proud that day. I knew it wouldn't be safe to let anybody, not the Yankees or anybody, know that we didn't have a master any more. The laws weren't good back then and the courts were even worse. Somebody was liable to come take the land—my land—and make my workers farm it for just about nothing.

So I told them the master and his wife had gone to Tallahassee that very day to pledge their allegiance to the Yankee flag. Then I showed them young Courtney, my baby, and made sure they knew that my job was to take care of the master's heir. I forgot to mention that young Courtney was a girl and not entitled to own anything in her own name. I also forgot to mention that she wasn't white, so she wasn't entitled to anything in this life at all.

Nope. There was no answer on this page. After this passage, Cally had rambled on about her life since the Yankees left, but there was no mention of Elias Croft on those final pages. Faye's sanity breathed a sigh of relief, but Faye herself wasn't done. She was sure that she remembered a Croft figuring into Cally's story somehow. The reminiscences of old people don't flow with the predictability of carefully composed history, so she flipped back a few pages, looking for him, and there he was.

Excerpt from the oral history of Cally Stanton, recorded by the Federal Writer's Project, 1935

When I heard that the Yankees was coming to Joyeuse Island, I knew I was going to have to give a little so that I wouldn't lose a lot. I'd hid the valuables, but I couldn't hide all the food, being as how a lot of it was still walking around on four feet. I thought maybe if I showed the soldiers a bit of hospitality, they wouldn't take my livestock and raid my garden and leave us to starve.

It's a good thing that boats move slow and armies move slower. One of the young'uns was out fishing that day afore the sun was up good, and she come running with the news. Men in blue coats was gathered on the shore, making ready to get in their boats. The hurricane washed away everything on Last Island years afore that, so I knew there was only one place they was planning to go in those boats. Here. To Joyeuse Island. And there ain't never been a group of men that big that wasn't hungry.

I sent the young'uns to take the pigs and cows into the woods. Wasn't nothing I could do with the chickens but let 'em run wild and hope the Yankees wasn't fast enough to catch 'em or stupid enough to shoot at 'em and risk killing folks standing nearby. I told the women to each one pack a basket of food from the larder — sacks of meal, slabs of salt pork, bags of dried peas — and to high-tail it into the swampiest land they could find. I wanted it to be hard for the soldiers to find the food but, more'n that, I wanted it to be hard for them to find the women.

Then I told the men to arm themselves with what they had, which was farming tools. A strapping field hand will make you think twice if he's standing there holding a scythe or a sickle or even a good stout rake. My field workers and their rakes met the soldiers at the shore and, when their commanding officer asked them who was in charge, they brought him to me.

Captain Croft treated me respectful. He listened to my lies about how the owners of Joyeuse was loyal Union citizens who'd be coming home any minute now. He seemed as concerned as I was about how those loyal Union citizens wouldn't be too happy if they come home and found that their very own soldiers had left the place in a mess. Then he told me his soldiers was hungry and asked me what I'd do in his shoes.

I was ready for him. I showed him a big crate full of rags his men could use for bandages and another crate loaded with moonshine to ease their pain. All my life, I'd tended everybody on the island when they was sick and I knew he had men who was bad wounded and needed more 'n that, but it was all I had. Then I took him into the workyard where the cooks were stirring great pots of hominy. I told him to tell his men to get in line with their cups in hand, because there was enough in those pots for everybody to have some. Then I pointed to a great big pile of roasted sweet potatoes and said they could have one apiece. It was a feast for a bunch of men who'd been living on hardtack, and I hoped it was a big enough feast to buy their friendship.

Captain Croft touched his cap—and me not a white woman!—and went to give his troops the good news. We had some lean times that winter when we wished for those sweet potatoes and pots of hominy, but that food did its job. The Yankees went away and nobody got hurt. Not even any of the pigs.

Faye saw nothing in this account to suggest that Cally ever changed her mind and murdered the man who had touched his cap out of respect for her...if this Captain Croft and Oscar's ancestor Elias were one and the same. Maybe Oscar could help her figure out whether their families were linked by the meeting Cally described. More likely, Delia was the one who could make the connection, if it existed, but Faye didn't want either of them examining every twig on her family tree. She wanted privacy, time alone to heal. She wanted Oscar and Delia to go away and leave her alone.

Faye was glad that she'd procrastinated about publishing Cally's story. She had no professional or personal obligation to share it with Oscar or anybody else. She put the pages back in her satchel, leaned back against the tree, and rested while the sun finished going down.

Chapter Fifteen

It was completely dark outside, except for a moon that was just past full. Michael was asleep, so the house was quiet. Joe had no idea where his wife was, nor his father. He was alone.

Faye had been gone for hours, but Joe couldn't go after her now. Well, he could, but it would require waking up Michael and walking through the dark woods with him in his arms.

Alone, armed with only moonlight and instinct, he could have found Faye's hiding place. But carrying a squalling two-year-old? He would only find her if she wanted to be found. If he'd known that his father would be so late coming home, he would have tried to find Faye while the sun was up and their toddler was awake and happy.

Maybe it was just as well that he hadn't gone after Faye. Before he went looking for her, he needed to decide what he was going to say.

◇◇◇

The gentle knock at Emma's front door surprised her. She had been tired from being out on the water, so she'd bathed and dressed for bed before the sun was gone. It embarrassed her to think that someone might see her in her nightgown so early. She might be an old woman, but she didn't like to act like one.

Emma didn't recognize the knock and she had no notion of who might be at her door. Her heart fluttered a moment, reminding her that Douglass had died at the hands of intruders in their home, but she told it to settle down. Her husband's murderers had not knocked politely and waited for him to answer the door.

A stout replacement stood in place of the door destroyed by those killers. It had a deadbolt that shot deeply into the doorframe to hold it shut, because Sheriff Mike had made sure of it. There were little wires on her front door jamb, attached to a security system that was monitored by people who wouldn't hesitate to come when called. A heavy-linked chain hung above her head, and there was a peephole right at her eye level that she never remembered to check before she opened the door. Tonight, she checked it.

She couldn't see her visitor's full face, but she could see enough to know that it was Oscar Croft. What to do?

On the one hand, the man had asked her out, and she had already decided that she would say yes if there was a second invitation. There was no more danger in opening the door now than there would be when she got in a car with him to go to dinner.

On the other hand, though her bathrobe covered her from chin to toes, she wasn't comfortable letting a man see her in clothes that in any way suggested a bedroom. Also, she had the sick feeling that always came when something wasn't right. She'd felt it, hard, on the night when she came home to a busted-down door, before she went downstairs and found her dying husband.

Tonight, she just felt a twisting inside her chest that asked why this man couldn't wait until she returned his call before he showed up on her doorstep. There was eager and there was too eager.

She waited, just on the other side of the door, as he tapped gently again. After a third knock, he went away, but Emma was no longer sure that she would accept any invitation that Oscar made in the future.

It was late. Faye doubted Joe was asleep yet, but she had to go home sometime. Maybe she would get lucky and find her husband snoring. She pulled a small flashlight out of her satchel and started heading to the house. After twenty minutes of picking her way, keeping each step within the circle of light cast by the flashlight, she could sense open space ahead. In the center of that open space was her home.

Just before she came into the open, she smelled smoke and saw a faint glow through the underbrush. Sly had built yet another fire at yet another random place in the woods. Before she could back up and find another route home, she heard a deep, quiet "Hey," in a voice that wasn't quite Joe's. She stopped in her tracks. Out of reflex, she thumbed the flashlight off to make herself harder to see, but the effort was futile. If she stepped off the path to flee, he would be able to follow the sound of her crashing through the underbrush. If she stayed on the path, he would be able to follow it straight to her. But why did she care whether or not her father-in-law could find her?

"I been looking for you since I got off the boat," Sly said, "but I stopped when I saw your little light way across the island. I knew if I stayed right here, sooner or later, you'd have to come to me on your way home. I'm sitting out here by this fire, 'cause I can't go in that house and look at my son when he's this tore up."

"Did he tell you where he was going when he went ashore today?"

Sly used a long stick to poke the fire. Sparks flew. "Didn't ask him. I think he'd answer his wife if she asked him."

Faye didn't say anything.

Sly used the silence to pull out a cigarette. He reached his hand toward the fire and lit the cigarette on a hot coal. "I don't know why you won't just ask him, but I know you two ain't happy. I never seen you happy together, but I never seen you before that baby died, either. Something tells me you was happy before, so I'm guessing you can be happy again, but it won't be the same. Might be better, might be worse, but it won't be the same. When you love somebody that dies, you ain't never the same after that. You and Joe both lost somebody, so you're both different now. That's just how it is."

If this was supposed to be comforting, Faye's tears suggested that Sly had failed.

He tapped his ash onto the dirt, grinding it into the ground to make sure every last spark was dead. Then he kicked sand onto his campfire, scattered its coals, and doused them with a bucket of water sitting by his foot. "Go on in there. Even in the dark, I can tell you need some sleep. My son wouldn't ever make you talk until you wanted to talk. I'm gonna stay out here and make sure this fire's out. While I'm at it, I'm gonna smoke half a pack of these, so you two can have a little time alone. I think you need some."

◇◇◇

The whooping alarm of Emma's security system woke her. In her drowsy confusion, she couldn't remember the code that would shut it up.

She shook her head to clear it. A few seconds passed as she remembered that shutting up the alarm was not her problem. Her problem was figuring out how to spend the time until the security company sent someone to help her.

Should she go out the window and risk showing herself to the intruder who had forced open a window or door? Or should she go trap herself in the closet or under the bed and begin counting the seconds until help came?

She crept to her closed bedroom door, not sure whether she wanted to hear the intruder or not. Hearing footsteps would tell her how far away she was from danger, but the answer was already obvious. It was "pretty damn close."

Not hearing footsteps might mean that the intruder was far away, which was good, but it would leave her with no information whatsoever. Or it might mean that this was a false alarm. Emma decided to hope for no sound other than the screaming alarm. She rested an ear against the door.

This was how Douglass had felt during those moments after his killers broke into their home and before the attack began. Lost in the dark, weightless, helpless, she was near a breakdown, but she had to fight back. If she sobbed, she would give away her location and, what is more, she would be giving power to someone who might want to hurt her. She breathed in calm, then she breathed it out.

She kept a rope ladder designed for emergency escape under her bed in case of fire. It tempted her, but she didn't know who might be waiting at the bottom of it and she wasn't even sure how long it would take her to unreel it and hook it to her windowsill. Using it seemed like a foolhardy plan. So did rushing blindly out the bedroom door without knowing what was on the other side.

After a moment's thought, she decided that her reading alcove was the place to be. She would be near the door and shielded from view. If someone came through the door and moved to the right toward the bed, thinking she might be hiding underneath it, she had a shot at darting behind the intruder and getting out of the room. If the intruder came through the door and moved to the left, she would be pinned in place, hoping they didn't see her lurking behind the curtains. It wasn't much of a plan, but it only had to work until help came.

Again, she breathed in calm, and she breathed it out.

Chapter Sixteen

Emma thought that Sheriff Rainey was doing an excellent job for such a young man. He probably wasn't even forty yet. She also thought that the sheriff himself probably wouldn't be personally responding to an attempted break-in if she weren't Douglass Everett's widow and if he didn't know that her husband had been killed during a robbery gone wrong. Her husband's robbers were both dead, but that wasn't keeping her from having flashbacks to the night she lost him.

She had crouched in her reading alcove until the deputies arrived and after. They'd had to come up the stairs and show her their badges before she could feel assured that it was safe to come out. They had been patient, even sweet, about settling her nerves before they brought her into the living room to talk.

"Ma'am, your laundry room window's busted," Sheriff Rainey began. "The leaves under the window are scuffled up, but we haven't found any prints so we don't know how many people were out there. You keep a nice cushy lawn, so there may not be any prints to find. We can't see any evidence that a car was here, so somebody could've come in on foot. I've got people checking the roads and your neighbors' yards and the beach behind your house for footprints or tire prints or places a car might have been parked. Do you remember hearing a boat motor?"

"Not before the alarm started howling. I couldn't hear anything after it started going off."

"I'm guessing you were asleep before the alarm started."

She nodded.

Everything about the sheriff's wide face said, "Trust me.' This was the kind of face that got people elected sheriff. He laid his hands, palm-down, on his widespread legs and said, "Bottom line. We don't think anybody got into the house. Probably the alarm spooked 'em. We found this outside, and it may explain why somebody—or some somebodies—were bold enough to break a window that any fool could see was wired for an alarm system. I'm thinking you don't use it these days."

He put a plastic container on the coffee table in front of her. Inside it was a teardrop-shaped piece of plastic smaller than her palm.

"It looks like—is that my fob? The one I'm supposed to use to get into my house when I come home?"

"But you don't."

It wasn't a question. He knew her habits, which Emma found a little spooky.

"I just never got in the habit. My old alarm system didn't have a fob, so I always use the keypad to come and go. That fob's been on my keychain for years and I never even think about it."

"You've had the system serviced lately."

Again, a statement, not a question. Spooky. "Yes. Something went kaflooie with the wiring and the whole thing had to be reprogrammed."

"But neither you nor the technician thought to reprogram your fob, because you don't use it."

Emma was trying to figure out how he could know all these things about a malfunctioning device lying outside her laundry room window. There was only one answer that made any sense and it wasn't a comforting one.

"Somebody stole my fob. They were planning to deactivate my system and just waltz in. Not through the front door, because it was deadbolted and chained, but a window? Yeah. That would have been easy. Click the fob to turn off the alarm, break a window, and you're in. It would have worked if my fob had been up-to-date."

Emma pictured the back of her house. The laundry room window wasn't within sight of any of her neighbors, so it was an obvious choice for a break-in. It was directly beneath her bedroom. This insight made her queasy. If she had climbed out of her window on her emergency ladder, she'd have been handing herself over to whatever criminal was down there breaking her window.

Emma had a momentary vision of Douglass, lying in a pool of his own blood, but she shook it off. Things hadn't gone that way tonight, and it was best not to dwell on what could have happened.

"Had you noticed that your fob was missing?"

"No, but it didn't do anything but hang on my key ring. I never used it. It could have been missing for weeks and I'd have never known."

Sheriff Rainey stroked his close-cropped brown beard until she finished speaking, then he immediately contradicted her. "I don't think it was missing for weeks. I think it was probably stolen today."

"What makes you say that?"

"Because the thief had no way to know that you never used it, not unless that thief was your best friend who watched you come in your house, day in and day out."

There was no one like that in Emma's life. Every day, she came home alone.

"Say this thing got stolen today," the sheriff said, picking up the container and studying the fob through its clear walls. "If you used it regularly—which you don't—you would've tried to use it when you got home and noticed that it was gone."

"That's what the thief would have presumed."

"Exactly. So say you got home today and it didn't work. You wouldn't have rushed out and replaced it at the end of a long day."

"Not unless I was completely paranoid."

"Exactly," he said again. "You would've thought, 'Darn. I lost my fob. I better get another one.' Then you would've have turned the system off at the keypad and made yourself a note to call your security company. Maybe you'd have done it tomorrow or the next day. All the crook knows is that you were more likely to get that replacement with every day that passed. The security technician would probably reprogram the system when you did that. The thief had to act right away for the best odds of getting in your house."

"On the very same day."

The sheriff nodded.

The night air coming in her broken window was cold. Emma felt a shiver start between her shoulder blades. "Why? Why would somebody want to get in my house?"

He shrugged. "Probably wanted to clean out the house of Douglass Everett's widow. Everybody around here knows you've got nice things. But maybe there was more to it than that. A nice lady named Liz got killed not so very far from here, and she had a lot less to steal than you do. I don't like to think about what might've happened if somebody had gotten into your house tonight."

Emma wondered what it was going to take for her to get warm. She didn't think that nailing a board over that open window would do it. She was cold on the inside.

"Miss Emma," the sheriff said, in a tone of voice that suggested that he was repeating himself. How long had he been calling her name? She was feeling too tired and cold to focus. "Who did you see today? Who could have taken the fob?"

"Today?"

Emma tried to trace back through her day, but it wasn't easy. She had never been one of those people who could remember what she'd had for lunch. "Um…Joe came to see me this morning, but I know he didn't steal the fob. He wouldn't have had to. If he'd asked me for it, I'd have given it to him. Then there were a bunch of people in and out of the museum, like always, but I didn't know any of them. After lunch, Oscar Croft and Delia Scarsdale came to talk to me and I saw Joe again. Oh, and I saw Sly Mantooth. He took me fishing. And there was somebody else…hmm. Who was it?"

Sheriff Rainey had started taking notes on his tablet, probably because there were too many names on her list for him to keep in his head.

"Oh, yeah. It was Oscar again. He came by my house this evening, but I already mentioned him, so he doesn't count."

"Why was he here?"

"I don't know. I wasn't expecting him and I was wearing my nightclothes," she gestured at the robe she still wore, "so I didn't open the door. Which means that he couldn't have stolen the fob then. Maybe he could have done it earlier in the day, when we were chatting at the museum, but not tonight."

The sheriff swiped his finger across his tablet screen. She imagined that he was bolding Oscar Croft's name, because of the man's effrontery in paying her a visit without calling first. Being a crime suspect seemed like a harsh punishment for bad manners.

He clicked the tablet off. "I'm leaving a deputy here for the rest of the night. You'll be in touch with your security company first thing in the morning, I presume."

"I will."

"Let's talk again after that. You look like you've done all you can do today."

It was true. Emma let him introduce her to the deputy who would be babysitting her, and then she took herself to bed.

"I can't think of any good reason for you to go to shore without telling me and then come back empty-handed. If nothing else, you could have said, 'Need something at the store?' I'm supposed to not notice when you do something strange? I'm supposed to pretend like it's not happening? Joe, that doesn't make any sense."

Anybody listening to them fight would have conceded Faye's point, because it *was* unusual for either of them to burn enough fuel to get to shore without checking with the other one. Truthfully, it was unheard of. There were few things more frustrating than spending half a day buying groceries and coming home to find that your spouse drank all the milk while you were gone.

Married people learned each other's ways. Changes, even small ones, stirred up insecurities. Wives asked themselves what else their husbands were doing that they didn't know about. Husbands asked themselves the same thing about their wives. The fights of married people are many-layered, and even the most trivial ones rest atop the deepest fear of all: "Am I losing you?"

Anybody listening to the fight would also have praised Joe's self-restraint in refusing to say, "And I'm supposed to not notice when *you* do something strange? Because it's been weeks since you did anything that *wasn't* strange."

Yes, his trip to shore had been out-of-character, but it bore no comparison to Faye's recent behavior. He could have fought back, blow by verbal blow. He could have said, "How is what I did different from what you've been doing? Maybe you don't get in a boat and leave, but you walk away every day without a word about where you're going. For all I know, you're going to shore every day without telling me. It's what you did today."

Joe knew that if he said these things, he might have won the argument, but he would have lost in the end. Maybe he would even have lost Faye.

Over the course of a marriage, a wife can draw invisible lines that her husband knows he cannot cross. Maybe Faye's had moved and he didn't know it yet. He felt like he didn't know her anymore.

Joe was human, so he had invisible lines, too, and Faye was tiptoeing near them. He knew one of them needed to maintain control or they were in real trouble, so he held his tongue and took the punishment she was dishing out.

He considered telling her that he'd met Oscar and Delia. She might respond by telling him everything, which was what he wanted more than anything, but the risk was too great. If she knew he'd been talking to Emma, she might stop talking to Emma. She might stop talking to anyone. Joe had no wish to watch his wife explode from her pent-up pain.

In the end, he said only that he'd gone to have a cup of coffee with Sheriff Mike and that he was sorry he'd forgotten to call her. Sheriff Mike would back him up, because he, too, had a complicated wife whom he loved to distraction.

Faye quickly got tired of pummeling him with words. She was a quiet woman. She loved quietly, never saying much about her feelings but always managing to say enough, and her anger was quiet, too. She listed his errors and yelled at him a while, but then she was done.

Fortunately for them both, the phone in Faye's pocket rang and saved her from ending the argument the way an introvert does it, by mumbling "So there! You're wrong!" and hurrying away.

Instead, she thumbed her phone on and he heard her say, "Oh, Emma!" as she backed into her office and closed the door between them.

◇◇◇

Faye knew she should go to bed. She had failed to convince Emma to stay with them on Joyeuse Island until her intruder was found. The very idea that someone had stolen the fob that controlled her friend's security system was going to keep Faye awake all night, so going to bed seemed silly.

She was exhausted by her time spent worrying over every move Gerry Steinberg and Nadia Lombardero made, and she was emotionally flattened by her argument with Joe. The longer she stayed holed up in her office, the more he would worry about how mad she was.

Let Joe worry. She had already spewed out most of her anger, but she didn't know what to say to him, so let him worry himself to sleep. (Yeah, that was a good plan. Faye knew how compatible worry and sleep were.)

While she waited for her husband to exhaust himself, she made good use of her time. Gerry Steinberg had said that he would love to see some photos of chemical storage on the grounds of Tommy Barnett's business. Faye had years of photos of Liz's dock and marina. She knew she could grant his wish.

Chapter Seventeen

Sheriff Ken Rainey loved getting to work early. The air was crisp and his mind was crisp. Too often, that crispness was wasted on administrative chores while his deputies got to do the interesting work. Not today. There was an unsolved murder in Micco County and an unsolved break-in. When one considered that Liz Colton and Emma Everett were about the same age and that they had lived fairly close to one another, Emma's intruder was more disturbing than a single broken window suggested. These things gave Rainey a good excuse to be personally involved, and he liked that.

The rumor mill said that both Sly Mantooth and Oscar Croft had been seen flirting with Liz not long before she died. Both of those men had spent time with Emma on the evening of her break-in. (Never mind that Emma hadn't spoken back to Oscar as he lurked on the other side of the front door of a woman who hadn't invited him to drop by.)

It was possible that neither Oscar Croft nor Sylvester Mantooth would talk to him. He had no probable cause, so it wasn't like he could arrest them, but maybe they'd talk anyway. Maybe they'd think that being cooperative would keep them from looking guilty.

There was no sense in calling ahead and giving them time to think. He wanted a partner with him as a second witness, on the off-chance that one of the men, each cagey in his way, was foolish enough to incriminate himself. Detective Gerry Steinberg was sharp, he was personally interested in Liz's murder, and he was already on Joyeuse Island getting his team started for another day of work on the contamination assessment.

Steinberg might grouse about leaving his field team for the Mantooth interview. He would certainly grouse, and loudly, about leaving them again while he came ashore to help interview Oscar Croft, but that was too bad. His performance evaluations were signed by both the Micco County Sheriff's Office and the Florida Department of Environmental Protection, so he had to serve both masters.

Rainey rather liked being sheriff. It meant people did what he said with precious little backtalk. Rainey hated backtalk. It wasted time. He got Steinberg on the phone.

"I'm in the mood to make a couple of suspects miserable. Why don't you come help me do that?"

Faye heard the boat coming. Of course she heard the boat coming. She lived on an island. Boats and all their sounds colored her days. The bumping of a boat's hull against the dock signaled bad weather coming, and it told her that she needed to go tie it up more securely. A faraway whine on a day when Joe had gone to shore told her that he was coming home. It was a fluke that he'd gotten off the island just the day before without her hearing him. The comings and goings of Gerry and his technicians must have masked the sound of Joe and his john boat, making its motor seem like just one more departing vessel.

Before she'd heard the coming boat, she'd been heading west across the island, hoping to get a little time to look at the work of Gerry and his crew before they arrived and started making a bigger mess. A light drizzle had set in and the rain was coming down harder by the minute. She'd turned around, not anxious to get caught far from the house during a rainstorm.

As she neared the house, the sound of the distant motor was growing steadily louder. When she first heard it, she'd been a few strides from the house, near the biggest of the five cisterns that captured the rainwater her family drank. It was shaped something like a missile or a fairytale tower—a two-story tall cylindrical tank, built of cypress wood and topped with a conical roof covered with handhewn cypress shingles. There had been a time when it was the house's sole source of drinking water but, as the plantation reached its peak pre-Civil War population, her great-great-great-grandfather had built four slightly smaller versions that stood at the house's four corners. They all collected rainwater from the gutters that drained the expansive roof.

The largest cistern's eaves stuck out just enough to block a little of the rain, so Faye paused beneath them, positioning herself so that the old water tank shielded her from the newcomers' view. She had no idea who was in that boat.

Fortunately, she was on her own turf, so she could hide and watch. After sizing up the situation, Faye walked quickly to the dark shade beneath the grand staircase that led to her front door and disappeared from sight.

◇◇◇

Joe answered the knock at his front door, secure in the knowledge that nobody had ever paid an unannounced social call on Joyeuse Island. Nobody since the Yankee Army, anyway, and Joe didn't really think of that as a social call.

This was the best thing about living on an island. Before anybody, even your best friend, showed up on your doorstep, you got a phone call first. Or a radio message, back in the days before Faye had a cell phone. What kind of a fool would take a boat all this way without being sure there would be somebody home at the other end of the trip? An unannounced visit to Joyeuse Island's big house, also called Joyeuse, was no casual thing.

Somehow, he wasn't surprised to see two lawmen when he opened his front door. He also wasn't surprised when they asked to speak to his father. He realized that he had been waiting for this visit from the law ever since Sly Mantooth got off the airplane from Oklahoma. Maybe he'd been waiting for it since he was a little boy. When a kid's father is trouble, that kid knows it.

◇◇◇

Faye considered how she could best exploit the home court advantage. After the sound of the sheriff's approaching boat had sent her into the darkness beneath the staircase to her home's front door, she had listened while he secured his vessel. Then she had watched as Gerry Steinberg and Sheriff Rainey emerged from the woodsy path that led back to the dock and house from the contamination site.

The main entrance of her old house sat at the head of this staircase, a full story above her head. Crouched beneath it, she couldn't be seen, but she would be able hear every word said before the sheriff and Deputy Steinberg disappeared into the house.

Behind her, inside the big house's basement, a sneak staircase had been built to make it easier for slaves to serve their masters unseen. It rose to the dining room and then to the master bedroom, serving the two rooms where the slaves' labor would have been most needed. Since she and Joe preferred to live in the cozier quarters in the basement, most of the rest of the house was empty and unused. This meant that she had a good shot at being able to lurk in the sneak staircase and hear anything that was said indoors, too. She just hoped that everybody talked loud and didn't mumble.

Looking into Sylvester Mantooth's eyes, Sheriff Rainey knew what it was like to be one of those wild animals that Mantooth's son Joe stalked. There was more intelligence behind those dark eyes than the man let on. There was a guardedness there, too, and how surprising was that in a man who had survived prison? But there was also a flicker of anger in those eyes, and Rainey knew no better tool for an interrogator.

Mantooth had suggested that they talk on the porch, so that they could smoke. Sheriff Rainey didn't smoke and neither did his deputy, but he had no objection to Mantooth doing so, as long as he did it outside where they wouldn't have to breathe the vapors secondhand. They settled into some rocking chairs so simple and sturdy in design that the sheriff suspected that Joe Wolf Mantooth had built them himself.

Rainey saw no reason to drag his feet and possibly let Sly Mantooth get control of the conversation. He went straight to the point.

"So you took Emma Everett out fishing."

"I would have told you that. I guess she already did tell you, since you already knew it before you came here."

"Just the two of you."

"Isn't that the way most people go out on dates? Just the two of them?"

"So you took Mrs. Everett fishing because you were interested in her as a woman?"

Sly Mantooth rocked back in his chair and let out a short laugh. "Son, you get to be my age, I guarantee that you will still be interested in women as women. I ain't even sixty, but I can guarantee you that I'll keep liking women when I am. When I'm seventy, too. Emma's a pretty lady. Hell, yeah, I took her fishing because I was interested in her as a woman. I don't mind saying it. And I know for sure that Emma told you that I behaved like a gentleman, because I did and she wouldn't lie."

"Did you come straight back here to Joyeuse Island after you left her house?"

"Pretty much. Stopped halfway back to watch the sun go down. You may forget how pretty it is when the sun hits the water, living here like you do."

"No, we don't." These were the first words Deputy Steinberg had contributed to the conversation. "We don't forget. It's pretty, every time."

Sly focused those black eyes on Steinberg. "That's why you do what you do, ain't it? Environmental work. That's why you do it, because you want to keep things the way they should be. Blue water, clean-smelling air, plenty of fish and birds. It's good work you do. I got no quarrel with it. But can you try not to bankrupt my son while you're doing it?"

"I'm trying to help your son. He loves this island and wants to take care of it."

Sly nodded at the deputy while putting a match to the cigarette held between his lips. He took a lungful of air in, then let it go.

"I don't know what else to tell you two gentlemen about last night. Emma called my daughter-in-law and told her about the sorry loser that tried to break in her house. You fellas need to find him. A fine woman like that needs to feel safe all the time. All women do."

Sly fiddled with his matchbook for no good reason, since his cigarette was already lit. If Rainey had to guess, he'd say that Sly was covering feelings awakened by his own words. Talking about women and safety had accidentally reminded him of Liz's death. Those words had done the same thing for Rainey, reminding him that a woman-killer was walking loose.

Sly's words also reminded the sheriff that he himself had failed to protect Liz. They made him ask himself whether he was failing to protect Emma even now. Something in his chest seized up at the thought of Liz's wounded chest and Emma's vulnerable eyes. If Mantooth had purposefully manipulated his emotions on this subject, he was a cagey suspect indeed.

Rainey worked to wipe his brain clean of the images of Liz, and maybe Emma, battered and dead. He decided it was time to ask the only question he'd come to ask. "What time did you get back here last night? Can Joe or Faye confirm that time?"

The cigarette made a trip to Sly's mouth. "I got back here right after dark. Took me a few minutes to tie up the boat. Then I went out in the woods and made myself a little fire to keep me warm. I sat beside it and smoked a while. Like this." The cigarette made another trip to his mouth, exaggerated and slow. "It was real late when I went in the house, so don't you go bothering my son and his wife with your questions. They can't help you and they got enough on their minds."

"Were you outside smoking for much of the night when Liz was killed?"

"I already talked to you about that night, back when I first found Liz. I ain't going to talk to you about it any more, so you can trip me up on my own words and tell me I changed my story. I know how you people work. I talked to you and told you all I knew. I've been helpful. If you want me to be helpful some more, you're going to have to wait until I get myself a lawyer."

The cigarette made yet another trip to Mantooth's lips and, again, away. "I don't have anything left to say to you two gentlemen. If you have hearts in your bodies, you won't go in there and bother my son and his suffering family. Don't you agree that this conversation is over?"

◇◇◇

Faye crouched below the porch where Sly sat with the two lawmen. She believed her father-in-law, which surprised her.

It wasn't that she had ever suspected him of killing Liz or breaking into Emma's house. She hadn't, not seriously. Sly was mercurial. He was self-centered and inconsiderate. He was totally lacking in boundaries. But was he dangerous? Was he a killer? She didn't think so, despite that mysterious penitentiary stay. Until this moment, she'd had no basis for her opinion. Now she did.

She was convinced that he hadn't broken into Emma's house the night before. She had spoken to him herself, not long after sundown, which wasn't long before the break-in. This wasn't to say that he hadn't hopped right in a boat and headed back to the dock behind Emma's house. It would have been odd for him to leave Emma, come back out to the island, then rush back to shore and try to break into her house, but it was possible. This illogical behavior could even have been intended to provide him an alibi, but it didn't. Not really.

Regardless of any other evidence, Faye didn't believe that he had climbed back in one of their boats as soon as she was out of sight. If he had, she would have heard him. She was an islander and she was never unaware of the sounds of boats.

There had been no boats coming and going after her encounter with Sly Mantooth the night before. If Sly had gone back to shore, Faye believed wholeheartedly that she would have heard him start the motor. Even if he had been crafty enough to paddle far from the island before starting it, Faye believed that she would have heard an unexpected bump when the boat hit the dock as he maneuvered it into open water. She didn't doubt that she would have heard repetitive splashes as paddle hit water.

If she testified in court, would these observations stand up? Maybe not. But Faye knew what she heard and didn't hear.

Reaching back to the night Liz was killed, she considered whether Sly could have left the island without her knowing. She thought not. She hadn't slept that night. That was a certainty. On the day she heard about Liz's death, she had thought back to the night it happened, remembering how she'd lain in bed looking at the moon all that long night. Sly would have been hard-pressed to get out of the house, kill Liz, then come home without her hearing him. She just didn't believe he could have gotten a boat away from the island without a single bump or splash reaching her ears.

Faye's ears never rested, not when a squall could blow in and trash a boat that was poorly secured and not when her family's lives might rest on the condition of that boat. Island dwellers slept lightly, listening for the next storm and, lately, Faye slept so little that it hardly counted. She couldn't prove Sylvester Mantooth's innocence, but she believed in it.

What if he needed her to prove it? What if Sheriff Rainey was set on pinning those crimes on the nearest ex-con?

Faye understood that Sly rubbed her husband the wrong way. She knew there was history between them that they needed to work out, but she couldn't help them with that, not when she was hardly keeping her own head above dark emotional waters. She hadn't realized it until this minute, but she didn't share Joe's irritation with Sly's coarse jokes and the buffoonish behavior that cried out "Like me! Please like me!"

When Faye looked at her husband's father, she saw a man who knew he'd made mistakes and wanted to fix them, but he wasn't sure how. Joe saw the man who had failed his dead mother.

Faye couldn't fix their relationship. Joe and Sly would have to do that for themselves. She could, however, do her best to keep her father-in-law from being railroaded for murder. She could honestly provide alibis for him for both crimes, but those alibis required a jury to believe her when she said that she would have heard him leave the island. So there would be no airtight alibi from Faye that would save Sly. This left her only one way to ensure that her father-in-law wasn't wrongfully accused: Find the killer herself.

Chapter Eighteen

Sly and his cigarette waited on the porch while the lawmen ran through the rain to get back to the dock. It was so damn quiet on this lump of land in the middle of the water that he could hear everything. Just everything. A tree full of birds tweeted to his left. The shushing sound of waves hitting the shore came from all around him. Before long, he heard the tap of hard knotted rope hitting the deck of Sheriff Rainey's boat. The wordless murmur of two men's voices drifted up to him, as did the quick cough of a boat motor coming to life.

He was not surprised to hear the house's front door open behind him as that motor raced for a second before the sheriff shoved his throttle forward. Joe had been listening, making sure they were gone before coming outside to have a long-overdue talk with his old man.

The boy—who was past thirty and a family man, so he should stop calling him a boy—lowered himself into the rocker beside him. Their chairs were conveniently located so that they didn't have to look each other in the face, and Sly was glad for that. After a time, and not a long time because Joe had been waiting to ask this question for years, Sly heard his son take a deep breath and say, "How did my mother die?"

Faye was trapped, as surely as if she were a mouse who had wanted a suspicious hunk of cheese a little too much and had paid the price. If she came out from under the porch now, Sly would know she'd been eavesdropping on his talk with the sheriff. That might have been okay. The more pressing matter, the thing that was going to keep her lurking under the staircase until they quit talking and went inside, was this: She couldn't interrupt Sly while he was answering the most important question of Joe's life.

This was going to be a problem. Joe was a hunter, so his ears were as attuned to the sounds of animals as hers were attuned to the sounds of boats. And Faye, technically, was an animal. To keep Joe from hearing her, she was going to have to sit still and try not to breathe. Or to sneeze.

Oh no, now she'd thought about sneezing. She raised her eyebrows and flared her nostrils and did every other facial contortion that might distract the reflexive part of her brain that wanted to sneeze. Just as she thought the urge would never pass, Sly started to talk and she forgot all about sneezing.

"What do you mean? How'd your mama die? Son, you was there. Didn't you hear anything the doctors said?"

Silence.

Sly only let the quietness hang for a second. "I guess you didn't. Or you was too upset to pay any attention. Son, your mama had cancer. Of the ovary."

"I never heard of anybody getting cancer and dying the same week. You were gone on a long haul. A real long haul. You came home and she went straight to the hospital and died."

"It was more than one long haul. That's what shames me. I was gone two...three...months. I think it was just three. I hope so. I should've asked her more questions before I went. She should've told me more than she did, too, but it ain't right to blame the dead."

"You're saying she didn't tell you everything. What part did she leave out?"

Faye heard a long sighing drag on a cigarette.

"Patricia left out the part that said she was dying. She—"
Sly's voice had ramped up until he was nearly shouting before he

stopped himself and started again, quietly. "She did tell me she had cancer. She did. But there's the way she said it and there's the way I heard it and there's the way it really was. She said the doctor said she didn't need any operation, which I was real glad to hear, since we didn't have any insurance. She said the doctor had give her some pills that would do her for a while, then maybe she'd need some radiation. Or chemo. Or something."

"I don't remember her getting chemo or radiation."

"She didn't, but them words scared me, because I knew I couldn't pay for 'em. All I could think of was the money and how I could get enough to pay her bills. And I'll tell you for true, I wasn't even nice to her about it. I wasn't thinking about how she felt at all."

"You weren't real good at that."

Another deep breath was filtered through a cigarette. "Nope. And I didn't do any better by you. Years probably went by that I didn't say a nice word to neither one of you. I never got happy unless I was on the road. I was a big man out there. They knew me at the truck stops and the pool halls and the bars. They knew I was always happy to buy a man a drink or tip a waitress enough to make her smile, because five or ten dollars can make you look like a big man when everybody's been drinking long enough. Coming home to that shitty house I'd rented for the two of you only reminded me how I wasn't big. I was little. And I always would be. Thinking about them doctor bills I wasn't going to be able to pay just made it worse…made *me* worse."

There was silence again and this time Faye noticed something special about it. It was truly silence. There was no clacking of beer bottles hitting wooden porch tables. Neither man had twisted off a bottle top and tossed it on the floor. She heard no sips, no swallows.

Joe was a light drinker and so was she. There was wine and beer in the refrigerator and they'd offered it to Sly when he arrived, then they'd failed to notice when he drank nothing but coffee for two weeks. She wondered how long he'd been sober.

"Women don't just up and die because their husbands are mean to them. If she didn't need surgery or chemo or radiation for the cancer, how bad could it've been? Dad. She *died*. She passed out and we took her to the hospital and she never woke up again."

"You think you're telling me something I don't know? I came home from all those hauls, bringing more money than usual but surely not enough to pay for cancer. And she was hardly there. You didn't see it?"

"See what?"

"Son, I don't think she'd ate a bite since I drove away."

Now came the slight whistling intake of breath, the little choking sound that was the only sign that Faye's husband was crying, and Faye knew that she was going to have to find a way to start eating again. Knowing what he knew now about his mother, it would kill Joe if he had to keep watching her waste away, just as it was killing her to hear him cry.

She'd heard this sound during the whirlwind emergency that had been Michael's birth. She'd heard it on the day Amande was kidnapped. And she mustn't think about this now or he'd hear her weeping, too, but she'd heard it on the day they lost the baby.

"Mama was always skinny. And tall. Must've been almost six foot. I was near fifteen before I passed her up. I didn't see it. I didn't see how sick she was."

Sly's voice lowered a tone, deep and warm, and Faye heard the note Joe used when he was talking to little Michael. "When you passed her up, you passed her up. You was a half-a-foot taller than her by the time she went, and you only eighteen years old. When you looked down at her, she just looked little. How was you supposed to see that she was getting littler every day? I should have been there. I'd have seen it."

"But you said the doctors thought she didn't need any medicine. I don't understand."

"That's not what they thought. When I finally met her doctors—and they musta thought I was a genuine asshole not to have come met them before that—they told me what they really thought. She was too far gone for surgery when they first found it. Maybe for chemo, too, I don't know. But radiation would've shrunk it. It would've shrunk it up. Eased her pain. Given her some more time. She thought it was stupid to pay for radiation that wasn't gonna save her, so she told them to give her some pain pills and send her home."

"For three months? She hurt for three months with just pills to help her? Dad."

This time, there wasn't even the sound of a man sucking in smoke. There was nothing to crack open the quiet night.

"No, Son, she didn't hurt for three months with just pain pills. She didn't take them. For three months, she didn't take 'em. She saved 'em up until I'd got home and she knew you wouldn't be by yourself, then she took 'em all. So, you see, a woman *can* just up and die, when things get bad enough."

Chapter Nineteen

Sheriff Rainey was not surprised that Deputy Steinberg agreed with him on his strategy for dealing with Oscar Croft. Both men thought that this was one occasion when it was more effective to give away information than to keep it close to the vest. Rainey could tell by the expression on Steinberg's face that he, too, had enjoyed the moment when Croft found out what they knew.

They'd probably enjoyed it more than they should have, in a professional sense. It was possible that Croft was responsible for the break-in at Emma Everett's house and it was possible that he'd killed Liz, so Rainey had professional reasons for wanting the upper hand in any conversation with him. Beyond that, though, Rainey simply didn't like him. He had the entitled air of a rich man, and he had the pushy ways of a man who didn't know how things were done in small-town Florida.

Worse than that, he acted like a man who thought he was the smartest person in the room, merely because he was the richest person in the room. And probably also because he wasn't from small-town Florida. Therefore, Rainey had really enjoyed beginning their talk by dropping a conversational bomb in Croft's lap.

"Why were you at Emma Everett's house yesterday evening? Did she invite you?"

Croft's mouth gaped. He definitely didn't look like the smartest person in the room.

"Who told you that?"

Rainey was under no obligation to tell the man that Emma Everett had been peeping out her peephole when Croft made his unannounced visit. Since Croft wasn't under arrest, Rainey wasn't even under obligation to tell him the truth. He opted to give Croft a look that said, "I'm not telling you how I know. Maybe I'm psychic. Don't be stupid enough to lie to me."

Rainey was successful in staring the man down. Eventually, Croft fussed with his Rolex and said, "Yeah, I stopped by to say hello to her. It's not illegal."

"Did you also maybe stop by Liz's place to see her on the night she died?"

"Not that night, no."

Shooting a look at Steinberg would have let Croft know that he'd just said too much, so Rainey kept his eyes on the man wearing a Rolex.

"You and Liz were friends? Why else would you be at her place? You don't look like the kind of man who hangs out in bars. Not when you can drink whatever you like here."

Rainey gestured at the fully stocked bar behind Oscar. It was a nice bar, the kind seen in houses designed for parties. It had shelves loaded with high-end liquor, racks of cut-crystal glassware, a sink, a tiny dishwasher, stainless steel muddlers and reamers and shakers. It was built for a hired bartender with a catering staff who roamed the expansive house with trays of cocktails and finger food.

In Micco County, a house like this would have been a corporate rental, used by companies who courted clients with alcohol-soaked fishing weekends. The only private home that approached it belonged to Emma Everett. Rainey knew that there was a dock out back as big as Emma's, with a party boat and a speedboat sitting in lifts that would drop them into the Gulf at the touch of a switch. Oscar had been in town for a while, so he must have rented this house for at least a month, maybe for the whole winter. Rainey doubted the landlord had ever before had a renter who wanted it for so long.

"I like a little nightlife. Always have. Besides, Delia's not a big drinker. Who wants to drink alone? So, yeah, I went over to Liz's place now and then, before she…when it was open. It was the only bar in town. People are going to miss it, now that it's gone. They still need a place to go. Somebody's going to figure that out and make themselves some good money. Not sure I'm up for starting something so far from home, but I've been in business all my life. It's hard to walk past an opportunity like that."

"I can't see you running a little dive way down here when you have businesses to run in Ohio." Delia said this in a calm and professional voice as she stepped out of a bedroom, but she looked surprised to see guests. Or maybe she was just surprised to see Oscar being questioned by the law.

She looked fresh out of the shower, so she must not have heard Rainey and Steinberg come in. Her cheeks were pink and she was running a brush through damp hair, but she was fully dressed and Rainey was glad. It would have been awkward if any woman had walked into the room wearing a towel, but it would have been especially awkward if the towel-wearing woman had been this pretty.

Delia was actually very professionally dressed for a glorified tour guide. She wore a crisp, button-front shirt, loose linen slacks, and dressy flat shoes. She hadn't come out of the same bedroom where Oscar had gone to fetch his glasses after they arrived, so it appeared that their relationship was a strictly professional one. Rainey had been wondering.

He was pretty sure that all of Micco County had been wondering, but his own professional ethics would keep him from spreading the news that the two tourists slept separately, despite the fact that doing so would damp down the gossip. Or it should. People only heard what they wanted to hear, and if Micco County wanted to believe that this fresh-faced woman was an old man's paid escort, there was nothing he could do about it.

"I'm in no hurry to get back to Ohio," the old man said. "I like it here. Maybe I'll stay in Florida until Delia gets another client and I don't have a personal historian to help me find the interesting sites to see." He grinned up at Delia, who didn't grace him with an equally flirtatious response. In fact, she rolled her eyes at him. She was one of those women who had learned to manage male attention with an air that said, "This far and no further."

"You said you had business to do today, so I thought I'd do some shopping," she said. "They tell me that the closest mall is in Tallahassee, so I'm driving up there for the afternoon. While I'm in town, I'll check out that restored mission you wanted to visit. If I think it's something you'll want to tour, we can drive up there tomorrow."

She turned to leave the room but Oscar called after her. "Buy something pretty!"

He got no answer, but her body language spoke for her. Rainey heard it loud and clear: "This far and no further."

A safe moment after the door closed behind Delia, Oscar said, "Not bad, right?"

Rainey emitted a grunt intended to signify that he didn't speak disrespectfully about ladies but that Delia's looks were, indeed, not bad. This was a lot of information for a single grunt to carry, but he thought he pulled it off. Steinberg just sat there and looked uncomfortable.

"I prefer a woman who's lived a while, myself," Oscar went on, "but there's nothing wrong with having a traveling companion who's nice to look at."

Emma had lived a while. So had Liz, but not long enough. Rainey couldn't point to a specific reason why he was uncomfortable with Oscar Croft and his relationships with the women around him, but he was. There wasn't necessarily anything wrong with appreciating a young female employee, although it was more respectful to keep your appreciation to yourself and Oscar was pushing the boundaries of sexual harassment. There was certainly nothing wrong with politely appreciating the company of a woman of a certain age, like Emma or Liz, particularly if you were yourself of a certain age.

It was only natural that Oscar would like Liz's verve and Emma's composed wit. Going to Emma's house unannounced was a little awkward, but it wasn't a crime. Going to Liz's bar for a drink wasn't even awkward. She was in business to serve drinks to people who were looking for company. Still, Oscar made the sheriff's creep detector go ping.

Chapter Twenty

Faye had thought about going into the house. She really had. She had sat under her own porch and listened to her husband and his father rip the patches off their torn relationship, and considered how she could make sure that they never knew she'd been there.

The basement door behind her had been an option. She could have backed quietly through it. Their bedroom was a few feet down the hall. She could have crawled in bed and let Joe presume that she'd come home to take a nap, although she couldn't recall ever having done that so early in the day. Maybe she'd done it when she was pregnant or when she had the flu. If Joe found her napping, he'd probably think she had a terminal illness. Not a good thing, considering the conversation he'd just had.

No, she needed an unobtrusive way to communicate, "Who me? Eavesdrop on the most intimate moment in your life that didn't involve me? Why would you think I'd do *that?*" A fake nap wasn't going to work.

She could have backed through that basement door and walked all the way down the hall into the kitchen. Joe would have found her there, chomping on a sandwich. Or she could have crept up the sneak staircase and pretended to have been sitting in the cupola for hours, looking out to sea.

The problem with any plan that took her inside the house was that it would require her to look Joe in the eyes while he wondered what she might have heard. There was no way she could do that without giving herself away. He would know. He would know that she'd heard his father's story, and Joe needed to tell her that story himself, in his own time.

So she had ruled out the basement door and stayed put until she heard their rocking chairs slide against the wooden porch floor above her head. She had listened to Sly give the slight groan of a man stretching out his aging ankles before walking into the house. She had listened for the non-sound of Joe's moccasins as he followed his father without a word. Then she had waited.

After a time, the rain eased. Gerry's crew arrived and started unloading the day's supplies at the dock. Faye took the opportunity to walk swiftly in their direction. Unless Joe or his father was watching at the exact moment she stepped out from under the porch, there would be nothing odd about her presence among these busy workers.

She had been ready all morning to walk across the island and watch them work. She had loaded her satchel with all the usual things. Field notebook. Pen. Gloves. Camera. A few small, light tools, like brushes and dental picks and tongue depressors.

As usual, she carried her trowel in a scabbard at her waist, but she otherwise traveled light, knowing that she could walk back to the house if she needed something. A couple of bottles of water had gone into the satchel, too, and enough calories in the form of a banana and a protein bar to keep her alive, but probably not enough calories to maintain her body weight.

She was ready to go watch the environmental scientists work.

Since Gerry and Nadia and their contractors had started their environmental cleanup, she had spent most of her days doing just that—watching them work. If she was going to be paying for this project, she wanted to fool herself into believing that she was its manager.

For days now, she'd also been carrying a copy of Cally's oral history and, today, she added another research source, her tablet computer, because she wanted more convenient Internet access than her smartphone gave her. She also wanted a bigger screen and she wanted the wireless keyboard that made the tablet so much more functional.

The laptop she used at home would be still more functional, but she shared that computer with Joe and this was research that she didn't want him to see. Using it would require her to believe that its "clear history" command worked flawlessly, and she didn't.

It was time to see what the Internet could tell her about Sylvester and Patricia Mantooth. And, because she had decided that Sly was innocent of Liz's murder—granted, she had no proof—and that Oscar was a suspicious character who deserved investigating as a possible suspect—again, no proof, just intuition—she planned to see what the Internet could tell her about Oscar, too.

Faye plopped to the ground and opened her tablet's case, typing "Sylvester Mantooth" into the browser's search bar. It was an unusual name, so Faye got a dozen or so hits that all referred to her father-in-law. As usual, it was amazing to see how much information the various "white pages" sites offered for free. She quickly confirmed Sly's age, fifty-eight. She learned that the World Wide Web knew that he had been married to Patricia, even though she'd been dead more than ten years. Her throat closed when she realized that Patricia had died when she was hardly older than Faye was now.

The web also knew that Sly's son's name was Joe Wolf. She found several addresses in for Sly in Oklahoma and she knew that one of those addresses was probably the house where her husband grew up. She was relieved to find that her father in-law was not a registered sex offender.

Probing a little deeper and paying a search site to get more closely held information, she learned that Sly's conviction had been for transporting drugs across state lines. If Joe ever wanted to know the name of the penitentiary where his father had served his time, Faye had the information. She found no other convictions.

There was a bankruptcy Sly hadn't mentioned, but there was no deceit in not answering a question no one had asked. Based on its date, the bankruptcy had occurred when Joe was six, so he might not know about it but he would have seen the financial belt-tightening. He would also have seen the kind of stress-fueled money arguments that broke open marriages.

Sly and Patricia had stayed married twelve more years after the bankruptcy. It was anybody's guess whether this was because they loved each other or whether it was because they were too scared to split. Maybe it was just because it was too expensive to live in two houses when they couldn't even afford the one they were in.

These things were sad, but they didn't speak to the question of who killed Liz. They just confirmed that Sly was who he said he was.

Faye closed the browser and walked over to kill some time with Nadia. The environmental chemist didn't take many breaks but she was standing at the waterline, relaxed and holding a cup of coffee.

"You're willing to drink coffee so close to an environmental disaster?" Faye asked.

Nadia laughed. "We're outside the exclusion zone. It's safe to eat and drink here."

"And breathe?"

"Oh, yeah. Your nose is a pretty decent detector for airborne petroleum-related chemicals. Do you smell anything?"

"Nope, but you can't smell arsenic, can you?"

The Spanish-inflected laugh took the edge off Nadia's talk of nasty chemicals. "I wouldn't worry about the arsenic, not unless we find a lot more. Gerry just wants to find out where it's coming from, because it's his job to make sure that we're not missing a bigger problem nearby."

"Where is he, by the way?"

"Chasing criminals with the sheriff. He was not happy to leave this job for the day, but he's a worrywart. I can manage these people just fine."

Faye believed her. She asked, "Do you see a lot of sites like this one?"

"Yes and no. I spend most of my time at petroleum sites, but this one is tiny compared to my ordinary jobs. If it weren't so close to the Gulf, I think we could have sold the department on leaving the kerosene leak alone. But the arsenic...now that's weird."

"Because of the low levels?"

"Yeah, sort of, but I've seen levels like these lots of times. It always turned out that the arsenic was a natural part of the soil, but not here. The background samples came up clean. Also, when we find arsenic and it turns out not to be natural, we can usually figure out where it came from. Agricultural chemicals. Wood preservation treatment. Electronics manufacturing. Those kinds of sites are likely to be huge and heavily contaminated. Here? We just have a little spot of arsenic with no reason to be here. It's interesting."

Wishing Nadia had found interesting work on somebody else's property, Faye excused herself and focused on her tablet again. She wondered if she could be as successful at digging up Oscar Croft's secrets as she had been at peering into her father-in-law's past.

◇◇◇

Tommy Barnett hit the end button on his cell phone, hanging up on a call that had brought the possibility of financial gain. He enjoyed calls like that.

Wilma Jakes, the worn-out hag who had operated the marina's fueling operation for Liz, had been on the phone, saying "I have a proposition for you."

She might have meant to say more, but Tommy had butted in. "You're old and ugly. I ain't listening to any propositions from you."

"Well, I ain't a hooker. You might consider giving a second chance to a girl who don't have any diseases to give you."

Tommy said, "Don't talk about Lolita like that," but Wilma knew what she knew, and Tommy didn't know how she knew it.

Yeah, Tommy and Lolita had each received a course of antibiotics at the county health department, not six months before. And it wasn't the first time. Tommy had no reputation to ruin, so having this information was of no direct value to Wilma, but knowing his medical secrets established Wilma as a woman with eyes in the back of her head. She wanted him to know that it wasn't safe to double-cross her.

Her witchy voice slithered out of his phone again. "About my proposition."

"I'm listening."

"I'm thinking that you need that marina running again, or your maintenance business is shot. And I need it running again, or I'll never put another gallon in another boat. I'm also thinking that there's not all that much money in fueling up boats or fixing their motors. We should think bigger."

"I said I was listening. But if you know so much, you know I'm looking at jail time. Or a big fine from the environmental people, at least. And there's some that's trying to say I killed Liz."

"Lucky you. You got me on your side. I'm willing to lie my ass off to say you didn't do it."

Tommy liked the sound of this, but he only said, "Why would you do that?"

"We need to buy Liz's place off the bank. Nobody else wants it. I think we can get it cheap and I think we can make money with it."

"What part of 'Maybe I'm going to jail' didn't you understand?"

"First of all, I can get you off the top of the sheriff's list of suspects for Liz's murder."

This would be nice if Wilma could make it happen. "I said I was listening."

"I live right by the marina. I see what happens there. I can tell the sheriff that I saw a real big man hanging around the parking lot at about closing time on the night Liz died. I'll say I've been afraid to speak up, because I live alone right here next to where she got killed."

Tommy was five-foot five in his work boots. He was built like a fire plug, but he wasn't a big man. He saw the value in this offer.

"Nobody's questioned me. Not the police. Not the environmental people. Nobody," she went on. "So it ain't like I'm changing a story I already told."

"Seriously? How did they miss you?" Tommy had thought they questioned everybody, and Wilma's house was right next door to the marina. She should have been high on the cops' list.

"It's damn shoddy detective work, if you ask me. Granted, maybe they didn't come to my house because it looks like nobody lives there. Well, maybe I let it look that way on purpose. Maybe it's a good way to get the cops to keep their distance. Anyway, if I tell them about my imaginary big dude, it'll get 'em off your back long enough for 'em to find the one that really did it. It wasn't you, was it?"

"No! Hell, no."

"Well, then, let's move on to your other problem, which we need to solve if you and me are going to go into business together."

Tommy had that sick feeling he got when he was missing something. "My other problem? You mean that environmental dumping charge? How you planning to solve that one? They're talking big fines. They're talking jail time. I never thought dumping a little waste oil now and then was that big a deal when I was doing it."

"That shows how brilliant you aren't. If it wasn't that big a deal, people would have been dumping their own waste oil, instead of paying you to do it. You got anything left that you didn't get around to dumping?"

"As of yesterday, no."

"You got records of how much you dumped and who you did it for?"

"Now, why would I keep something they could use against me?"

Tommy thought Wilma should be happy with that answer, because she had availed herself of his services on occasion. Sometimes a customer had spilled a gallon of something that she'd soaked up with kitty litter. Why would Wilma want to pay to get rid of the stinking kitty litter? And also, every now and then, she had to empty a tank and the sludge that came out of the bottom needed to disappear. Any business dealing with petroleum had waste sometimes. If Tommy had kept a list of his clients, she would have been on it, so she should be glad that he didn't.

"I ain't a lawyer, Tommy, but it seems like maybe you could've spread the blame around if you'd kept records. But it's too late, so never mind that. You still got a chance to spread the blame around. Tell 'em that you was working for Liz. Tell 'em she paid you a little salary and kept the rest of the money. Liz did a big cash business in the bar and the bait shop. If she'd been running a dumping business on the side, it would have been easy for her to hide it, don't you think?"

"You think I should tell 'em that I was the little guy? Took all the risk, didn't make much money?"

"It's worth a shot. And I'll back you up."

"Why?"

"Because we're going to put all our money together in one big pile and put in a bid on the marina. The bank don't want it. Nobody else wants it. It'll need to be in my name, so the law can't tap it to pay your fines, but I'll pay you a fair share. Thirty percent."

"And I put up thirty percent of the money?"

"No, you put up fifty percent of the money. Maybe sixty, if you keep talking. I can do this without you. It'd be hard, but I could round up the money. You, on the other hand—Tommy, you can't get nothing from a bank while you've got those fines hanging over your head. You need me more than I need you. But think about the money to be made. Liz wasn't a bit of good at running a business. She was too nice. You and me, we could rake it in."

"I want a bigger cut."

"Tough shit."

Chapter Twenty-one

Having consulted the Internet, Faye now knew that Oscar Croft had earned every cent of his money. A reporter had quoted him as saying, "I grew up in the house my great-great-grandfather built in 1852. It was drafty and the roof leaked, but we were glad to have it. It stayed in the family until my father lost his job at the hardware store. By that time, I had my building supply business, so Father came to work for me, but we couldn't afford to keep the house in the family. Three years later, I could have afforded any house in Ashtabula, any house in Ohio, maybe. But that one was gone, torn down to make room for a highway exit ramp. I'd give anything to have it back."

He'd gone on to describe its mid-nineteenth century wood-work and its plastered walls, and the historic preservationist in Faye had almost liked him. She stopped liking him when she probed a little deeper in Oscar's Internet persona and got a look at the news coverage for his sexual harassment suit. It had been quickly settled and a gag order meant that the truth was bottled up forever inside Oscar and his accusers, but he would always be a man who had been accused of rubbing himself all over women who depended on him for a paycheck.

"Innocent until proven guilty," Faye reminded herself. Then she read that Oscar's wife of thirty years had left him as soon as the suit was settled. He might or might not have been guilty, but the person who knew him best had behaved as if she believed the accusers. Or maybe Oscar was just a garden variety son of a bitch whose wife had been waiting for an excuse to walk out. There was no way to know.

In the years after the divorce, websites of lifestyle magazines based in the big Ohio cities—Cleveland, Columbus, Cincinnati—showed an unbroken stream of photos of Oscar at formal fundraising galas, wearing bespoke tuxes as he got ever older and his dates got ever younger. And ever blonder. Faye wondered how he'd managed to find a historical tour guide who wasn't just young and pretty, but also blond.

A casual web search for Delia's name turned up the website for her business, *Journeys of Self-Discovery*. The site was very simple. If Faye had to guess, she'd say that Delia had built it herself, but it didn't look amateurish.

Delia was a historian, and historians tend to possess writing skills, so her company's stated philosophy was straightforward: "They say you can't go home again, but they're wrong. I can take you there." This statement was backed up by photos of Delia with happy customers who had given her quotes like, "Delia found a half-brother I didn't know I had!" and "I was adopted, but now I finally know where I come from. I can't tell you how much peace that gives me."

A photo of Delia did its part to sell her services. It is useful to be beautiful. But the photo was taken in a library where Delia sat behind a computer and surrounded by paper. It said, "I'm not just eye candy," while also saying, "If you care about how your tour guide looks, this face hasn't stopped any clocks lately."

Next to the photo was a bio stating that she had studied for her PhD at Ohio State. Having a PhD of her own, Faye recognized this to be code for "I took a bunch of classes, but I never finished my dissertation." In other words, she was letting people think she had a credential she didn't. This seemed a little underhanded for a woman who cultivated an image that said, "I'm wholesome and sweet. Is there an illegitimate child or a convicted murderer on your family tree? Was your great-aunt abandoned in an asylum? Trust me with your family's darkest secrets."

Delia gave Faye only an instant to feel judgmental about her shaky credentials as a historian, because the next sentence in her website bio said, "When I lost my husband, I couldn't face the stresses of academia, so I started this business. Five years later, I couldn't be happier, and my clients seem happy, too. Let me take you on your own journey of discovery."

Very young widows carry a certain kind of tough memory. Car wrecks. Soldier husbands killed in the line of duty. Rare and quick cancers.

Whatever her story was, Delia had found a way to move ahead. At the moment, she was moving ahead by putting herself in close proximity to a man who had been accused of some pretty serious things. Faye hoped Delia was as smart as she seemed, because she herself wouldn't be anxious to go on an extended business trip with Oscar.

While walking from Oscar's rental house to his car, Rainey checked his phone and saw that he had a voice mail. He hit the phone's touch screen. A high and reedy woman's voice said, "My name is Wilma Jakes and I can meet you at the marina any time you want to talk. It's where my business is. Was. Ain't been much business since Liz got killed. I want to talk to you about what happened to her. I don't know who killed Liz, but I do know somebody that didn't."

Steinberg was studying his own phone, but Rainey didn't wait for him to finish reading his e-mail. "We need to get back to the marina." Then he hit the button that would return Wilma's call so that he could tell her to meet him at the marina in an hour.

Steinberg, still reading, said, "Damn straight, we need to get back to the marina. I need to find Tommy Barnett." After a quiet moment spent staring at the little screen, he slid the phone in his pocket. "I sent some divers out to retrieve the cans of waste that I watched Barnett throw overboard. They just sent an e-mail to say that that they found the spot easy, even without the GPS coordinates I gave them. It's marked by a long oil slick heading out toward the islands. And while they were out there?

They found another big slick marking the spot where somebody threw some more crap into the Gulf. They're pretty sure it just happened. Is Barnett really dumb enough to keep doing this?"

Steinberg backed out of the parking slot much faster than necessary and slammed the car into gear. Rainey thought this was hot-tempered behavior for a scientist.

"I'm not sure it's a question of dumb," he said to the angry scientist. "It may be a question of desperate. It may be a question of a man trying to get rid of something he can't let anybody see."

"Hazardous waste? Or evidence of a murder?"

"Maybe both. Maybe we're really lucky that some of the stuff he dumped has floated to the surface. Maybe that slick is leading us to something else Barnett is trying to hide. Tell your divers to take a lot of pictures. And tell them to bring us everything they see that doesn't belong under the water. Every last thing."

Pulling up his own e-mail, Sheriff Rainey saw that Faye Longchamp had overloaded his inbox. Each message contained a link that highlighted something sketchy about Oscar Croft. He would have been annoyed that she'd e-mailed him five times to give him information that was in the public record, but this would have been unfair. One of those e-mails told him something he didn't already know.

Rainey needed to speak to the detective in charge of the Internet arm of the investigation of Liz's murder. He needed to tell her that an amateur was doing a better job than she was.

Rainey had known about Oscar's sexual harassment charge since the day he started this investigation. He also knew that the timing of the man's divorce made his accuser look like the wronged party.

He had known about the high-profile lawsuit that had threatened to sink Oscar's business, too. His detective had gotten him a stack of details about the supplier who had sued Oscar's company for a fortune, claiming in vain that the man had cancelled a big order and refused to pay for the hefty expenses incurred before the cancellation. Oscar had won that fight, but was it because he was in the right or was it because he hired a bunch of expensive lawyers?

His detective had also done a good job of running down information on the driving-under-the-influence incident that had drawn a slap on Oscar's wrist, because that's how seriously drunk driving was taken in the disco years. She had not, however, found out about Oscar's other divorce, and she had not investigated the important difference between Ohio divorce law and Florida divorce law.

In both Ohio and Florida, two partners can dissolve their union with a graceful, no-fault dissolution, but angry Ohioans have another option that Rainey would call the take-no-prisoners approach. They can opt for a divorce that airs the wronged party's grievances and makes sure that they are always available to curious eyes.

Faye Longchamp-Mantooth had found out that this was what Oscar's wife had done. She had aired every grievance that had led to their divorce. Presuming Oscar Croft was capable of shame, he had to be sorry that she'd chosen that tactic. Anyone motivated enough to check the public record would know that the first Mrs. Croft had based her petition for divorce on Oscar's infidelity, and her private detective had provided reams of salacious proof. Public records in Ohio would, forever after, include evidence that Oscar Croft had enjoyed the company of a barely legal blonde more than he enjoyed the company of his wife.

Sheriff Rainey had seen a lot in his years on the job, but he'd rarely seen such graphic testimony in a file that didn't involve a criminal action. If Oscar Croft's divorce had been a movie, there was no way that the movie industry would let it sneak by with just an R rating.

Rainey was grateful for the information, because Dr. Longchamp-Mantooth was correct that it was pertinent to his investigation of Liz's murder and Emma's attempted break-in. Both incidents had occurred very near Oscar Croft's rented house and very shortly after he came to town. This proximity, combined with the man's undeniably uncomfortable history with women, made him a person of interest, and this didn't even take into account the fact that Rainey had witnesses saying that Croft had seemed attracted to both Liz and Emma.

If Sheriff Rainey had to choose between knowing his wife was in the presence of Oscar Croft or Sly Mantooth, he believed he would choose the ex-con.

It didn't get any easier for Faye, walking up the dock where Liz had died. Fish gathered around the posts under her feet. She wondered whether they heard her footsteps and were hoping that Liz had come back to give them their daily basket of stale dinner rolls.

Beer cans were starting to accumulate in the parking lot. This place had been her friend's life and now it was a hangout for underaged drinkers. The windows of Liz's upstairs apartment overlooked that parking lot. Faye could see Liz now, hanging her bright orange head out the window and bellowing at beer-swilling loiterers. The window was closed, and it had been closed since Sunday night. The air conditioner hadn't run for days, so the apartment had to be sweltering and damp. If nobody had emptied the closets of her clothes—and who would have done that?—they were mildewing by now.

She had timed her arrival right. Gerry and the sheriff pulled off the highway before she'd walked the few steps from her boat to the parking lot. Faye had brought them information that she hoped might help them find Liz's killer. She hoped they were grateful.

Sheriff Rainey thought back to the e-mail he had sent Faye Longchamp-Mantooth, responding to her messages about Oscar Croft's divorce and his other legal woes. Had he mentioned that he was on his way to the marina? He must have, because here Faye stood, uninvited.

She shook his hand, then pulled her satchel off her shoulder. Reaching into it, she said, "I have those photos you wanted."

Rainey looked around for Steinberg. He was already standing in front of Tommy Barnett's maintenance shed. Just standing there. He was pretending like he was studying the padlock on the door and the oily stains on the concrete pad out back, but Rainey thought he really just wanted to get close to the greasy stains on the concrete pad behind the shed. He couldn't manage it because the pad was surrounded by a chain-link fence, but he looked like he wanted to cut that chain-link fence real bad.

"Detective, there's nothing to see over there. The man has taken his hazardous waste out to sea, and we're going to nail him for it. Come over here and help me look through some pictures taken before Tommy Barnett and his sludge flew the coop."

The three of them sat together on a bench, stomping down the dried grass at their feet. With Faye in the middle and a lawman on either side, Rainey and Steinberg watched as she flipped through a fat envelope full of family photos. The top one was a sucker punch, because it showed Liz hanging out the kitchen door of her bar and grill, the same door where Joe had found wet footprints on the night she died. She was leaning down to scoop up little Michael in mid-toddle. Sly was jogging to keep up with his grandson. Joe must have been holding the camera.

"I mostly just wanted to bring a picture of Liz," Faye said. "You know…to remind you that she was a real person who should still be here. But look at this," she said, pointing to the lower left corner of the photo. The person holding the camera had been standing on the dock and a small portion of Tommy's fenced-in storage pad could be seen. Two fifty-five-gallon drums were visible. Faye handed the photo to Gerry who was obviously dying to study the words printed on the side of the drums.

"Take it," she said. "Maybe it will help you figure out what kind of gunk he was dumping."

"You give him too much credit," Gerry said, holding the picture inches from his eyes. "You presume that the chemicals that are in the drums are the same as the chemicals that are on the labels. Who knows what Tommy put in there? But this is a start." He looked up from the photo and met Faye's eyes.

"Thank you. Thank you for going to the trouble of bringing these pictures to us."

"You said you'd tell me what you learned about the contamination on my property. I thought returning the favor was the least I could do."

"Yeah. Um…about that."

Faye said nothing, just cocked an eyebrow to encourage him to talk.

"Did Nadia tell you the lab results on the wood you wanted us to analyze?"

"No. She mentioned the background samples, but I forgot to ask about the wood. Arsenic?"

"Yeah. Not a lot, but that chunk of wood was definitely impregnated with arsenic, as if it had been soaked in a solution of it. You might find that in modern pressure-treated wood, but I don't have a clue what could have gotten into it before your grandmother was a kid. I'm listening if you've got any ideas. Hell. Maybe you have a picture from 1912 of somebody emptying a big can marked 'arsenic.'"

"If my great-grandmother had owned a camera and if the pictures had survived a few hurricanes then, yes, I might have that picture for you. My family has never had much, so they've never thrown much away. I'll keep feeding you information, if you keep doing the same."

The sheriff said, "We're the law. You're supposed to tell us stuff. We don't have to return the favor."

Gerry said, "Not to argue with you, Sheriff, but I'm required to include a summary of the site's environmental history in my report. Faye is the best source of information I've got. To get the best information out of her, I'm going to have to share at least some of what I know."

"If you must, Detective. Within reason."

Faye had felt powerless for so long. The loss of the baby, the loss of Liz, the expenses that would come due for Gerry's cleanup… all of these things had taken their toll. Feeling the power balance of one area of her life shift in her direction gave her an adrenaline rush so pronounced that she could feel her legs shake.

"If you tell me enough, Gerry, and if you're lucky," she said, "I might just write that report for you."

The sheriff looked like he wanted to distract her from her newfound power. He leaned over to look at the photo and pointed at a spot near its bottom. He asked, "Who's that woman standing by the fuel pump?"

"Her name's Wilma," Faye said. "As far as I know, every cent that passes through her hands comes from sales from that one pump. She must be hurting by now."

So this was Wilma Jakes. Rainey had thought so. That's why he'd asked. He studied her jowly face, her stout legs, her resolute stance. This woman might be able to take him in a fist fight, and she would probably fight dirty.

He looked at his watch. Wilma herself would arrive in half an hour with the evidence about Liz's killer that she'd promised. The timing could be tricky. He didn't want to interrupt Faye, who was voluntarily giving him evidence he could use in the Barnett case, but when Wilma arrived, Faye would have to go. Testimony about a murder trumped information about environmental contamination. It just did.

Together, the three of them thumbed through the snapshots, and Rainey tried to hurry things along. The faces of Faye and her family passed by, time and again. He saw Liz and her son Chip. He saw Tommy. He saw random strangers, dozens of them, with nothing in common except that they were standing near Tommy's maintenance shop. If Liz were still alive and if Tommy had kept his sludge to himself, these pictures would mean nothing to anybody who wasn't emotionally attached to the people caught by the camera.

"You can keep the pictures. I have copies," Faye said, and Rainey gathered them in his hand, stacking them neatly like a deck of poker cards.

The picture of Liz was on top. There was something profoundly vital about the way her muscled arm swung out to encompass Faye's little boy. Something alive. Sheriff Rainey couldn't look away from her face and, judging by their silence, neither could Faye or Gerry.

"Who's that in the background?" Faye asked, bringing her eyes close to the picture, then tapping a fingernail on its upper left corner. Five or six people were coming around the building, heading from the parking lot to the restaurant door. They would have been nothing but blurs, indistinguishable in the distance, if it weren't for Delia's bright hair blowing into the weathered face of the man at her side.

Sheriff Rainey watched the archaeologist pull her reading glasses from her satchel. After a few seconds' study, she gave a firm nod. "Yep. It's them. Delia and Oscar. This means that they ate breakfast at Liz's sometime in the past two weeks. Breakfast is when my family usually eats at the marina."

"These pictures are only two weeks old?" Gerry said. "You mean I've been staking out Tommy's operation for more than a year and I missed those rusty drums behind his shed?"

The sheriff said, "You weren't here every day. You had other things to do. I know, because I assigned them to you. You must have come on days when he didn't have any customers. Luck of the draw."

"I don't see a date on the picture," Gerry said. "You're sure it's recent? You were there?"

"No, I wasn't. But I know when it was taken because Sly has only been here for two weeks."

"Oh, I thought he lived with you."

The sheriff saw Faye flinch at the suggestion that her father-in-law might do something drastic like move in with them, but she said nothing. She only shook her head.

"Has your husband mentioned seeing Delia and Oscar here?"

"As far as I know, he doesn't even know who they are. You can ask him, if you like."

The sheriff noticed that this woman who had gone to so much trouble to bring him all these photos didn't offer to ask her own husband. This was interesting, but it seemed immaterial. He'd ask Joe himself, if he decided it was important. It was time to end this interview, so that Wilma could come tell them what she knew.

He shifted his weight forward and Dr. Longchamp-Mantooth unconsciously shifted forward in response to body language that said, "This interview is over."

She got up and said, "Let me know if I can help in any other way. Maybe I could look at the pictures again or tell you what I remember about Liz or…it doesn't really matter. If I can help you find her killer, call me."

As Faye turned to go, someone emerged from the woodsy area bordering the marina, as if she, too, was watching their body language and responding.

"Who's that?" Steinberg asked.

Sheriff Rainey tapped a finger on the bottom of the top picture in the stack in his lap, the one where Wilma stood by her fuel pump while Liz greeted little Michael Longchamp-Mantooth. If Steinberg's wits were about him, that finger tap would be enough to let him know who he was looking at.

Rainey himself would have known who it was, even without Faye's photograph. It was Wilma Jakes, arriving ten minutes ahead of schedule for their chat. Now it really was time for Dr. Faye Longchamp-Mantooth to get in her boat and go.

Chapter Twenty-two

Faye couldn't have guessed Wilma's age within two decades. Maybe she was sixty-five. Maybe she was forty-five.

Wilma wore dusty flip-flops that gave an aged shuffle to her walk, but her shoulder-length hair was still more brown than gray, so Faye guessed that she was on the young end of that twenty-year span. Her worn facial skin was hollowed at the cheeks. Faye watched her watery eyes shift from the sheriff to Deputy Steinberg to Faye, then back to the sheriff for another visual sweep. They were an odd color. Like her hair, Wilma's eyes were brown going to gray. Even her face was tanned to the gray-brown of an unpainted wooden house.

Aged shuffle or not, Wilma was upon them before Faye had shouldered her satchel and walked away. "I saw somebody. The night Liz got killed. I saw somebody."

Faye saw the sheriff catch her eye, and she knew what he was trying to communicate. He wanted her to walk away.

So that's what she did. Or it's what she tried to do. Wilma had other ideas. The woman seemed to have come to the sheriff, ready to talk, and she wasn't interested in waiting until they were alone.

"The guy I saw, the one I told you about. The one I saw on the night Liz got killed? He was prowling around the outside of the building, peeping in the windows. I saw him walk over to Tommy's shed, too. It was a little bit after Liz closed up shop for the night, so there wasn't nobody else around."

"Did you recognize him?"

"Naw."

"Would you know him if you saw him again?"

"Naw. Didn't see his face, but he was a big man. I know that. Tall, for sure. Looked like a man with some muscle. Liz kept the parking lot lit up every night until she went to bed, so I got a good look at his back, but he never turned his face in my direction."

"Did you see a gun?"

She shook her head. "All I can tell you is that he was big and he was wearing blue jeans. And work boots."

Faye didn't look around, so she couldn't see the sheriff's eyes boring into her back. He wanted her gone. She was cooperative to a point, meaning that she kept walking, but she wasn't totally cooperative. She walked slowly and she took small steps.

The sheriff had eyes. He could see that she wasn't moving with any speed, but there was nothing he could do about it. He didn't dare interrupt Wilma to bark at Faye. What if Wilma decided to stop talking?

"Was anybody with this mysterious big man?"

First, Wilma said "Naw," but then she gathered herself to her full height and spoke again, clearly this time. "No."

"Did you see him leave?"

"No." Her voice was firm. "First, I saw him in the parking lot. Then he walked around the far side of the bait shop, and I didn't see him no more."

"What time was this?"

"Ain't sure."

"Was it before or after you heard the gunshot?"

"Didn't hear any gunshot."

Faye slowed to a trudge, knowing that the sheriff was probably wishing he could shoot *her* right about now.

"If you were close enough to see somebody, then you must have been close enough to hear a gunshot." Rainey's voice sounded so reasonable that he must be working hard to make it sound that way.

"I didn't like the look of that man sneaking around. I got in my car and drove to the Sunset Lounge. It's in Panacea. I stayed till closing time."

"Can somebody confirm that you were at the Sunset Lounge?"

"Sure. I'm there a lot of nights. They know me."

"Did you see Liz on the night she died?"

Wilma gave him a firm no.

"Have you seen any suspicious activity since then?"

Again, she said, "No."

When he said "Had you ever seen any suspicious activity before that?" Faye wondered if he was just trying to exhaust all the possible questions that Wilma could answer with "No." Anyone could tell that the woman had come to tell the sheriff only so much and no more.

Faye picked up her pace. She'd heard all that Wilma was going to say. If she put enough distance between herself and the sheriff before Wilma walked away, he wouldn't be able to yell at her for dawdling.

As expected, Wilma quickly drew away from the two lawmen. By the time Faye reached her own oyster skiff, Wilma was gone.

Faye had dawdled away the afternoon, walking the trails that circled her island until she was too tired to move. She had no destination. She just couldn't stand to see anybody, not the environmental scientists at their dig site on the other side of the island and not her family in the house at its heart. After a lot of walking, she had found a place where she could sit on the ground and lean against a tree. It was a good spot to do yet more timekilling web searches. The Internet wasn't going to tell her why Liz was dead or why her baby was dead, and it sure wasn't going to tell her how long she was going to feel this way, but it certainly was distracting.

At some point, she remembered that it had been a long time since she ate, and the banana and energy bar that she'd thrown in her satchel that morning were long gone. Since she'd promised herself that she would eat more, if only to keep Joe from worrying so much, it was time to go home.

As she walked quietly into the hallway of her home's ground-floor basement, her satchel felt so heavy in her hand that it seemed to drag the floor. She could smell chicken frying somewhere ahead of her, so she knew where Joe was. The slapping of bare feet on brick floor told her that Michael was on his way. She set down the satchel and dropped into the widespread crouch that usually kept her upright when her son launched himself into her arms.

As she waited for Michael to leap, his grandfather came into sight. "I knew you was home by the way the little fella's face lit up."

When Faye saw that Sly held a wooden locomotive in one oversized hand and a coffee cup in the other, she realized two things. She realized that he was a big man who wore blue jeans and work boots. And she realized that she loved him for his coffee cup. She loved him for deciding that coffee was a better bet for him than whiskey. Every day, he made that decision again.

Maybe that love showed on her face, but all Sly said was, "Welcome home, Daughter. I believe my son has intentions of putting some meat on your bones. He's frying chicken *and* okra. And also some corn. He just slapped the pulley bone out of my hand 'cause he says it's your favorite piece of the bird. You better go eat it so's he'll quit yelling at me."

So she did. She sat at the kitchen table, so close to the stove that Joe could fork food out of all of his skillets, straight onto her plate. She gnawed the rich meat of a chicken thigh right down to the bone. She used her fingers to pop crispy rounds of cornmeal-coated okra into her mouth like candy. Joe's corn, cut off the cob and fried in butter, dripped off her fork.

He didn't say anything. He just kept giving her food.

The pulley bone, a palm-sized hunk of white meat clinging to a wishbone, was an odd dessert, but she saved it for last. Then she wrapped the clean wishbone in a napkin and tucked it in her satchel for later. The time would come, sooner or later, when she would know what wish should be made with it.

The gargantuan meal had put Faye in bed before sundown. She had slept hard for five hours straight, and that was a better night's sleep than she'd had in a month, but now she was done. It would be a long time before the sun showed its face, probably more, and she needed something to occupy her mind.

Joe had been in bed maybe fifteen minutes. He was now sleeping like a man who'd cooked up ten thousand calories. She eased herself out from under the covers and found her satchel. Once out of the house, she opened it and pulled out her flashlight and Cally's oral history.

The flashlight led her out the basement door and up the stairs to the grand front porch of Joyeuse Island's big house. Curled up in a rocking chair, she read her great-great-grandmother's stories. Faye hadn't given up on finding Elias Croft.

She wondered whether Elias had been a common name in those days, because she remembered Cally mentioning a man named Elias who had lived on Joyeuse Island. She'd never had any reason to think that this man and the respectful Yankee captain had been one and the same. In fact, she had presumed that Elias had been one of the freed slaves who worked for Cally, but now she was beginning to wonder.

Cally's memoirs started before the Civil War and they stretched to the Great Depression. Based on what she remembered of Oscar's story, she hadn't had the impression that his Elias had lived into old age. Oscar's great-great-grandmother had received letters about her Elias for years, it was true, but she had died prematurely of consumption and she'd still managed to outlive him. So he'd likely died after the Civil War, but before the turn of the twentieth century.

The question to be found in Cally's journal was *when* a man named Elias had lived on Joyeuse Island. If Cally had known an Elias during the Depression, then he wasn't Elias Croft. If she knew him during Reconstruction, then perhaps he was.

Not sure where in the sheafs of paper to look for him, Faye flipped to random pages until a familiar passage showed itself. This story of Cally's Elias was overshadowed by a crisis that had nearly killed everyone on Joyeuse Island. It was a wonder that Faye had remembered his name in the first place.

◇◇◇

Excerpt from the oral history of Cally Stanton, recorded by the Federal Writer's Project, 1935

It was my job to keep the island provisioned, always. It was my job when the old Master was alive, and it was my job when my husband Courtney took over after the old Master died. After my husband Courtney died, it was still my job to stock the stores on this island, and it would be for all the rest of my days.

Young Courtney don't know she still needs me to keep things running, but she do. We raise most all our food, always did, but there ain't never been a time when we wouldn't have sorely missed the supply boat if it didn't come bring the other things I sent away for. Even during the War, the supply boat got out here now and then, and it was always a happy day when the boat come out here to Joyeuse Island.

Tea. Coffee. The supply boat brought us wheat flour and sugar, when I had the money. Most medicines, I could make for free out of weeds I found in the woods, but some of 'em needed to be bought and paid for. Castor oil comes in handy, sometimes, and cod liver oil, and Elias swore by something he said was a distilled homeopathic oil that come all the way from India. "Jowl mooker" is what he called it, and I do think it was a help to him at times.

The supply boat brought yard goods to sew up into clothes. Kerosene. Newspapers and books. Records, after we got the Victrola. It was all I could do to keep everybody on the island from a-gathering at the dock as soon as that boat come into sight, but I always shooed 'em away. How was I supposed to keep my accounts straight if I had a hundred people watching me tally up the deliveries?

I met the boat when it come in the rain and in the cold. I met the boat the day after we put my husband

Courtney in the ground. I met the boat the morning of the day young Courtney come into the world. Many's the time I carried her on my hip down to the dock, my account books in my free hand. I go with her now, never mind how much she fusses when I mess with her bookkeeping. Only one day did I miss that boat, and it was the day I was in the bed with the yellow fever, me and everybody else living in my household and in the workers' cabins out back. Everybody on the island was down with yellow fever but Elias. I guess it was the only time he was happy to live all by hisself.

I was as scared as I ever been. I'd tended many a soul with yellow fever and I knew what it was like to die from it, blood a-running out your eyes and your mouth. Still, I think I would've crawled to that boat on my hands and knees out of nothing but habit, if I could just have got out of bed. Sometimes I think it's habits that keep us a-going. Breathing's a habit, and that's a fact.

Elias went down there to the dock, wrapped up in a scarf and hat in the full-out summertime—I told him not to go, but he did—and he told the boat captain how it was. The captain went straight back to shore and sent us a doctor.

We all lived, and I credit Elias and the captain and that doctor for a miracle. Nothing I ever done for Elias in all the years I knew him could add up to what he done for us that one day. He took a risk to do it, and he shouldn't have. I told him not to.

So there he was. Elias. Was this Elias Croft? Was the Yankee Captain Croft named Elias? Did anything in Cally's stories connect the two men? No, not that Faye could see.

Did those stories suggest that Cally killed either man or kept him captive? No. Did they clear Cally's name? No. She revealed no murderous feelings for the man she called simply "Elias," and she'd seemed to have warm feelings about her encounter with "Captain Croft." but that proved nothing.

Could Faye put a date on the story of Elias and the supply boat? Not really. Cally herself had said she met that boat for her entire adult life. But what about the part of the story that mentioned yellow fever? Faye remembered that the last big yellow fever epidemic in America had happened in New Orleans, sometime after the turn of the twentieth century, and this gave her an idea. She shot off a text to Magda:

> Can't sleep, so I'm sitting on my front porch worrying about really important stuff like when the last big yellow fever epidemics came through this area. Late 19th-century, right? Were there any particularly bad years?

Magda turned her phone off at night, so she would wake up to this question. If Faye had resisted off-loading the question onto Magda, she would have lost any slender chance that she might go back to sleep, but now her mind could rest. More likely, her mind could find something else to fret about.

Faye re-read the passage about Cally's Elias one more time, then she did it again. The second reading gave her another question for Magda, who had gotten used to Faye's weird texts years before. She typed a particularly random question into her phone and sent it to Magda:

> Still can't sleep. Were there any popular homeopathic remedies imported from India in that same time period, the late 19th century? Were any of them named "jowl mooker"? Or something like that. I don't know a word of Hindi or Sanskrit, so you could tell me it was another word for hog jowls and I would believe you. I would also start getting hungry for hog jowls, which I do believe is happening right about now. Hope you're sleeping well.

Magda might bark at her for bothering her with weirdo questions, but Faye knew it was an act. Her best friend and former professor lived for weirdo questions.

Chapter Twenty-three

Sometime during the night, Faye had figured out how to curl herself into a ball that fit comfortably between the wooden arms of her rocking chair. Almost comfortably.

She hadn't slept. Sometimes she'd surfed the web on her phone. Sometimes she'd made notes on Cally's reminiscences and how they might relate to Elias Croft. Sometimes she'd just studied the porch ceiling over her head. She knew it was blue because she'd painted it that color, but everything outside the circle of her flashlight was rendered in shades of gray. The luminescent screen of her phone was so out-of-place that she sometimes flicked it off, just to let her eyes rest.

Water sounds reached her ears. The sound of water slapping the bottom of her dock told her drowsy brain that the tide was high and the seas were rough. Wind on her face told her that the rough seas were driven by a storm far away. She didn't have to think about these things. She just knew, just as she knew that a faraway buzz, growing louder, was a boat coming her way.

Her eyelids slid open and shut a few more times before she could rouse herself enough to check her phone for the time. It wasn't seven yet. Even Gerry's workaholic remediation crew wasn't dedicated enough to get out here this early. Who was out there and why were they coming at this hour?

Faye hated unannounced guests, which was fine, because she never got them. The only good explanation for the coming boat that Faye's sleep-addled brain could manage was a surprise party. Her birthday was weeks away and so was Joe's. Michael's was months away. So was Amande's, and she wasn't even home. She had no idea when Sly's birthday was, and she had no idea if he had friends who might throw him a party. If he did, they were in Oklahoma.

She shook off fatigue and stood up. From this angle, she had a better line-of-sight to the dock. It was still obscured by trees, but she could see water glinting through their leaves. When the unidentified boat pulled alongside her dock, she could see the movement of more than one person as they secured it and walked her way. Unseen strangers made her think of Liz and Emma, and she wished very much not to be alone.

Faye was on a porch that stood a story above the ground. Joe was below her, surrounded by the thick masonry walls of an above-ground basement. She could scream her loudest and he would never hear her. Fortunately, she had a cell phone in her pocket.

She dialed his number and prayed he hadn't silenced his ringer. Rewarded by the rumble of his sleepy voice, she said, "Somebody's here. More than one somebody. Come up here on the porch now, and bring your dad."

◇◇◇

Faye and Joe had been sent back into their own house. They sat downstairs in their living room, surrounded by four cold thick walls lit by a single window. When they'd converted the basement of the big old plantation house into living quarters that they could afford to heat and cool, they'd cozied up this room with yellow paint and shelves of books. Somehow, being ordered to wait downstairs by people who had taken over their own front porch had caused "cozy" to quickly shift into "claustrophobic." Michael was still asleep and neither of them was hungry, so they'd had nothing to do but sit and wait.

Sheriff Rainey and Deputy Steinberg had asked straight out to talk to Joe's father alone. Sly had given a quiet nod of assent, so Faye and Joe had backed away. They'd left him on the porch standing in a wary position, legs flexed and both arms slightly extended as if to ward off an attack.

Joe sat across from Faye, looking afraid, and she couldn't think of anything comforting to say. She had just put her hand on his knee and held it there while he covered it with his own.

Neither of them asked the obvious questions, "What do they want with Sly? They were just here yesterday. What's changed since then?"

Joe managed to sit still for three minutes, tops, then he hopped up and said, "Dad's gonna need some coffee when this is over. I'll go make some."

Faye felt the same need to do something useful, but what would it be? Maybe she should go fetch a carton of cigarettes and a lighter so that she and Joe could meet Sly at the door with both caffeine and nicotine for comfort?

No, that was going too far. Michael and Amande deserved a grandfather who wasn't crippled by emphysema or dead of cancer.

As it turned out, she wouldn't have had time to find the cigarettes. Sly was downstairs before the coffee had brewed. He sank into the soft cushions of the easy chair that Joe had just left and asked, "Do you know who Delia Scarsdale is?"

"Yeah. She and a man named Oscar Croft are here on vacation. They've been around for weeks. You haven't met them?"

"Nope."

Remembering the photo of Sly chasing Michael toward the back door of Liz's restaurant while Oscar and Delia approached from the parking lot out front, she said, "You probably saw them one of those times when you and Joe were eating breakfast at Liz's. Older guy? Young woman, long blonde hair?"

He shrugged. "Maybe. I spent most of my time joshing with Liz while she slung hash. If Delia and what's-his-face was there, I might not have noticed. Anyways, the sheriff wants to know what I was doing last night when somebody broke into her bedroom and attacked her. Delia, I mean. It was Delia that got attacked."

"Was she hurt? What happened?"

"I don't know." Sly fumbled in his pocket and came out with an empty pack of cigarettes. The defeated slump in his shoulders made Faye almost sorry that she hadn't brought him some.

"What did the sheriff say to you? Does he have any idea who did it?"

"They showed me a belt the guy left behind and they asked if it was mine."

The intruder had taken off his belt. This didn't sound good.

"They don't think it was you, do they?"

"They came straight here, so they must think it was me. I told them hell, no, it wasn't my belt, because I was wearing the only one I owned. Then I didn't tell them no more."

"They're already out here talking to you, right after it happened? Sly, you need to get a lawyer."

Sly shook his head. "I might've told 'em I was gonna call my lawyer, but I didn't mean it. I had a lawyer once, and he didn't do me a damn bit of good. How could he? That time, I did the crime. This time, I didn't. And I can't afford a lawyer anyway. I believe I'll take my chances."

"You didn't give them an alibi?"

"I was in bed. By myself. Asleep. What kind of alibi am I gonna give?"

"I have one for you."

And Faye was out the door, brushing past her husband, who was standing in the door with a brimming cup of coffee in his hand.

◇◇◇

Hurry, hurry, hurry.

Faye told herself to move fast, because she needed to talk to Sheriff Rainey right this minute, before Sly solidified in his mind as the most likely suspect. She dialed Sheriff Mike's number as she ran. He was retired, so he didn't officially know anything about current criminal activity in Micco County. In reality, he knew everything.

The tone of Sheriff Mike's voice told her that the crime hanging over Sly's head was disturbing him. This was significant. Sheriff Mike had seen almost everything in his long career.

"Yeah, I heard about what happened to the nice tour guide lady." Sheriff Mike's voice was quiet. "Bad thing. It was a real bad thing."

Faye was running and breathing hard, but she could gasp out short sentences. "Was she hurt?"

"She's okay, but it could've gone another way. Somebody busted in her window. Ripped the bedspread off her bed before she was good and awake. Wrapped it around her head so she ain't gonna be able to identify anybody on sight. Tried to use the sheets to tie her to the bedposts, but she got away long enough to open the bedroom door and make some noise. The bastard went out the window before Oscar came running."

Faye tried to shake the image of Delia, sprawled across her own bed while a man she couldn't see removed his belt. "When did this happen?"

"It ain't been long. Sometime in the wee hours, a long time after midnight."

"That's what I thought. Thanks, Mike."

Her feet pounded the dock's wooden boards as she turned off her phone. Sheriff Rainey and his deputy were already in their boat, pulling away, but they looked up when she bellowed, "Wait!"

Sheriff Rainey idled the motor and reached out an arm to keep the boat from banging into the dock. The water was rough and it wasn't easy for him to keep his grip, but he hung on and waited for Faye to speak. She leaned forward, hands on her knees, and held up a hand while she tried to catch her breath.

"I know where he was. Sly. I know where he was. I can give him an alibi for last night. It wasn't Sly who tried to hurt Delia."

The sheriff said, "I'm listening."

If they figured out she'd talked to Sheriff Mike, he'd never give her insider information again, so she couldn't let them know that she knew the timing of the attack. She had to act like she was guessing.

"It can't have been long since Delia was attacked. My father-in-law is under the impression that you came straight here. Even taking into account that you had to respond to her call and question her and look for evidence, I'm still thinking that the attack came well after midnight, right?"

The sheriff gave her a look that could only be described as a non-response.

Her breath came ragged as she pointed to the white-painted walls of Joyeuse, clearly visible through the trees. "I've been sitting on the porch of that house since midnight, right after my husband came to bed. I didn't see Sly come or go. I didn't hear any boat come or go, not until I heard you coming this morning."

"What about before you got out there?"

So they were going to try to keep her guessing about when the crime happened. Sheriff Mike had told her that Delia was attacked long after she walked onto that porch, but she could play that game.

"I'm sure my husband was with him till bedtime. They like to stay up and play cards. Come in and ask Joe. Between the two of us, I think we can vouch for Sly's whereabouts for the whole night."

Gerry Steinberg spoke up for the first time. "Meaning no disrespect, but I have to point out that we're talking about your husband's father. I understand that you want to protect him, but this evidence isn't all that compelling. All you're telling me is that Mr. Mantooth's family is willing to say, 'Coincidentally, we didn't sleep a wink. We can vouch for him.'"

Faye locked eyes with Gerry as she pulled her phone out of her hip pocket. She opened the thread of texts that had passed between her and Magda and handed the phone to him. Beautifully and clearly time-stamped, those texts proved where she'd been and when.

"See? At 1:32 am, I sent a text to Magda that began, 'Can't sleep, so I'm sitting on my front porch worrying...' At 2:14 am, I followed it with, 'Still can't sleep. Were there any popular homeopathic remedies imported from India in that same time period, the late 19th century?'"

She took the phone back and opened up her record of outgoing calls. "Oh, look. At 6:47 am, I called Joe's phone, which is pretty decent evidence that we weren't sitting together in the house when you got here. See?" She held it out just long enough for them to confirm what she said, then jerked it back. "My testimony that I was still sitting on the porch, saw you coming, and called Joe to come outside jives with this phone call just fine. It explains why all three of us were waiting on the porch to meet you, doesn't it?"

Sheriff Rainey tried to speak, but she said, "Wait. I'm not finished. I don't like even a suggestion that I'm a liar. Look here." She held out the phone again. "Here's an outgoing phone call to Emma at 12:07 am. After her break-in, I promised myself I'd call her every night at bedtime, just to make sure she was okay. And here I'd already failed, just two nights later, because I went to sleep right after supper. She didn't answer when I called at midnight to apologize, so I'm guessing she was asleep. If you hurry to her house and check her phone before she deletes my message, you can hear me say I'm sitting on my porch and thinking of her."

"Are you finished?" asked the sheriff.

"No." She tapped the Notes icon on her phone. "For the rest of the night, I sat in that chair and made notes about my great-great-grandmother's oral history and Liz's murder and Emma's break-in."

She showed the men her phone's screen again then pulled the phone back and scrolled through her notes with her thumb.

"Here they are, all of them time-stamped. Two forty-nine. Three-oh-two. Three-sixteen. And so on. You can try to say I saw Sly come and go and I'm lying about it. You can try to say that I spent all night faking this paper trail...a paper trail that I didn't know I was going to need unless I was conspiring with Sly to help him break into Delia's room. But do those things sound logical at all?"

She looked up from the phone's screen. "Oh, let's just say what we mean. Sly told me that you found a man's belt in her room. You can say that I was conspiring with my father-in-law so he could have an alibi for raping somebody. But to say those things, you will first have to clearly say that you think I'm a liar."

The men's gazes drifted down away from her eyes, but just for a second. They were professionals. They got over it.

Gerry said, "Well, strictly speaking, that phone is not a paper trail."

"No, it's not. It's an electronic trail," the sheriff pointed out.

If the phone hadn't been so expensive, Faye would have thrown it at them.

"We're sorry if we insulted you," the sheriff said, "but we're paid to be skeptical. Your testimony and Joe's…and your phone's…support an alibi for your father-in-law. But the alibi isn't iron-clad. He could have slipped past you, coming and going, while you were making those notes. He could have hidden a boat on the far side of the island, slipping out the back door. If he did that, you wouldn't see him go from where you were sitting on the front porch."

"That doesn't make any sense unless he knew I'd be sitting there."

Sheriff Rainey inclined his head in assent. "You are correct. Your evidence makes him a weaker suspect. It doesn't eliminate him as a suspect, but it does help him. He's lucky to have you on his side."

"You ever thought about going to law school, Dr. Long-champ-Mantooth?" Gerry asked.

"I have a PhD, so I have spent quite enough time in school. Go out there and find some real criminals. None of them live here."

Chapter Twenty-four

Tommy sat at his workbench, looking out of his maintenance shop's one window. He doubted that he could be seen unless somebody walked right up to the greasy glass and peered in, but he could see out just fine. He avoided law enforcement officers on general principle, and he most definitely did not want to speak to Sheriff Rainey or Deputy Steinberg today, unless forced to do so by law.

It took the officers a little while to tie up their boat, and they were deep in conversation by the time they walked past where he sat. He watched them move his way, one step at a time.

Step. They approached his shop, so close that either of them could have reached out a fist and punched its wall.

Step. They passed the window without looking inside where Tommy sat.

Step. They passed the door without noticing the telltale sign that someone was on the other side of it. Its padlock was missing. Tommy had unlocked it and put it in his pocket with the key, which is where they always stayed until he finished working and locked the place behind him.

And another step. Tommy was home free. There was no way now that they would notice that he was here. He had arrived by boat, so there was no truck in the parking lot to give him away. He'd had the forethought to hide his boat a quarter-mile east, in a tiny inlet obscured by tree branches hanging so low that they brushed the water. They hadn't seen it as they came in from the island where the good-looking archaeologist woman lived, and that was a good thing. He'd been out to that island himself, just the day before, and he needed to hide all evidence of his trip.

He'd needed to wait overnight, so that nobody would see a light on at his shop, but he'd gotten here at the crack of dawn. Who would've thought that the cops would already be out and about? Didn't they have doughnuts to eat?

As soon as he was sure they were gone, he'd finish the task they'd interrupted. He'd come here to fetch some rags and two buckets of the best industrial solvent money could buy. He knew the law wasn't through with him, and he couldn't let anybody see his boat in this condition. He needed to get it so clean that they'd never be able to find a trace of the things he'd been hauling. Suspecting a man of something and proving it were two different things, and boat mechanics owned solvents that could clean anything off anything.

Tommy figured it would take him a couple of hours to make his boat cleaner than it had been the day he bought it.

◇◇◇

Wilma listened to Tommy's phone ring until it went to voice mail. He wasn't out of bed yet.

Of course, he wasn't out of bed yet, and he probably wasn't alone there. He wasn't working these days, which gave him time and energy for drinking himself into a stupor with Lolita. She really must love him. At the moment, Tommy didn't have any income to pay for the liquor or for her services.

He sounded half-drunk in his voice mail message, so Wilma knew that she was going to have to be the public face of their partnership. People who knew her would laugh at the notion of Wilma investing in a marina, but people had been underestimating Wilma for fifty years. She had some money saved. She had enough cash to buy herself a dress to wear to the bank when she went to negotiate the loan. She could pay somebody to cut her hair and fix it. She could buy all the makeup she needed at Walgreens, and she did in fact know how to put it on.

More importantly, she knew the name of the bank that held the mortgage on Liz's business. Many nights, she'd sat with Liz after the bar closed, sharing drinks and competing for who had the saddest story. She'd heard all about the bank and its antics.

Wilma knew that Liz had sweated every check she sent that bank. It was never a sure thing that any of her checks would clear until they cleared. Anytime a check didn't clear, Liz knew to look out for letters and calls from the entity that she called Asshole National Bank.

More than once, Wilma and Liz had taped a nagging letter from Asshole National Bank to the bar's dartboard and had some drunken fun. There had been many months when Liz got behind on her payments, but she had always found a way to catch up. Wilma felt sure that Asshole National Bank was missing Liz's almost-regular payments and her late fees. Especially the late fees. They were practically pure profit.

Deep in her heart, Wilma believed she could step right into Liz's shoes and run her business, because Liz had told her all about it. Those nights in the bar had been like tequila-fueled management training. Wilma's best guess was that Asshole National Bank was sweating over Liz's outstanding loan. How easy was it going to be for them to sell a business that had never been profitable? Wally had turned to crime to support himself when he owned the marina. Liz had dealt with the problem by living for years without a dime to spend on herself.

And now poor little Asshole National Bank was making do without that income. Wilma wasn't half-bad at math. Since Liz had been getting by, Wilma figured she and Tommy would be in good shape if they got hold of the marina, because they already had income from their own businesses. If they rolled the marina rentals, the income from the bar and grill, the boat ramp fees, the fuel sales, and the boat maintenance into an entity that they could manage and promote as a single business, they would be sitting pretty.

Interest rates were lower than when Liz got her loan, so she and Tommy wouldn't be struggling under the same payment schedule. They could even make a few hundred dollars a month by renting out Liz's apartment.

Wilma had run the numbers. This could work.

To most banks, Wilma and her partner might seem like low-lifes and bad credit risks, but Liz had been rough around the edges and Asshole National Bank knew that she'd always found a way to get her bills paid. Wilma figured that, with the help of a new dress, a haircut, and the Walgreens cosmetics department, she could manage to look like as much of an upstanding citizen as Liz ever did.

And, best of all, Tommy would have to be satisfied with thirty percent because she was going to keep him out of jail. For the first time in her life, Wilma had the upper hand in a business deal. She had waited fifty years for the chance to say, "Screw you," to the world that had ground her under its heel because she'd been born poor and ugly. Liz's death had given her that chance.

Faye had watched the sheriff's boat disappear into the distance and still she stood on her own dock. She didn't want to be where she was. Where did she want to be?

She wanted to be in her boat.

Where did she want to go?

It would be a while before Gerry and his crew showed up for work. Faye had a sudden desire to be at the contamination site in the daylight, alone, so she indulged that desire. Newly appreciative of a smartphone's power to put a time-stamp on a person's whereabouts, she shot Joe a text:

> You and your dad should go ahead and have breakfast. I'm taking the boat out for a few minutes and I'll eat when I get back.

Faye rounded the far end of the island and cut the motor, drifting silently into sight of the live oak that marked the contaminated area. She'd hoped that seeing the trouble spot from the water would give her a miraculous mystery-solving perspective, but she was disappointed. Between her boat and land, she saw nothing but an expanse of shallow water. Beyond it was a sandy shelf of land between the water and the excavation. This sand-and-grass beach was narrow now, with the tide high. It would be wider later in the day.

She had seen these things before. They were not news.

Beyond the overgrown beach was an open area of about an acre, centered on the excavation. The big live oak gave the only real shade in that acre. Faye would have guessed it to be hundreds of years old. Nadia had taken one of her background samples at its base, on the presumption that the soil beneath that tree had been undisturbed by anything but its roots for a long, long time.

Behind the open acre was the lightly wooded area where she had found the piece of an old wooden trough, the basis for some of her grandmother's scariest stories about The Monster Man. And now she knew that it was tainted with arsenic, but again, this was nothing new. What could she learn, right this minute, by looking carefully at this trouble spot?

She looked down at the water, glad that she could see clear to the bottom. There was no oil slick on its surface, where there had been an obvious rainbow sheen just a few days before. Maybe she'd done the right thing by calling in the cleanup crew. Maybe they were doing a good job, earning every penny of their eventual bill.

Raking her eyes over the scene, she saw only one thing that surprised her. The cupola of her house rose above the far tree-tops. The distance from her home to the spot where she sat was a decent walk, but she sometimes forgot how massive the big house at Joyeuse Island really was. Two stories, surrounded by porches on all sides, sat atop an above-ground basement, and the whole thing was topped by a cupola the size of a large bedroom. The view from that cupola was breathtaking, blue-green water dotted by islands and hugging a dark coastline. It had been a long while since Faye'd had enough free time to sit up there and do nothing but look.

If she went there now, she would see that her great-grand-mother Courtney had been right when she remembered seeing this end of the island from the top floor of her house. If there had ever been a Monster Man's cabin here, or any cabin at all, little Courtney could absolutely have sat in the cupola and seen lamplight shining out of the monster's cabin door. When Courtney, Faye's great-grandmother, was a little girl, that lamp would have been lit by burning kerosene.

Had Faye really dug up The Monster Man's fuel tank?

Before she gave any thought to what she was doing, Faye had beached the boat. Trowel in hand, she sidled up to the excava-tion that she really wasn't supposed to revisit until Gerry had signed off on its safety. He had greatly enlarged the unit where she'd been working, removing the old tank and the kerosene-saturated soil near it. The contaminated soil had been placed in fifty-five-gallon drums that sat nearby, waiting for disposal. Soil that had been screened but tested as clean sat in piles, waiting to be returned to the excavation as backfill.

As Faye surveyed the piles of clean soil and thought that "screened" was a funny word. If she'd been the one doing the excavation, looking for artifacts instead of contamination, her technicians would have used actual screens to check out this soil. They would have methodically run this backdirt through progressively smaller screens to separate it from the tiny things that archaeologists loved. Seeds from garden plants, fish bones left from somebody's dinner, buttons—any of these things could help tell the story of the way people used to live.

Faye squatted next to Gerry's screened soil and thought. If this dirt was clean enough, environmentally speaking, to go back in the ground, then why couldn't she screen it again her way? When she saw Gerry, she'd ask his permission to do that. In the meantime, she figured he wouldn't even notice if she disturbed his dirt.

There was no stratigraphy left to preserve. This soil was totally churned. Since she couldn't do much more damage than Gerry had already done, Faye stuck her trowel in the pile at a random spot and started scraping.

It would have beggared the imagination if she'd found something interesting right away, and she didn't. Faye had spent a lot of her life digging and finding nothing. This had fine-tuned her already considerable capacity for patience. She used that patience to keep scraping at Gerry's backdirt for two hours until she heard the boat bringing him and his crew back out to Joyeuse Island.

During that time, she found only a triangular shard of blue glass and a chip of white china, neither of them as big as a dime. They had the look of age, but she saw no identifying marks on them to tell her anything more without the aid of a lab. Nevertheless, they had their value.

Faye had never heard any mention of someone living on this end of the island. There had never been a garbage pit here, because nobody was going to haul garbage to this end of the island when it was so easy to bury it behind the house. She could construct any number of narratives that would bring these bits of trash to the west end of Joyeuse Island—hurricanes, wayward pirates, messy picnickers—but one of those narratives was her grandmother's tale of a forbidden cabin. It presumed that someone really had lived in a cabin right here. It presumed that The Monster Man stories were based on truth.

After eating the pancakes Joe had saved for her, after doing the breakfast dishes with him, after leaving Sly with his coffee, Faye put Michael on her hip and she took Joe's hand. They walked up the sneak stair to the second floor. From there they stood on the landing below the cupola and Joe lowered the staircase that would take them up there.

It wasn't the original cupola. They had lost it in the big hurricane that had almost taken the whole house and the two of them along with it. Together, they had reconstructed it, building the wooden framework and roofing it and fitting new windows into all four sides. For a while after they finished the renovation, they had brought their morning coffee and bedtime snacks up here, but business and children and everyday chores had distracted them, and those relaxed days seemed a long time in the past.

As Joe listened to Faye's stories about The Monster Man, he looked out a window and followed her pointing finger with his eyes. She showed him where the tank had been and where the arsenic still was. She told him about the bits of china and glass, and she asked him to imagine where the old cabin might have stood.

He scrolled through her phone's displays as she talked, and he listened to her tell him how she'd shown Sheriff Rainey and Gerry Steinberg that they were wrong about his father. Then they'd just sat for a while, side by side, and watched the sun on the water. Faye could have convinced herself that there was no trouble out there in a world so beautiful, until Joe spoke and interrupted the silence.

"I hear what you're saying about how you were out on the porch all night, and I appreciate you telling the sheriff about it."

"But?"

"But it's not proof that you didn't go to sleep for a little while. Or that Dad didn't find a way to slip past you, real quiet."

"I would have heard—"

"Probably you would've heard. But probably ain't proof."

Joe wasn't looking at her. He was looking out at the water where his father would have been navigating a boat in the dark, if he'd taken a surreptitious trip ashore to attack Delia.

"It ain't proof," he repeated. "I guess what I'm trying to say is this. I'm real grateful that you're defending my dad this way. I believe every word you say. I believe everything you showed me on your phone. Still, all of those things added together don't make me as certain-sure as you are that he ain't guilty."

Joe had taken Michael back downstairs, leaving Faye to look out at the water, alone, wondering how Joe could stand to let his father stay in the house if he thought the man might be a rapist. Or a killer.

The vibration of the phone in her pocket interrupted her thoughts.

When she answered it, Sheriff Mike's voice said "Hello."

"Long time no talk. How's Magda?"

"Working too hard. She needs to retire, so she can do nothing but drink coffee and gossip. Just like me. She says she's too young to retire, and she is, but that don't mean I'll quit pestering her to stop working and start sitting around, passing the time of day with her loving husband. Anyway, I've got some more gossip for you."

"Lucky me."

"Since you were so interested in poor Delia Scarsdale's situation this morning, I thought you might want to hear the latest scuttlebutt. It's about Liz this time. You knew her a lot better than Miss Scarsdale, so I thought you'd be even more interested in this piece of gossip."

Faye looked toward shore, as if she could see the marina from where she sat. As if she could see the shallow water where Liz met death. "Have they found her killer?"

"No. But Tommy Barnett has been running his mouth."

"About what? Does he know who killed her?"

"It's not about who killed her. It's about who was the mastermind behind Tommy's waste dumping business."

"I thought Tommy was behind it, if it makes any sense at all to call Tommy a mastermind. He was the one getting paid for it."

"Well, that's just the thing." Sheriff Mike paused, like the true storyteller that he was. Storytellers made people wait for the good stuff.

"*What's* just the thing?"

"Tommy says that he wasn't the only one getting paid for dumping. He says that Liz was the one who ran the operation. He said people would come to her with their chemical problems. She would put them in touch with Tommy and then he'd make those problems go away, no questions asked. He claims that she took most of the money and let him take the risks and do the scut work."

"Does that even matter?" Faye asked in a voice loud enough to overload the Sheriff Mike's phone speaker. "He's guilty. Gerry Steinberg and those other deputies saw him break the law with their own eyes. Why are they letting him accuse Liz when she's not here to defend herself?"

"You asked if it mattered whether Liz was involved? No, it doesn't. Yes, it does. It's complicated." He took a breath, but kept talking without taking a real storyteller's break, probably because he didn't want Faye to yell at him again. "Realistically, I doubt he'll serve jail time. He was flagrant about his dumping, but compare the results to the Deepwater Horizon spill and you'll get a sense of scale. And it's technically a first offense, especially if he tries to claim he didn't know he was breaking the law until Steinberg chased him down."

"So. No jail time. What's he worried about? Fines? Penalties?"

"Yes. There's a fancy formula for calculating his fines. It will look at environmental damage Tommy caused. It will consider how much he gained, money-wise. It will consider whether his violation was deliberate or chronic—"

"Yes to both. Deliberate. And chronic."

Sheriff Mike continued as if she hadn't interrupted him. "And then the powers-that-be will run all those factors into a blender and come out with a number that says what Tommy has to pay for his environmental sins. If they don't think his crime is worth the expense of a big court case, they have an incentive to keep the penalty low.

"Define 'low' for me."

"If the fine is under ten thousand dollars, they can handle things administratively without going to court."

Was ten thousand dollars really "low" in the environmental world? What did this say about the cost of the work Deputy Steinberg was doing on Joyeuse Island? Faye and Joe could soon be as broke as Tommy Barnett.

"You know they're never going to get ten thousand dollars out of Tommy," she said.

"Hell no. But the penalty can't be too low, because the state wants to make Tommy an example to other people. Penalty calculations are a dark art. The fine goes down if the environmental damage is considered to be low, but how do you judge that anyway? Sometimes community service or public education can substitute for the dollars-and-cents fine. And I think that's what he's aiming for, myself."

"Who's aiming for what?"

"Tommy. You'd think his case is black-and-white. Guilty or not guilty. But not really. If he's not going to jail, and I don't think he is, his whole game comes down to one thing. Getting that fine as low as possible. So why not shift the blame onto a dead woman? Make himself look like the little guy she took advantage of. Hell. I think he went out as soon as the sheriff finished questioning him and tossed the rest of his sludge inventory."

"Why would he do that?"

"So he don't get caught with so much stuff that he looks like a major player. It was a stupid move, but his best defense is to make himself look as stupid as possible."

"Which won't be hard."

"No, ma'am, it won't. The powers-that-be know that he doesn't have any money to pay a fine, so he's hoping they'll think 'Why not just sentence this dumbass to get some education and do some community service? Case closed.'"

So Tommy was going to try to save himself by dragging Liz's name through the dirt. Faye was not amused.

"Faye, you knew Liz and you know Tommy. Do you think he's telling the truth? Was she involved?"

"Nope. I've got no proof. I just don't think she'd do what he said. She loved living on the water. I don't think she'd have been willing to pollute it."

"I don't, either," Sheriff Mike said.

Faye looked out the cupola's windows, over the roof of her old home and over her island and out to sea. She didn't have anything left to say, not even good-bye. She just sighed and said, "Lying about the dead is really bad karma," then she hung up.

Sheriff Graham and Gerry Steinberg had started Faye's day shortly after dawn. Faye's morning had been stressful and busy and it wasn't even over. What was she going to do with the rest of her Friday?

For the first time in a long while, the answer wasn't "Go dig some random holes and see what you find." Today, the answer was "Go find out the truth about Liz."

Her husband's father was at risk of being railroaded for attacking Delia and maybe for killing Liz. Liz herself was in danger of being labeled as an environmental criminal, and she wasn't here to defend herself. The person who broke into Emma's house was still at large, leaving her vulnerable. Any fool could see that there was a good likelihood that all Micco County's unsolved crimes were related.

All those crimes swirled around Sly Mantooth, but they also touched Oscar Croft. Faye had a photo proving that he'd been at the marina shortly before Liz's death. He had asked Emma for a date on the very evening of her break-in, then he'd showed up unannounced on her doorstep when she was slow in returning his call. He was only a room or two away from Delia when she was attacked.

Or was he?

Delia didn't see her attacker. Could it have been Oscar who came in through her window and blindfolded her with her own bedclothes? Then, when she got away and went looking for him, did he do nothing more than slip out her window and come back inside through a door?

Connecting Oscar to Tommy was more of a reach, but no matter. Exploring the connections between Oscar, Liz, Emma, and Delia was the important thing.

So how was she going to do that?

Oscar had been trying to get an appointment with Faye for weeks to talk about his ancestor Elias, but she'd been dodging him. As much as she hated to admit it, Faye knew that the time had come to stop avoiding Oscar Croft.

Chapter Twenty-five

Faye couldn't believe that Oscar had agreed to see her that very afternoon, inviting her to the same house where Delia had just been through so much. She kept her surprise to herself, since she knew more about Delia's attack than she was supposed to know. The news had already hit the Internet, but the reports had shielded the victim's identity and the location of the crime. Still, this was Micco County and even people who weren't best friends with the former sheriff's wife had already figured out what was going on.

The mere fact that the victim had been a woman staying in a rented house near Panacea gave away a lot. There weren't that many tourists hanging around the Florida Panhandle in November. Anyone who had met Delia probably suspected she was the victim, but Faye was going to pretend that she wasn't one of them.

Faye was also going to pretend that she didn't know the sordid details that hadn't reached the Internet rumor mill—the sheets twisted into ropes, the wrists tied to bedposts, the man's belt abandoned by the intruder. She was riding herd on her own imagination, working hard to block the image of a sheet over her head, tied into a cowl that blocked all vision and clung to her face when she inhaled. This was a place where sanity did not want her to go.

As far as Oscar was concerned, Faye knew nothing when she picked up the phone and dialed his number.

"Dr. Longchamp-Mantooth!" he had said. "Thanks for getting back to me! I know your work keeps you busy. I can meet with you any time you like. Today, even!"

So here she was, standing on his doorstep, and she had only just realized as the door swung open that she had been visibly pregnant when she last saw Oscar Croft. If he asked her about the baby, she might have to run away and hide.

He didn't. He was far too focused on his hope that Faye could solve the mystery of Elias Croft and his fate. The intensity of that focus struck Faye as over-the-top, even abnormal.

"So," he said, anxious to begin questioning Faye before her butt even hit the couch, "we haven't talked for awhile. Have you had any thoughts on my search for Elias Croft? What's my next step?"

They sat together in the living room of Oscar's rented house and, from her perch on its comfy couch, Faye could see the kitchen and four doors. Behind those doors were at least two bedrooms, probably three, and a bathroom or two. And behind one of the bedroom doors was probably Delia, curled into a fetal position and recovering from a waking nightmare. It's where Faye would have been, in her place.

Maybe Delia was nursing abrasions on her wrists and ankles, where sheets had rubbed hard against her skin as she fought against being tied. Maybe her knees were black with bruises from throwing herself off the bed and crawling to the door, still bound and crying for help.

Oscar seemed happy, even chipper. Even if he and Delia were nothing more than friends, how could he be having this calm conversation with Faye when his friend must be suffering?

Oscar was wearing short sleeves and shorts. Faye searched his arms and legs for bruises that might have been sustained while struggling with Delia, but there were none. And how paranoid was it for her to think of this annoying but harmless old man as a rapist? If she planned to go fully down the path of paranoia, she needed to consider whether Delia could have tied the sheets to her own wrists, then rubbed the skin raw. Could she have thrown herself on the floor, hard, to give herself bruises that would back up her claim of an attempted rape?

What was it about these two people that made her imagine such horrible things? Before they had arrived in Micco County, her suspicions about an attack like this one would have centered on sleazy characters like Tommy Barnes, not on a retired businessman or, dear God, on the victim herself.

Oscar crossed his legs at the knee, like a man on a 1960s talk show, and went straight to the point. "So where were we? How much did I tell you about the mystery of what happened to my great-great-grandfather after the Civil War?"

"You said he didn't come home, but that his wife received many letters over the years. She got letters from Elias himself during the war, and they were the kind of passionate letters a wife expects to receive from a husband who is away at war. She had no reason to expect that he wouldn't come home to her. Then the letters stopped without warning, about the time the war was over."

"Well, to be honest, whether she had warning is in the eye of the beholder."

"What do you mean?"

They were sitting at either end of the long couch. Oscar scooched toward the middle, leaned just one centimeter too far into Faye's personal space and said, "I'm sorry, I should have offered you something to drink. Would you like a soda? Some coffee? Some water?"

She politely declined, but he didn't retreat to his side of the sofa.

Leaning back a centimeter and hoping this sent the right signal, she said, "You were going to explain that maybe Elias' wife had warning that he would disappear, but that the warning was in the eye of the beholder. Or something like that. What, exactly, are you trying to say?"

Oscar held his ground. He had staked a claim on the sofa's center pillow and he wasn't giving it up. Faye's butt was up against the sofa's arm and she was leaning back on it hard.

"My great-great-grandmother grieved over her husband's last letter till the end of her days. It didn't survive, so I've only heard about it third-hand. Fourth-hand. Whatever. Her son told his son, my grandfather, about it. I think she interpreted Elias' last letter as being a typical wartime love letter, at least when it first came. He said he loved her and he missed her and he said some version of the thing that so many soldiers say, 'If I don't come home, remember me but find a way to be happy.'"

"Had he said this kind of thing before?"

"Yes. She said he had, and that she didn't see that this letter was different until she realized it would be his last. Years later, after his sword was delivered, she read the letter again and saw that he had been saying good-bye."

"And then after that letter came, she started getting letters from a woman demanding that she come down south and get her husband, because he was living in sin on an island with a woman of color?"

"So I was told. Are you sure I can't get you something to drink?"

Oscar looked suddenly uncomfortable, maybe because he had realized that he was having this conversation with someone who was herself a woman of color, but he didn't back away.

Faye pressed him to keep speaking. "Years later, she got another letter, this one claiming that he was being held prisoner."

"Yes. By a woman named Cally Stanton. Have you heard of her?"

"I've searched every official record I can find. There's no mention of Cally Stanton in any of them." This evasion was conveniently true. He'd asked if she'd heard of Cally Stanton, and this was a name she'd heard all her life, but she knew Cally to be invisible in the official records, because she'd checked, over and over again.

Failing to tell Oscar the whole truth was a lie—a lie of omission, but still a lie—but she plunged ahead. "You don't have anything? None of the letters? Not even the sword?"

"The sword? It's the only part of the story I can hold in my hands. Yes, I have it."

Oscar fetched the sword quickly from a room that she presumed was his bedroom. It was wrapped like a mummy in yellowing linen. He laid the bundle across his lap, unrolled one layer of the linen, and pulled out a pair of cotton gloves stored there. Faye thought that keeping the gloves so handy was a clever way to keep himself from ever being tempted to touch the old sword with a fingertip laden with destructive oils.

With the gloves on his hands, Oscar finished unwrapping the sword, folding the linen and laying it beside him on the sofa cushion. Pulling the sword from its sheath, he held both sheath and sword out toward her on flat palms, as if he were a servant offering it to a master going to war.

"It's a Model 1860 Light Cavalry Saber. Brass guard. Steel scabbard. Most of the leather wrapping the grip is still intact." He laid the sheath in his lap, turning it over to show her the other side, then he leaned over the sword. Still gazing at the sword, he ran a gloved finger lovingly across the flat side of the blade and the grip.

Faye didn't think he realized that he was too close to her. He seemed less like a lecher than like a man with no sense of personal space. She would guess that this deficiency had gotten him slapped a few times.

"Custer carried a sword like this. So did Jeb Stuart."

Faye pulled away from him, but he and the sword leaned forward into the space she'd vacated. She wondered what he would say if she called his attention to the fact that Custer and Stuart had both died of battlefield injuries, but this would have been unfair. Their swords might not have been to blame for the famous generals' sad ends.

Instead, she said, "You told me that Cally Stanton sent this sword to Elias' wife. What did you say that her letter said?"

"Only that Elias had used his dying breath to ask Cally to send his sword home to his wife, and that he had asked her to send his love with it. I couldn't tell you why Cally Stanton was there when he died, not unless the other letter-writers were right.

If she had imprisoned him and tortured him and killed him, she would have been there at the end."

Faye's eye raked over the slight curve of the saber's blade. She was speaking more to herself than to Oscar when she said, "But why would she have written his wife to send her his love? Wouldn't a woman so evil have taunted her? To tell you the truth, I don't think somebody evil would have sent his wife anything at all. True evil would have left her wondering for the rest of her days."

Something about the pile of linen was drawing Faye's eye. There was a stroke of green across one end of it, made out of silk thread with tiny even stitches. The fabric had been adorned with a garland of embroidered leaves, and Faye had seen this pattern before.

She was about to ask him to let her take a closer look at the old linen, but she was startled silent when one gloved hand reached toward her. Oscar touched her hand, then slowly brushed the back of his index finger up her bare arm. Oh, yes. This man was completely aware that he was invading her space.

She jerked her arm away from his finger and leaned back until the sofa's arm caught her in the lower back and she could go no farther. Even then, this man was too close to her.

She heard the sound of a door opening behind her, and Oscar cried, "Delia! How was your nap? Are you feeling better?"

He was immediately out of Faye's personal space and into Delia's. Taking the young woman by an arm, he guided her into an easy chair. "Can I get you something? Some tea? A sandwich?"

Unlike Oscar's unmarked wrists and forearms, Delia's arms did show battle wounds. Her hands were bruised, and the skin around her wrists was raw. Another bruise showed on her forehead, beneath a fluffy fringe of hair. Delia hadn't had bangs before. The thought of Delia in front of the bathroom mirror, snipping just enough hair to hide her wounds, went straight to Faye's heart.

Oscar patted the brand-new bangs tenderly, saying, "Faye came to talk to us about the sword and about Cally Stanton. Do you feel up to joining us?"

"Yes. If you'll get me a cup of tea."

Delia smiled and Faye was impressed with her resilience. Faye herself had shown a noticeable lack of resilience lately.

"You can help us track down Cally Stanton?" Delia was indeed resilient. She was already looking Faye coolly in the eye, while backing her into a commitment she didn't want to make.

"I'm afraid I can't do any more than what you've already done. You're the historian, so your skills at tracking down primary sources are at least as good as mine. I haven't found any trace of Cally Stanton in public records. Have you?"

"No. But if I know Oscar, we'll be living in this house until somebody does. You don't pile up accomplishments the way Oscar did without being willing to chase your goals longer than you probably should. He's really a very impressive man. Don't you think?"

Faye wanted to say, "Impressively sleazy," but Oscar arrived with a cup of hot water and a tea bag, saving Faye from having to answer. She studied Delia as the woman reacted to Oscar fussing over her tea.

Delia hadn't drawn back when Oscar leaned too close. She had worn a tender twist of a smile while she watched him stir sugar into her tea. Most telling of all, she had accepted the cup with an open hand that lingered on the timeworn hand offering it.

Faye might have been disturbed by Oscar's inappropriate invasion of her space, but Delia was not. This meant that his manner toward Delia wasn't inappropriate at all. She liked it. She liked him.

Faye needed to think again about Oscar's relationships with Liz and Emma and, given his excursions into her own personal space, with Faye herself. Mostly, though, she needed to revisit her prejudices about Oscar's relationship with Delia. So he was forty years older than she was. Big deal. Some people would remind her that it wasn't all that usual for Faye to be eight years older than her husband.

"I'm glad you were able to come talk to Oscar about our research, Faye," Delia said. "I know you're busy, but is it possible you could meet us at Mrs. Everett's museum sometime? She has access to some databases there that are way too expensive for me to buy on my own. Besides, only a fraction of her collection is on display and she's given me access to the archived pieces. So many of those artifacts was found right here in Micco County. There could be things in Emma Everett's museum that Cally Stanton herself touched."

"Or Elias Croft." Oscar stroked Delia's hand absentmindedly as he spoke. Delia let him.

Faye and several crops of interns under her supervision had curated everything in Emma's museum. If Delia found a relationship between Cally Stanton and any physical object in that museum, Faye would eat that object.

But she couldn't swear that there wasn't something in the museum that was related to Elias Croft. She'd never even heard of him before Oscar and Delia showed up in Micco County.

"We can go over there now." As she spoke, Faye remembered what had happened to Delia that morning. She almost added, "If you're feeling up to it," but she remembered at the last minute that she wasn't supposed to know anything about Delia's attack.

Delia set her mug down so firmly that a little tea sloshed over its rim. "If I have to sit here for another minute in this house with its locked doors and its fully armed alarm system, waiting to hear whether the police have arrested anybody, I will scream."

So Delia didn't mind admitting that she was the woman whose story had been all over the news that morning. This meant that Faye could stop worrying about accidentally revealing that she had known this for hours.

Delia pulled the sleeves of her cardigan down, but they weren't long enough to fully cover the red marks on her wrists. "Shall we go?"

Faye watched Oscar spread the old linen across the ottoman in front of him, carefully laying the sword on it. It looked like a piece of a bedsheet. As he swaddled the weapon like a baby, she got a close look at the green leaves embroidered along one edge of the linen in a pattern that she'd seen before.

They formed a garland, caught up at intervals with flowing yellow ribbons to make a scalloped design. She owned a few pieces of china, all of them old and most of them broken, with that design painted along their rims. Stamped on the bottoms of those teacups and plates were the words "Turkey Foot Hotel." Most of them had been found buried among the ruins of the hotel owned by Cally's husband Courtney Stanton. A few of them were uncovered by a hurricane that came more than a hundred and fifty years after the one that destroyed the hotel.

Faye had tracked down the china company who had made them, and she knew that they had been designed and custom-made for the hotel. There were no others like them in the world. She tried not to stare as she tracked back through the only reasonable sequence of events that put a piece of linen from the Turkey Foot Hotel into Oscar Croft's hands.

The Turkey Foot Hotel had died young. It had stood on Last Island, which had been so close to Joyeuse Island that Faye could see its remnants from her cupola, and the hotel hadn't survived the great hurricane of 1856. Neither had the island. Last Island had been blown into so many pieces that the area was now called the Last Isles.

In her oral history, Cally had clearly said that she attended the grand opening of Courtney Stanton's hotel as a slave in 1856. While she was still on the island, probably within days of the grand opening, a hurricane destroyed the hotel and killed most of the people in it, including her master and mistress. Courtney Stanton had been her master's son-in-law, and he had inherited Cally, all the other slaves on Joyeuse Island, and the island itself. Eventually, Cally had become his common-law wife, living with him in Faye's house on Joyeuse Island until he died sometime after the start of the Civil War.

There was almost no way that a piece of linen carrying the Turkey Foot Hotel's crest could have survived the hurricane. Perhaps someone had found it floating in the Gulf afterward but, more likely, a shipment of linens had arrived after the hotel was destroyed. Even a week's delay in shipping would have meant that a shipment of sheets could have outlived the hotel.

Cally's husband Courtney would have found himself poorer by the value of a hotel and the island it sat on, but very rich in bedsheets. Faye imagined that even the slaves in their cabins slept wrapped in sumptuous linen.

Cally, frugal to the bone, would have used those sheets for years. Then, when it came time to send Elias Croft's sword home—two decades after the 1856 hurricane? three?—she would have used the worn but still serviceable fabric to cushion it for the trip.

Was she looking at a scrap of fabric that Cally had held in her hands, washed and hung out to dry, and maybe even slept under? Resisting the urge to reach out a hand and snatch it, she answered Delia's question. The words "Shall we go?" had just left the young woman's lips, even though Faye had spent that instant traveling to 1856 and back.

She dragged her gaze away from the linen, met Delia's eyes and said, "Sure. Let's go check out Emma's museum."

Chapter Twenty-six

Faye had come to her meeting with Oscar by boat, so it made sense for the three of them to ride together to the museum in Oscar's car. She sat in the backseat and listened more than she talked.

Oscar teased Delia while she smiled indulgently. "Do you think you could cram more paper into that briefcase?"

She laughed and teased him back. "If you'd focus on family mysteries that don't go back a hundred and fifty years, there would be a lot less paper and I'd be working a lot less. If you'd contain your curiosity to things I can find on the Internet, I could eliminate the paper altogether."

"But then you might finish your work quicker, and I'd have no excuse to keep you around."

"We can't have that!' She patted the hand resting on the stick shift between them.

This was not the kind of relationship that Emma had described during their endless conversations about Oscar and Delia and how to keep them out of Faye's personal business. Maybe Delia's near-escape had brought the two closer together.

At any rate, Faye needed to focus less on gossip about the feelings of people who were old enough to make their own decisions. The question at hand was not "Does Delia care for Oscar?" It was "Could Oscar have killed Liz or broken Emma's window or—and this was an awful thought—attacked Delia in a way designed to drive her into his own arms?"

Knowing the contents of Delia's heart couldn't answer that question for Faye. Nobody knew its answer but Oscar, but Faye was hellbent on finding it out.

Emma looked startled to see Faye enter the museum with Oscar and Delia, probably because she was the one who had been listening to Faye babble for weeks about how badly she wanted to avoid the two of them. Faye gave her an I'll-tell-you-later glance and settled herself at the work station next to Delia's.

Oscar left them to their work, taking a seat in Emma's office and launching a conversation with the not-creative gambit of "So…how've you been?" If Emma minded him interrupting her work, Faye couldn't tell it. She could see Emma listening intently. Sometimes, Oscar even took a breath and let her talk.

Whenever a new woman came into view, Oscar was captivated, at least for the moment. Did this bother Delia? Not that Faye could tell.

Sitting down to a computer, Faye logged into the museum's collection catalog and typed in a search term that she'd used many times before: "Cally Stanton." As a curator of the museum, she had access to more data than Delia, so Delia was hoping for new information. She was destined to be disappointed. Delia didn't know that, but Faye did.

Once Faye's computer screen showed the expected "No matches found" message, which she very helpfully showed to Delia, Faye was free to watch the other woman work. Delia certainly did know what she was doing. Faye could tell that Delia already knew about the Micco County courthouse fire in the 1890s, because she was ignoring local records and focusing on records from the U.S. Census. Faye would have done the same thing.

With a portal to the census records open on her screen, Delia pulled a file from her briefcase and unfolded several large copies of old maps. She smoothed their creases and spread them across their shared workspace. On them, Delia had highlighted every visible island in Micco County. Most of the islands were in the Gulf but, damn, the woman was thorough. She had even marked small islands in rivers and lakes, all over the county. If an island was visible at the scale of any of her maps, she had highlighted it in yellow.

Next, Faye watched her unfold another set of maps, one for every publicly available census after the Civil War, ending with 1940. When Faye saw what Delia had done with these maps, she stopped being impressed and started panicking. Delia had used detailed historical maps, along with the cruder census maps, to figure out which of the censuses' Enumeration Districts had contained islands.

This was huge. Delia was no longer looking for Cally Stanton on a list of everybody who had lived in Micco County over an eighty-year stretch. Now Delia could focus her laser-like attention on lists of people who had lived *on islands* in Micco County in those years. How many could that possibly be? A hundred? Two hundred, tops.

Delia still wouldn't find Cally herself. Faye already knew she wasn't listed in any census report. But there was one faint thread that could possibly take Delia's search to Joyeuse Island. And then to Faye, who would have an interesting time explaining why she had failed to mention that she had inherited her island from ancestors named Stanton.

Cally was invisible to history for so many reasons. She had been a slave without a birth certificate. Her "marriage" to her legal master, the first Courtney Stanton, had been an illegal thing forged between two people who loved each other, so there was no marriage certificate.

Courtney Stanton had torn up the deed showing his ownership of his wife, so it was long-gone. For the rest of her life, Cally had retained her suspicion of the government that had let people own her, so she had never once filled out a census form. In Cally's day, it had been possible to get away with that when you lived on a remote island.

Since she had never had a birth certificate, there had been no pressing need to get her a death certificate. Her daughter, the second Courtney Stanton, had buried her on Joyeuse and her grave marker had washed away in a hurricane before Faye was born. Faye knew of no document in existence that gave Cally the surname of Stanton. She had never had any legal surname at all. Faye was as sure as she could be that there was no paper trail to lead Delia to Cally Stanton.

This was not true of Joyeuse Island.

Cally's daughter had been more law-abiding than her mother. She appeared as a resident of Joyeuse Island in the 1940 census, the first one taken after Cally's death. This was not a huge problem, as she was listed under her married name, Courtney Wells.

Faye's problem lay in the archives of the *Micco County Sun-Record*. Courtney Wells had been in a highly publicized court battle to keep property she had inherited, all of which had been located on islands off the coast of Micco County. It was not possible that a researcher with Delia's training and determination who was looking for an island in Micco County had missed newspaper coverage of a battle over ownership of most of its offshore islands.

Cally's name did not appear in the newspaper coverage—Faye had checked—but the name of Cally's husband Courtney Stanton did appear and he was identified as Courtney Wells' father. Oh, how Delia's eyes would light up to see someone named Stanton associated with a lawsuit over islands.

After reading that article all Delia had to do was reach back a single generation and look for the first Courtney Stanton. More accurately, all she needed to do was to reach back a single census report. She had to do something not obvious—look for a man named Courtney Stanton living on an island years before Elias was supposed to have been imprisoned by someone named Cally Stanton.

If Delia looked at the 1860 census, she would see Courtney Stanton living on Joyeuse Island. Pairing this with the knowledge from the newspaper article that Courtney Stanton had a daughter named Courtney Wells who was making trouble in court in the 1930s would give Delia almost everything she needed. She would have a set of data with a single fascinating, woman-shaped hole: Who was Courtney Wells' mother?

The mysterious woman would have been an adult when Elias Croft went missing. As Courtney Stanton's wife, she would have carried the surname Delia was seeking. And she would have lived on an island. A woman with a PhD in history could mate this information with Oscar's oral history and make a compelling case that she had found Elias Croft's Cally Stanton. Then she could write a hell of a research paper with a title like "Documentary Evidence Supports Oral History: Union Hero Was Kept Prisoner for Years by a Confederate Woman."

Even worse, Delia could take her story to the public. With any public relations savvy, and Faye did not doubt that Delia had it, she would make piles of money by publishing a lurid book from Oscar's point-of-view. The notoriety would bring in well-heeled private clients for the rest of her career. Faye might live to see the nonfiction bestseller listed topped by *Imprisoned, Tortured, Sexually Abused, and Murdered by a Madwoman named Cally: My Ancestor's Story!*

But before all that happened, Delia would come for Faye and she would ask her this: "You knew I was looking for Cally Stanton and that she lived on an island. Why didn't you tell me that there were Stantons on your family tree and that they lived on your island?"

Faye wouldn't blame her if she went on to say "What are you hiding? And why?"

Faye didn't know the answers herself. She was acting on instinct, and that instinct was to protect Cally.

Her instincts were urging her to do something...anything... when Delia reached out a graceful hand toward the keyboard and said, "I've been reading some interesting stuff in the *Micco County Sun-Record*. There was a lawsuit involving the Last Isles and some nearby islands. It made me think I should go back a little further in the census. To 1860, at least."

Faye was never sure how long she sat there watching Delia wade through the 1860 census of Micco County. The younger woman was oblivious to Faye's misery as she checked her maps and scrolled through on-screen data. Faye sat waiting for her to turn her wide blue eyes on her and ask, "Why didn't you tell me that you've known the answers to our questions all along?"

Oscar, too, had been oblivious to Faye's silence as he leaned over Delia's shoulder to watch her work.

Faye needed to say something. It wasn't her way to let trouble lie. She needed to address the problem while she was still in control. She reached for the file holding Delia's newspaper research. "Did you say that the woman in the newspaper article was named Courtney?"

Delia nodded, hunching over a map and tracing the route of a river with her finger.

"My great-grandmother's name was Courtney. It's an unusual name for a woman."

The finger stopped in mid-river. "Where did she live?"

"Not far from here, on Joyeuse Island. My home."

"When did she die?"

"My mother was a teenager, so probably in the late 1940s."

Delia's fingers flew to the keyboard and she pulled up the 1940 census. Checking the map to see which Enumeration District included Joyeuse Island, she searched through the names in that district.

Several minutes passed, then both Delia's hands dropped into her lap. "Her last name was Wells. She's the woman who sued for ownership of those islands, and the newspaper said that her maiden name was Stanton. Faye. Your great-grandmother was born with the name Courtney Stanton. "

Her statement didn't demand an answer. By not giving one, Faye was neither confirming nor denying that she had already known her great-grandmother's maiden name.

Delia backed through the census records, finding Courtney Wells on Joyeuse Island in 1940, but nobody named Stanton, because Cally had died in the 1930s. Crawling through time, she found no census records at all during the years when Cally would have been in charge of filling out the forms—1920, 1900, 1880. If she'd stopped then, Delia would have had nothing but a woman on an island who had been born with Cally Stanton's last name. But she didn't stop.

Census records from 1860 were on the screen when Delia's composure finally slipped and she squealed out loud. As Faye had already known, the first Courtney Stanton had been scrupulous about filling out his census forms, at least when it came to reporting the existence of people who weren't slaves.

"What is it?" Oscar asked.

"There was a man on Joyeuse Island in 1860. His name was Courtney Stanton, also. The female Courtney Stanton doesn't show up, because she hasn't been born yet."

"But no Cally?" Oscar asked. "You don't see her name there?"

"This is the next best thing. In two years another Courtney Stanton will be born, probably on the same island where she will live for the rest of her life. She didn't drop from a cloud. She had a mother, and that mother would be the right age to be your Cally Stanton. Make that *Elias'* Cally Stanton. And, like your Cally Stanton, she would have lived on an island. I don't know why she's not on the census—maybe they weren't married yet?—but I think the woman who married Courtney-the-man and birthed Courtney-the-woman is the woman we came here to find."

Oscar pulled Delia up out of the chair and gave her a hug. "You found her! The U.S. Census missed her, but you didn't."

He turned to look at Faye. "We need to go out to your island. If we see the place where Elias Croft suffered, maybe we can get to the truth of what happened to him. That's all I want. The truth."

Faye was being completely honest when she said, "I don't know the truth."

Chapter Twenty-seven

Faye couldn't believe she had spilled her guts. She had told Oscar and Delia everything she knew about Cally Stanton.

Well, no, she hadn't. She was emotionally damaged these days, and she'd never been much good at lying, but she wasn't stupid. Faye had told Oscar and Delia some of what she knew about Cally Stanton. She'd given them the highlights, so to speak.

She'd told them that Cally had been a slave to a man who was probably her own father. When he died in the Last Island hurricane, ownership of Cally had passed to his son-in-law Courtney, who eventually fell in love with Cally, freed her, and married her.

"Was that legal back then? She was a slave, so I guess she wasn't white." Delia had asked, though she should have known that the answer was no.

"No, she wasn't white and their marriage wasn't legal, but they considered themselves husband and wife. She wore his ring and ran his household."

"When?" Oscar had wanted to know. "After the Civil War?"

"During and after."

"So she could be the one. The one who sent my great-great-grandmother her husband's sword."

Oscar had leaned closer to her, closer than Faye had wanted him to be, and he had studied her face as if he were hoping to find Elias Croft's murderess there. His eyes crawled all over Faye's face. Most likely, he was studying her mid-brown complexion and imagining that biracial Cally had looked like Faye.

Faye only knew of one photo of Cally, taken when she was in her nineties. Minus fifty years of sags and wrinkles, she probably had indeed looked like Faye, but this was none of Oscar's business.

An odd moment had passed, while the old man got up in her face and the young historian hung back, regarding them with narrowed and thoughtful eyes. Faye willed herself to hold still, even though his nearness made a primitive part of her want to run. He said nothing.

Delia, too, said nothing, but her gaze unsettled Faye. Did she realize that Faye had been withholding information? Was she angrier about it than she'd been willing to admit? Or was she jealous? Was she thinking about the moment when she had watched Oscar trail an unwelcome finger down Faye's arm?

And then the moment had passed. Oscar had said brightly. "Well, this is just wonderful. Now we need to come out to your island and take a look around."

And that was the extent of the conversation about what Faye knew about Cally Stanton. They both seemed to assume that she'd been utterly upfront with them. They'd jumped to the conclusion that she hadn't known her ancestors' full names, and thus she couldn't have realized they were looking for her great-great-grandmother. This gullibility had let the conversation steamroll past the question of "Why haven't you been helping us?" and go straight to "Let's go to your house and see if we can find some skeletons in your closets."

And now Faye had to decide. Was she going to extend Delia a little professional courtesy and let her take her client on a historical tour that included her own home? Or was she going to cling to her obsession, probably irrational, with keeping Cally's name clear? How did Cally's actions in eighteen-seventy-whatever affect Faye?

They didn't. Even if Cally was a coldblooded killer, her sins didn't reflect on Faye, but she wanted to come to her own rational and provable answer to the mystery of Cally Stanton and Elias Croft. In particular, she wanted to do it before Oscar and Delia scraped together a cockamamie story that confirmed their pre-conceptions but was just flat wrong. She decided that she might learn something by letting Oscar and Delia tour Joyeuse Island, but that she wasn't obligated to tell them everything she knew. She would let them find out what they could on their own, and she doubted it would be much more than what they knew now.

"Okay," she said. "I love showing my home off to people who appreciate history. We have hours until dark. Let's go now."

It had been a quick trip back to Oscar's rental house where Faye's boat was waiting. Her text to Joe, telling him that they were coming, had prompted a single-character text in return:

?

She had just responded,

Tell you later.

and started the motor. Her home was remote enough that she was usually able to keep from revealing it to people she didn't know and like, but not lately. The week had begun with the invasion of environmental contractors wanting to empty her bank account with their enforced cleanup. It had been dotted with visits from law enforcement officials. And now it was ending with an invasion of people who wanted to turn her family's history into something tainted and ugly.

She felt like she should announce to the world, "Here's the password to my savings account and the key to my bedroom. Come on in!"

Instead, she pointed the boat toward Joyeuse Island and pushed it harder than necessary. She planned to aim it for the biggest waves she could find. She had weighed all the facts and come to the conclusion that it was time to show Oscar and Delia around Joyeuse Island. This didn't mean that she didn't intend to treat them to a very bumpy ride on the way.

◇◇◇

The dock at Joyeuse Island was clearly marked "Private," and Faye had counted three "No Trespassing" signs before she got there. The signs were copious all around the island, because Faye had made sure of it. Faye knew Joe hated all those ugly signs. She often saw him adjusting himself so that his eyes fell on nothing that was not natural. She had even seen him walk a few steps off a path, just to keep a tree between himself and something he didn't want to see.

Despite the fact that her nature-loving husband didn't like Faye's signs, they usually kept the number of unwanted visitors way down. Not today.

She helped Oscar and Delia out of the boat and asked, "Can I offer you some lemonade?"

Oscar wasn't interested. He seemed to have forgotten that Delia's body was probably stiff and sore. Faye's own wrists hurt in sympathy whenever Delia's bruises and abrasions peeked out from beneath her cardigan sleeves. Who knew what injuries hid under her clothes?

"Would you like a tour of the house?"

Oscar didn't answer Faye and he didn't give Delia a glance. He just stood on the dock, eagerly squinting through the trees at Faye's home. "Where do you think she kept him? In the basement?"

Delia said, "You told me that the letters said he was being held in a cabin."

"Oh. Right. We should start outside."

He looked around. Joyeuse Island went on in all directions, as far as he could see.

If Faye hadn't been under such stress, she would have been amused by his confidence that he could find the site of a cabin that had rotted down a century before. What's more, Oscar was confident that he could do it in an afternoon. No tools. No library research. No ground-penetrating radar, which would have been prohibitively expensive for Faye but maybe Oscar could afford it. He seemed to think he would magically know when he walked over the right spot.

Granted, this was how Faye had been conducting her work over the past few weeks, but at least she knew when she was being an idiot.

Delia put a hand on Oscar's shoulder. "Faye offered to give us a tour of her house. We should start with that."

The gesture was possessive. It also looked for all the world like a married person silently handling a spouse's social blunder. The words unspoken were "Dear, it's rude not to accept an invitation into someone's home."

Oscar looked down at her hand and said, "Yeah, okay, that's a good idea."

So Faye took them across the same front lawn where Cally had met Captain Croft and offered food to his men. The rules of hospitality said that Cally had also ushered him up Faye's entrance stairway, brought him inside, and offered him something to drink. In wartime, she'd probably had nothing to give him but water.

Faye showed Delia and Oscar around the main floor, designed as a public area for entertaining, and thought, "Cally and Captain Croft probably lingered at the door before sitting here in this parlor, or maybe that one, to hammer out a truce that would feed his men without starving her people. She probably walked him through the dining room and the ballroom, pointing out the hand-blocked wallpaper imported from France before the war. There would still have been draperies around the windows, pictures on the wall, rosewood furniture, and brass chandeliers designed to hold candles."

Faye told Oscar and Delia about the wallpaper and the chandeliers, but her gut told her to keep Captain Croft to herself. She listened to her gut.

Then she took them up the spiral staircase that she and Joe had worked so hard to rebuild after the hurricane. She showed them the hand-painted murals in the bedrooms and the music room. She took them into the cupola, but she didn't tell them that Courtney Stanton Wells had told Faye's grandmother that she remembered seeing The Monster Man's cabin from there.

From the cupola, they came down the ladder, down the sneak staircase, and took a quick tour through the basement.

Oscar latched onto every detail and made it lurid. "The sneak staircase...she could have used it to get Elias away from anybody who might hear him being kidnapped," was quickly followed by "Once she got him into that concrete-walled basement, there would have been no getting out unless she wanted him to get out. It would have been like a dungeon."

Faye responded mildly. "Tabby. The basement walls are tabby. It's like concrete, but made with shells and sand."

Delia kept patting Oscar on the arm to calm him down. Between pats, she admired the view from the cupola and asked Faye to show her how the house's casement windows worked. She was fascinated with the way the louvers shading the entire back porch had been designed to keep out heat and let in breezes.

After Oscar realized that the basement had been the business center of the plantation—office, storeroom, classroom, and butler's pantry, and all of them full of people by night and day—he knew that it would have made a terrible dungeon, so he was ready to go. Faye's tour had taken him past the living room where her family sat among their books and toys, but he didn't speak. He refused Faye's second offer of lemonade, and Delia gave him the warning look that wives saved for erring husbands.

Delia tried to make up for his rudeness, asking Faye questions about the basement door and its hand-crafted hardware, but Oscar was hustling her out of the house. Faye saw that it was time to take Oscar on the tour of Joyeuse Island that he wanted so badly.

But it was a big island. Where should she take him? Faye paused in the open area behind the house, which had been the work yard where Captain Croft's men were probably fed their hominy and sweet potatoes. Paths led into the woods in three directions.

She dithered about which one she should take. In the end, she led them down the one leading straight back behind the house first. It took them to the rows of slave cabin foundations she had excavated. Faye had always considered them an impressive sight, stretching for hundreds of feet in two straight lines.

Delia asked, "Can you tell me how they made the tabby cement for the foundations?"

Oscar interrupted Faye's answer with his own demand. "Did anybody live here after the slaves were freed?"

"Yes. Most of the freed people stayed on as paid workers."

"Then she wouldn't have kept my great-great-grandfather prisoner here, in front of all those people. Let's move on."

They walked to the second trail, which led left toward the remnants of the old outbuildings—kitchen, barn, smokehouse, grain bins, and chicken houses. Delia looked like she would happily amble around the ruins all day. Faye had a soft spot for people who liked old stuff as much as she did.

Oscar was not inclined to linger. He said, "She wouldn't have kept him here. People worked here. They would have seen him." So they moved on.

They took the third trail, a long path winding to the right, through the eastern part of the island. The island had slowly gone to trees as first Cally and then her daughter, Courtney, had farmed less of its land over time. This end of the island had returned to nature first.

After young Courtney died in the 1940s, Faye's grandmother had moved to Tallahassee to take a job as a secretary, and farming on Joyeuse Island had come to an end. Even its youngest trees had been growing for a long time. Nothing on Joyeuse Island except the house could possibly look much like it did in the years just after the Civil War. Faye wasn't sure what Oscar thought he was looking to find, but this wasn't it. He was obviously bored as they hiked through endless trees.

Faye was surprised that they found so few brambles growing across the path. She figured Joe must be keeping the weeds down with the soles of his moccasins. How often did he walk this trail to nowhere? Her husband was never going to spend a lot of time with a roof over his head.

They rounded the end of the island and walked back west toward the dock, where this path met the westbound one that led to the contamination site. As they traveled further and further west, Faye saw the trees thinning around her. Every step showed brighter sunlight ahead and, with every step, Oscar sped. He walked with a silent intensity that was unnerving. It was as if Faye and Delia weren't there.

The trail ended at the familiar clearing, with its big live oak and shabby beach. A collection of drummed soils, ready to be shipped to an incinerator, sat beside their ongoing excavation. The air still smelled like kerosene.

It was a depressing spot and there was an opening where a cabin could have stood, so Oscar claimed it. "This is where she kept him prisoner. It's close enough to bring him food, far enough away to hide him from the others. I can feel it."

Faye stifled the urge to say, "Give the man an honorary doctorate. He's such a good archaeologist that he doesn't need to go to school or even pick up a trowel." She also didn't say, "My grandmother told me there used to be a cabin here. Cally told her daughter a Monster Man lived here and threatened to take a switch to her legs if she came near," because Oscar would have taken her words as proof that he was right. She didn't say anything at all.

Neither did Delia.

The walk back to the dock was disturbing. There was no other word for it. Oscar wouldn't stop spinning fantasies about how Elias Croft might have been tortured.

"Do you think she fed him?"

Delia was moving like a woman who'd been assaulted about fifteen hours before. Her shoulders sagged and she kept adjusting the cuffs of her sweater so that they wouldn't rub against the wounds on her arms, but she never stopped answering Oscar.

"Of course she fed him. You said she kept him alive for years."

"Sure, but do you think she fed him every day? And what about water? Did she bring him enough water to bathe?"

"I guess. As often as anybody bathed in the nineteenth century."

Delia was starting to limp. She should have been home resting. Faye regretted bringing her.

Oscar stopped walking, stretched out both arms and spun around once. It was a move better suited to a fairy princess than to a seventy-year-old man. "This is perfect. It's the perfect place to hold a prisoner."

"Of course it is," Delia snapped. "It's an island and they owned slaves. You just saw the foundations of cabins where a whole bunch of people were held prisoner for years and years."

This time it was Oscar who reached out a hand and said something wordless by patting her on the shoulder.

Faye wanted to say, "Cally was one of those slaves. What would she have had against a Union soldier who fought against the people who had owned her? If you're so sure she hurt Elias Croft, say something to make me understand why." She thought it better to hold her tongue, so she walked in silence.

Faye had walked this path so many times. She knew that the dock was almost in view. She was glad. Faye was ready to load Oscar and Delia into her boat and take them home before either of them noticed that Sly Mantooth had been behind them ever since they walked out of the basement of her house. She might not have Joe's skills in woodcraft, but she knew when she was being followed.

He was still back there.

Chapter Twenty-eight

An ax rang, then Faye heard a tearing sound as its blade bit into wood. She had half-expected Sly to meet her at the dock when she got back from taking Oscar and Delia home, but this was the same thing. He knew she would be looking for him, so he was telling her how to find him.

There was another percussive noise as the blade hit the tree trunk again. Faye followed the sound and found Sly chopping a downed tree into manageable pieces for splitting.

Her foot broke a twig and he looked up. "Looking for me, Daughter?"

"You know I am. Why were you following my friends and me?"

"You're calling them your friends now? I don't think so."

Faye was silent for a moment and he let the silence be. Finally, she said, "I don't think so, either. So why were you following us?"

"Because I knew they wasn't your friends and I didn't like their looks."

"Thank you."

The ax swung again. Sly left its head buried in a stump. "I found something when I was following you around. Let's go take a look at it."

It was a short walk to a spot less than a quarter-mile east of the contamination site and a few feet above the high tide line. There, Faye saw a hole like a buffalo wallow in the sandy ground, hip-deep and too broad for her to jump. It was littered with two empty cans that had held housepaint and a lidless container labeled "mineral spirits." The discarded lid of a fifty-five-gallon drum, circular and red, lay atop the churned dirt like a giant penny.

The overturned soil looked pretty fresh. "When did it last rain?" she asked.

"Thursday."

"So somebody's been here since then. And it looks like they came here to dig up the kind of stuff that Tommy Barnett is accused of dumping." She pulled her phone out of her pocket and looked at it for a while without dialing. She spoke to Sly without taking her eyes off its screen. "I have to call Gerry Steinberg about this, don't I?"

"Looks that way to me."

"Damn."

She placed the call.

Gerry's hello sounded relaxed, which was the way a man should sound late on a Friday afternoon. Faye quickly described to him what Sly had found, and she heard a sigh that said she might have just ruined the man's weekend.

"Is there any water nearby?"

"Well, Joe could throw a rock and hit the Gulf from here, but I couldn't."

"Gee, that was helpful. Is there anything seeping into the Gulf? Can you see a sheen?"

"No."

"What about the excavation itself? Is there any standing water in there? Any visible chemicals? Stained soils?"

"Not really. I mostly just see trash. Do you want me to take some pictures and send them to you?"

Sly was squatting next to her, staring down into the hole.

"Yeah," Gerry said, "that would really be helpful. Can you take a quick video, scanning the bottom and sides of the hole? Then take some close-ups of anything that looks iffy?"

"No problem."

Still silent, Sly pointed at a few pieces of trash Faye should document, but he mostly stayed out of her way and let her work.

After she sent Gerry the video and photos, she called him and listened as he thought out loud.

"I don't see anything here that constitutes an emergency and it's nearly dark. We're already working out there, so we won't need to tool up if this turns out to be a big problem." He added quickly, "And I think it won't," and Faye was grateful for the reassurance.

"Tell you what," he said. "I'll come out there and look at it by myself tomorrow morning, but I don't see any reason to mobilize a crew, not based on the photos you just sent. I'll try not to take up too much of your time. We'll just walk out there, I'll look at it, then I'll leave you to your weekend."

Faye should have been as gracious as Gerry and left him to his Friday night, but she had a question that wouldn't wait till morning. "Do you think Tommy Barnett did this?"

He surprised her by giving a straight answer. "I do. My divers have been bringing up chemical waste containers and trash all day, after some of my people saw an oil slick floating on the water not too far from where you live. Remember that we've already arrested him for openly doing the same thing. My guess is that he went out to Joyeuse Island, dug up some incriminating evidence, and took it out into deeper water for dumping. Maybe he's not done. Who knows how many unpermitted waste dumps Tommy has?"

"If he'd buried it out here, why did he dig it up and haul it away?"

"Probably because he knew we were working out there on your island. He was afraid we'd find his dump site, so he dug up the stuff and dumped it into the Gulf. If he'd left it where it was, we might never have known it existed. In the water, the oil slick gave him away."

"No genius, is he?"

"Nope. And I'm going to make him pay. I'll see you tomorrow morning."

Stormy weather blew in that night. It was all wind and no rain, but it was as fierce as a summer squall. Faye slept beside Joe in fits and starts, like a woman who was worried that the wind would

harm her boats or that its sound would mask the movements
of someone who shouldn't be on her island.

Michael wandered into their room twice before midnight,
crying in his sleep. Joe dragged him under the covers to sleep
between them. Faye draped an arm over them both. If she slept,
she wanted to still be able to know they were there.

Sly wandered the dark house barefoot, having shed his boots to
keep from disturbing his sleeping family. His mind was set on
protecting them from whatever was out there.

Storm.

Polluter.

Burglar.

Rapist.

Murderer.

There was stale coffee in the coffeemaker, room temperature.
He poured it in a tall mug, doctored it well with sugar and cream,
then he set it on the floor next to a front porch rocker. Feeling
his way in the opaque night, he found the ax he'd hidden under
the staircase and brought it upstairs to keep with him while he
sat awake.

His son was a man and he could take care of his family, but
a man has to sleep. Sly figured it was his job to watch over them
until Joe woke up and went back to doing it for himself.

The caffeine did its job and the sugar didn't hurt. Sly was
awake at midnight and past, but he was nearly sixty years old.
The years when he could carouse at night and drive a truck all
day were behind him. Eventually, he slept.

Faye woke up hungry for breakfast, only to find out that Joe
wasn't making any. He handed around bowls, then put a box of
cereal and a jug of milk on the table.

"I'm going ashore this morning. I don't care how stubborn
Emma is. She doesn't belong by herself while all this crazy stuff
is going on. I'm going to get her. I should have done it days ago."

Shaking some corn flakes in her bowl, Faye said, "I'll come help you talk to her."

"No, you won't. You're so tired the wind would blow you over."

The storm was still blowing. She had been too tired to notice it. "Maybe you're right."

"I am right. Besides, you need to be here when Gerry comes out to look at that hole Dad found. Dad can watch Michael while you take Gerry out there. I don't want him making plans for another big cleanup without one of us there to calm him down."

Sly nodded as he slipped a parent-authorized spoonful of sugar into Michael's cereal. And another unauthorized one. Faye pretended not to notice.

Faye yawned. Joe's emptied cereal bowl was in the sink and he was out the door before she closed her mouth. She listened to his john boat's motor as he pulled away from shore. Playing in counterpoint to it was the familiar sound of a big boat that sucked in a lot of taxpayer-funded fuel. Gerry was on his way.

"So what's the verdict? Am I in twice as much trouble?"

Gerry shook his head at Faye. "You're not in trouble. Nobody's going to think you did this." He stood around the wide shallow pit where he stood. "I'm going to do my damndest to pin it on Tommy."

"So he can pay to clean it up? With what?"

"His charm and good looks?"

"It's not funny, Gerry. I don't know what your work is costing me."

"Maybe nothing. Faye, you've just got to let this play out. Liability will be assigned when it gets assigned. The government moves slow."

"I'm afraid it's going to roll all over me."

Instead of answering, Gerry leaned down and studied the soil around the empty container of mineral spirits.

"If we're lucky, we'll find something with an unusual chemical signature, and we'll find it in one of the places where I know Tommy's been operating—at his shop or at the spot where I watched him throw a bunch of garbage overboard. If the stars align, maybe I'll also find it at the spot where my divers found an oil slick and some more sunken debris. If I can tie all that together, it's Tommy that the government will be rolling all over."

"So what about all this? Are my problems twice as bad now?"

"It's not an emergency. I'll have Nadia run some samples on Monday and we'll know how bad it is—I mean, if it's bad at all. Seriously, Faye. Try not to worry."

That was easy for him to say.

Joe sat on Emma's back deck, waiting for her to come home. Emma was a predictable woman. It was Saturday so she had gotten her nails done, had lunch, and she was now at the grocery store. She would be home shortly before two. He wasn't happy about his friend's predictability, not when the sheriff was still coming up dry in his search for the person who had broken Emma's window and scared her to death. And now the sheriff's attention was distracted by the even scarier attack on Delia. Were he and his officers doing a good enough job of looking after Emma?

But was Delia's attack really scarier? Maybe the only difference between the two crimes was timing. Emma's alarm system had called for help. Maybe that alarm system was the only difference in the crimes. Maybe it was the one thing that had kept Emma from being blindfolded and tied up to her own bed. It only made things worse to realize that Emma lived alone, without someone like Oscar to hear her if she called for help.

Liz had lived alone. It would not help Joe's mental state to let his thoughts stray far down that path, so he didn't. Instead, he focused on what he had just seen while walking along the sandy bluff overlooking Emma's house.

A trail, covered in pine needles, ran along that bluff, and it gave the perfect hidden vantage point for watching Emma's every move. When Joe considered that vantage point with Emma's predictability in mind, he got the shivers.

As he'd walked that trail, he'd looked for tracks and signs just like he did when he went deer hunting. On the downhill side of the trail, he'd found three grooves in the sandy dirt. They were shaped like two heels and a butt. Somebody had been walking through these woods, leaving no trail on the thick bed of pine needles. When that somebody stepped off the path and onto bare soil, invisibility vanished. Three grooves showed where someone had awkwardly slid a few feet down the hill, then sat.

It had rained since Emma's break-in, so this butt mark had appeared since the sheriff's people did their investigation. They might have missed it anyway, since there was no guarantee that they'd have thought to look up here on this bluff. Even if they had, only the most savvy tracker would have understood the scene the way that Joe did, and Joe wasn't sure the sheriff employed anyone with enough skill.

Very few people would have known that the spreading width at the base of the middle depression showed that someone had sat in the sand and lingered. Even fewer would have seen the cupped dent left by an elbow used to support someone leaning to the right and peering through a gap in the underbrush. An inexpert tracker would not have known to look three feet above the ground for the branch that had been broken by someone wishing to widen that gap.

A person whose butt was sitting in that sandy spot could sight Emma's house through the opening in the underbrush. Joe was pretty sure someone had been sitting up there on that bluff watching Emma, and he was pretty sure it had been since her break-in. Specifically, it had been since the last time it rained, which had been Thursday morning.

He was absolutely going to let the sheriff know what he had found, and he was also absolutely not going to let Emma spend another night in that house. While he waited to explain these things to Emma, he sat in a deck chair behind her house, relaxed and alert and fully engaged in seeking a solution to the problem of his friend's vulnerability.

There was only one solution that suited Joe. Emma needed to come spend a few days with her good friend Faye. It would be easier, much easier, for Joe to keep an eye on the women who were worrying him—Emma and Faye—if he could get them under one roof. Magda had the sheriff to watch out for her (and the sheriff had Magda to watch out for him), but Emma and Faye needed Joe, whether they would admit it to his face or not.

For once, he was glad that Amande was far away. It gave him a pang to know that, until this thing was over, he wished he had someplace safe to send Michael.

There was a tiny flaw in his plan to gather Faye and Emma under his roof, in that he was not wholly convinced that his father was fit to be around them. Joe figured that he could think his way through this logical flaw before Emma got home, but thinking would have been easier if Faye hadn't made him give up tobacco. He usually concentrated with a wad of tobacco in his mouth or a cigarette he'd rolled himself resting in his hand.

After about twenty minutes of wishing for a cigarette, Joe remembered who had taught him to track and he knew it wasn't his dad who had been sitting on that bluff spying on Joe's friend. If Sly Mantooth had been the person watching Emma's house, he would have left no signs for Joe to find.

Joe didn't know who was stalking women in Micco County, but it was not his father.

Joe heard Emma's car door slam, so he got up off the deck chair and walked around to the garage. She was still driving the big boat of a car that Douglass had bought her for their last anniversary and she still paid somebody to keep its deep blue paint clean and shimmery. Joe could have sworn he detected new car smell when she opened the door, but he was probably smelling the freshly conditioned leather seats.

Emma dressed nice to go to the grocery store—flowery dress with a long flowing skirt, high-heeled red shoes, and matching purse—but those clothes weren't going to be very comfortable for their boat ride out to Joyeuse Island. She was going to have to change clothes.

"You're coming out to our house to stay for a while."

Emma hooked her forearm through the handle of her purse and got out of the car, saying, "You're telling me what to do? That's cute."

Joe reached down and took her hand. Emma was taller than Faye, but she was still little, so little. Joe believed he was going to a good place when he died, or at least he was trying his best to get there, and he believed that Douglass was already there. If Joe allowed harm to come to this woman, there was no doubt in his mind that Douglass would make his afterlife hell for all of eternity.

"Yes, you're coming with me, and not because I'm telling you what to do. You're coming because you're smart."

Carefully and in detail, Joe described what he'd seen on the sandy bluff overlooking her house. He explained the chronology—Liz dead on Sunday night, Emma's security fob stolen on Tuesday and her window broken that night, a butt-print in the sand sometime after a Thursday rainstorm, an attempted rape on Delia early Friday morning—and asked her to tell him honestly that she believed she was safe in her big house alone.

Then he hefted all six of Emma's grocery bags and took them to the kitchen while she went upstairs to pack her things for an extended stay on Joyeuse Island.

Chapter Twenty-nine

Faye stood in the kitchen where Joe was putting away the leftover gumbo. It had taken him a solid hour to clean and chop the tomatoes, onions, peppers, sausage, and okra for that gumbo, because knifeplay was one of her husband's favorite strategies for dealing with stress. She thought Joe should probably have warned his father that he was bringing Emma home.

Sly had spent the hour before dinner standing uncertainly in the kitchen with Joe, shifting around on his feet like a fourteen-year-old boy forced to speak to a girl. Emma had stayed with Faye in the living room, because a woman of her age and grace did not chase men. Sly had not even come to tell her hello. There had been no dinner table conversation, just a two-year-old babbling at four grown-ups who sat as silent as a pile of rocks.

After dinner, it had taken maybe three minutes for Sly to move his things out of Amande's room into the smaller but perfectly adequate room next door. Then he had fled for the woods while Emma arranged her things in the room he had just vacated. Faye had watched him out the back window, walking with determination and swinging an ax from his right hand. He'd obviously been handling axes for a long time. Otherwise, Faye would have worried more about a man this distracted handling a sharp blade.

She'd felt Emma's skirt brush her leg as the older woman came to the window and stood beside her. "It can't have been something I said, because I didn't say anything. What did I do to make that man act this way?"

"I don't know what his problem is, but it's not you."

Joe gave his father a half-hour to stew, then he went after him. Sly wasn't hiding. Joe followed the sound of his ax and found him working next to the ashes of yet another one of the camp-fires. He'd left them scattered all over the island, which made Joe a little nuts, but he hadn't said anything because he knew his father knew how to put out a fire. And also because when somebody got on your nerves as bad as Sly got on Joe's, you had to pick your battles.

"What's the matter with you, Dad? You weren't even nice to Emma. What are you mad at her for?"

Sly laid the ax on the ground and pulled a pack of cigarettes out of his pocket. Joe wanted one, but he waved the offered pack away.

"Ain't mad at her. I'm mad at you."

"For what? Have I been cooking your breakfast wrong? Leaving you and your grandson alone to play and get to know each other—have I been doing that wrong?"

"No, Son, it ain't none of that. But why did you bring that woman out here?"

"Emma? Because it's my house and I'll invite whoever I want. And because she wasn't safe. I told you about the tracks outside her house. You wanted me to leave Emma where she wasn't safe?"

"You think she's safe out here? Take a look. Behind me."

Then Sly stood with his back to Joe, so he could prowl outside the ring of bare sand surrounding the old fire without his father peering over his shoulder.

"When did you last have a fire out here, Dad?"

"Wednesday. Haven't been out here since." Sly didn't turn around, so Joe knew that there was something else he was supposed to see.

The area of dirt around the ashes had been scuffed by some-one's feet since the rain on Thursday, so since Sly's last visit. Most of the marks were indistinct, but one footprint stood out clearly. Its low-relief texture was highlighted by the slanting light of early evening. It was the unmistakable imprint of the treads of a sneaker and it was right in front of an overturned bucket that Sly had used as a stool. Somebody had been sitting in this spot, and for no good reason Joe could think of, since there hadn't been a fire to enjoy.

Faye wore boots for work and sandals to relax. Joe wore moccasins or went barefoot, unless he needed boots to protect his feet. On the rare occasions that Sly shed his work boots, he wore flip-flops. Emma and her stylish loafers had just arrived. Michael did own a pair of sneakers, but they were tiny. Nobody who belonged on Joyeuse Island had made this print.

"I never seen Gerry or any of those environmentalists leave the path between their dig and the dock," Joe said. "I don't think they did this."

"Me, neither. Besides, they wear safety boots. And Faye didn't bring that weirdo guy—"

"Oscar." Joe didn't like the way the name sounded coming out of his mouth.

"Yeah, and his girlfriend Delia—Faye didn't bring them over here."

"I saw you follow them out of the house yesterday."

"You didn't stop me."

Joe shook his head. "Nope. But I did go up to the cupola and keep an eye out. Can't see much through the trees, but the paths all come out into the open now and then. Sometimes I could see bushes move when they passed through them, but you move better in the woods than they do. Still, I could track you."

"I bet you could." Sly squatted outside the sandy ring, on ground strewn with a thick bed of pine straw. He stared at the dead ashes as though they were still aflame. "Why did you bring that woman out here, Son? Why did you put Emma in danger that way?"

"I told you. I saw prints on the bluff above her house. Somebody's been watching her. She's safer out here on the island, with you and me to look out for her—well, at least she's not

alone now. Even if the person who did all those things comes
out here, she's not alone."

It had been years since Joe heard his father's temper explode.
Sly's voice was cannon-loud, just as he remembered it. "When
you was little, I thought you was dumb, but now I know you're
not. Think, Son. Whoever it is *has already been out here.* Look
at that footprint by the fire."

Joe looked at the print. He couldn't argue with it. Maybe
a random trespasser had left it. He himself had first met Faye
because he was on Joyeuse Island when he wasn't supposed to
be. Deep down, however, he knew that his father was right.

His father wasn't finished yelling at him. "Look at that print real
good. Who was the person wearing that shoe looking for? Faye?"

Joe flinched.

"You like the idea of letting that little woman be in the same
place...the same world...as that animal what tied young Delia
up? And Emma? I can't do it. Never could. I can't do it."

"Can't do what, Dad?"

"Keep 'em safe. All of 'em. Emma, Faye, my grandson. The
granddaughter that's coming home on an airplane soon, the one
I ain't met yet. You."

*And my mother. You can't say her name, but this is about her,
isn't it?*

"I don't need you to take care of me, Dad."

"I don't care if you do or you don't. *I* need it. I needed to do
it a long time ago, and I couldn't figure out how. You and your
mama. You needed me to fix things and I didn't know how."

"That's over and done. Besides, we have the law to help us
this time."

"You talking about the same law that thinks I killed Liz and
hurt Delia and tried to hurt Emma?"

Joe recognized the belligerent set to Sly's jaw, because he had
seen it in the mirror. "I'm talking about the same law that we
should have called as soon as you saw that track," he said. "It's
dark now. What if it rains tonight? That track might prove you're
innocent and we need the law to see it."

"They'll just say that I made it myself."

"Let 'em say it. I'm calling Detective Steinberg and asking him to come out here and look at this. I'm asking him to bring a camera and the brightest lights he's got, because we've got to get a picture of this. He's been straight with us through this whole thing. He came out yesterday on his time off, just to look at that hole you found. He'll come look at this print. If we're lucky, he'll come before we get some rain that washes it away."

Joe wasn't just afraid of rain. He was afraid of a stray breeze that might kick up just enough dust to hide the details of the tread of that sneaker. It wasn't just proof that someone had been on the island. It could be evidence that would convict Liz's killer.

"You do that. You call the detective. Then you help me lock up the doors and shutters on the basement of that big house you live in. They're stout oak and the walls might as well be made out of concrete. If we put the women and the baby behind those walls, we can look out for 'em."

"Do either of those women seem like somebody who'll smile when you tell her you're locking her up for her own good?"

"They don't have to know. I spend a lot of nights outside with a cigarette in my strong hand. Tonight, I'll smoke with my left hand, because this will be in my strong one." He brandished the heavy ax. "We've got to get this problem cleared up. I'm looking forward to meeting my granddaughter, and I don't intend for her to set foot on this island until you and I have cleared it of vermin. You sure you trust the law to help us do it?"

"No, Dad. We're not keeping Faye and Emma in the dark. We're going to tell them what's happening. Faye can be dangerous with a gun, and they're both of 'em smarter than we are. We need them."

Joe opened the bag tied to his belt. He pulled out a leather sling and three heavy rocks that fit into the sling's pouch. Then he pulled out a hand-chipped stone blade lashed to a handle that was balanced for Joe's hand and Joe's hand alone.

"And, yeah. I do plan to trust the law, but not only the law. I also trust myself. And I trust Faye. My wife and I will look after the people under our roof. If you want to help us, you're welcome."

◇◇◇

Gerry was standing on their doorstep in less than an hour. He wasted no time setting up lights and getting photos of the footprint and zapping them through the Internet to shore. Joe's pictures of the butt-print near Emma's house went with them. Come what may, the sheriff would have these two weapons in his fight to find and convict Liz's killer.

Faye, Joe, Emma, Sly, and Gerry sat around the kitchen table.

"You agree with me, don't you, Detective?" Joe said. "You saw the footprint Dad found. You know somebody's been out here. Somebody's been watching us. And I'm telling you that I also saw prints uphill from Emma's house, right where somebody could keep an eye on her."

"I believe you about the prints at Emma's. I saw the pictures you took. I'd give a million dollars if you'd found a shoe print that matched the one here on Joyeuse Island, but I do agree," Gerry said. "It looks like somebody's been watching all of you."

"Or maybe not all of us," Sly said. "It was Liz that got killed and Delia that got attacked and Emma here that had a close call. They're all women. Maybe the person who left that footprint wasn't here to watch all of us. Faye's the only woman living out here. Maybe they was here to watch her. I won't stand for it."

"I won't stand for anybody being in danger, man or woman," Gerry said. "But you're right. Somebody does seem to be stalking women. They've been doing it on an almost daily basis ever since Liz died. It's only been six days, yet we've had a death, an attempted home invasion, an attempted rape. Now we have evidence that someone has been lurking—recently—near the homes of one of the victims and yet another woman. I don't blame you for being worried. Have you considered taking your family ashore?"

"Where?" Faye asked. "Emma's house isn't any safer than ours. Should we all go stay with Sheriff Mike and Magda? How long should we plan to sleep on their floor? Or should we go get a few hotel rooms and stay there until we spend what's left of our money?"

Joe had both hands flat on the table in front of him, his long thin fingers tapping a nervous rhythm. "We've got four adults out here—Emma, Faye, my dad, and me. Liz was by herself when she was killed. Emma was by herself when somebody tried to get in her house. Oscar was in the house with Delia, but she was alone in her room. I think we'll be okay."

Faye put a hand on Joe's, quieting the tapping fingers. "Gerry, if we're lucky, that footprint will help you find the person behind all this. It could happen tomorrow. Or maybe some other clue will come along tomorrow to help you crack this case. But that's tomorrow. We'd appreciate any advice you can give us on how to stay safe right now, tonight. The nights last a long time out here so far from people."

"I know they do," Gerry said. "That's why I'm not leaving all of you out here alone on this island tonight. I'm staying. It's my job to serve and protect. Tonight, I think you need protection."

It rattled Joe to know that a law officer thought the situation was so serious that he wanted to stand guard over his family. This meant that the law officer agreed with Joe that the danger was real. Joe would have preferred to be wrong.

Joe looked at Faye and she gave a little nod, so he said, "Thank you, Detective. We're grateful for your help."

The sky was going quickly dark and Emma had carried a drowsy Michael to his bedroom for a story. Sly had positioned himself on the front porch and Gerry had let him, telling Joe, "I'll take the back porch. You take the cupola. You'll have a line-of-sight in all directions up there. With eyes like yours, you'd see a boat coming before your dad or I would."

"If that boat's got its running lights on."

"The moon won't be up for a good long while. It'll be pretty damn dark till then. You think somebody could get all the way out here without lights?"

"I could do it. Dad could do it. Lots of people could do it, if they were brave enough or stupid enough. Or patient enough to go slow and pay attention."

"I'm guessing that would be your strategy, to go slow and pay attention."

Joe nodded. "That's the way I do a lot of things."

"So you're okay with taking the cupola?"

Joe wanted to be on the front porch, waiting for trouble like the hero in an old Western, but he said, "Yes."

"The porches face north and south. Up top, you can see in all directions, but the trees block a lot of your view of the ground. We need some ground-level visibility to the east and west."

"Emma says she's staying the night in my son's room. She'll be watching out that window without me telling her to do it, but I'll tell her anyway. My wife will have some ideas about where she wants to keep watch, but I'm thinking she'll be up a story on the other side of the house, sitting at the parlor window."

Joe looked outside at the gathering night. The house was lit up like Christmas morning. He'd fired up the generator, so they weren't just depending on battery power from the solar panels. When they'd done the electrical part of the renovation, Faye had insisted on wiring the whole house with outlets and overhead lights that they never used, because they lived ninety percent of their lives in the large and practical basement. She dreamed of having parties in the ballroom and Thanksgiving in the dining room and family Christmases in the parlor, and what good is a Christmas tree without lights? Faye's dreams fueled all the hours they had spent on the restoration, so Joe wasn't about to argue about running a few extra wires. One day, they'd get around to buying furniture to sit on for those family holidays.

Even the porches were lit up, because Faye had wanted lights to welcome all those guests she was going to have someday. Joe doubted that the person spying on them would try anything on a night when anybody could see that the house was full of people who weren't sleeping.

Who was out there? A SWAT team? Because that's what it would take to storm the house tonight and take them all out without a fight. Nothing that had happened suggested that there was more than one stalker…one killer.

Still, Joe didn't have eyes in the back of his head. Just because the cupola had windows in all directions, it didn't mean that he could see in all directions. What if someone came across the water while his back was turned? What if someone charged the front porch and his father had to confront a gun with only an ax? What if they came in a window and overwhelmed Faye, despite the gun in her hand, the one that they liked to pretend they didn't own?

Joe hated guns. He hated the way they looked and the way they smelled, and he hated the things they did to human bodies.

Tonight, he wished he owned more than one.

He needed to get up in that cupola before dark, but first he was going to take a few minutes to talk to his wife.

Chapter Thirty

Faye was sitting on a stool by the parlor window. Its seat was hard and her butt already hurt. The windowsill was wide enough for her to rest both forearms on it, hands clasped. There was room at her elbow to rest the handgun that she had hoped she never had to look at again.

She had aimed this weapon at a person before, someone she believed had killed Joe. Her bullet had missed, but it had torn into a gasoline engine and the explosion had done the killing for her. In other words, if she wasn't a killer, it was only because she'd gotten off on a technicality.

She heard Joe walk up behind her. She knew he was making noise on purpose. Joe's motions were ordinarily soundless, but he knew it was dumb to sneak up on an armed woman, particularly when that woman's nerves were shot. He leaned down, his lips brushing the hair behind her ear.

"Dad thinks the person who left that footprint by the campfire was out here looking for you. I think he's right. Faye, if something happened to you, it would kill me. Or I'd have to go kill the person that did it. Or both. We haven't been talking lately—"

"Tell me about it."

"Is that my fault?"

"No."

He was squatting beside her and his hand was resting on her thigh. She reached for it, rested her hand on top of it. He let her do it, but he didn't take her hand in his.

The lips at her ear said, "You're my wife and you're also the smartest person I know. Who do you think is doing these things?"

Faye pulled her hand back and rested it on the windowsill, next to the one holding the gun. "Well, it could be a stranger who just came to town to hurt women. If that's true, then there's no way to know who it is and we're wasting our breath. So let's think about people we know."

"There's Tommy," he said. "I think he's scum. With him spending all that time with Liz every day, anything could have passed between them. I can see him killing Liz."

"That's a terrible thing to say about a person, but I can, too."

"You're in and out of the marina all the time, Faye, so maybe Tommy had his eye on you, too. The same goes for Delia for the past few weeks. But Emma's never at the marina these days. What about Oscar? He was around all of them."

"I have a picture of him at the marina, so he probably met Liz before she died. Emma said he asked her out, then came knocking on her door, uninvited. Who knows what his relationship with Delia is like? That's three women in his vicinity who have had some serious trouble."

"He doesn't have a lot of connection with you, other than meeting you a couple of times."

Faye didn't respond.

"Faye?"

"I didn't want to tell you, because it seemed like nothing. It knew it wasn't nothing, but I still felt dumb about telling you."

"Telling me what?"

"Oscar sort of…he…well, I guess the word is groped. My arm. Just my arm. When I saw him yesterday, he sat way too close to me and he was just starting to rub his hand up my arm when Delia came in the room and interrupted him."

Joe looked like he wanted to go break a seventy-year-old man in two. "If somebody's been sitting out there watching you—*targeting* you—Oscar just went to the top of the suspect list, because he's the only one who's crossed that line with you. Isn't he?"

"Yes."

"Then go tell Gerry what you just told me. No, don't. We need you at the window and, as soon as I tell Gerry what you just told me, we need me upstairs. I can't stay here much longer." Finally, he reached for Faye's free hand, dragging it off the windowsill and putting it inside both of his. "After I tell Gerry what you said, he may want to send somebody to get Delia out of there."

"She may not want to go. I think she cares for Oscar, although I'd think a woman who'd been widowed would steer clear of older men. A thirty-year-old widow starting something with a seventy-year-old man is just asking to go through the same thing again."

"Her husband died? I figured she'd gotten divorced."

Faye knew Joe didn't snoop around on the Internet the way she did, so she asked him, "How'd you know she'd been married?"

"I saw the mark on her wedding ring finger. It takes a long time for the dent to go away. You saw that, too?"

No, she hadn't noticed a micrometer-deep dent on Delia's finger, because she did not have Joe's eyes and attention to detail. "I didn't pay any attention to her hands, but I did look up her business on the web. Delia's husband died five years ago, according to her website."

"He's been gone five years? That means there's been another one."

"Another what? Another dead husband?"

"I don't know if he's dead, but that dent on her finger ain't five years old. She's been wearing rings on that hand lately, so there's been another husband."

Joe pulled Faye's phone out of her hip pocket. "I know what you and the World Wide Web can do. You could find the lost treasure of Captain Hook, if you set your mind to it. See what you can find out about Delia and her husbands. Text it to Gerry and me."

"While I also keep an eye out the window, in case I need to shoot a bad guy?"

"Yes."

Faye was pleased to know that her husband thought she had magical powers.

"We should've been talking," Joe said. "You should've told me that Oscar put his hands on you. Not because I'm jealous, but because I should know when you're upset. And if we'd been talking, I would've known Delia was married a long time ago and you would've known that she just got finished being married again."

"Do you think it matters?"

"It depends on how that first husband died. And on what happened to the next one. She's young to be a widow. She's real young to be a widow twice. Maybe Oscar's not the creepiest half of that pair. Maybe it's not just one killer out there. Maybe they've been working together. I'll let Gerry know about Delia and her husbands. You start web crawling and find us some answers."

Joe was still holding her left hand. He gently disengaged the right one from the gun and pulled her to her feet, wrapping her in his two long arms. Then he kissed her. Joe was so tall, a foot and a half taller than Faye, that a simple kiss required him to stoop his shoulders and crouch low while she stretched up to meet him. She knew they looked a little bit stupid when they kissed, nothing at all like the cover of a romance novel. Well, this was her romance, and it didn't matter whether anybody else thought it looked like one.

"We're going to make it," Joe said, and Faye didn't know whether he meant they were going to make it through the night or whether their marriage was going to make it through this dark time. Whatever he meant, if Joe said it, Faye believed it.

Faye's phone beeped. She had just sent Gerry an extended text with information on Delia's husbands, with links to both marriage licenses and both death certificates. These things showed that Delia liked her men old. Old and rich.

Her first husband had been the heir to a family chain of drugstores, the old-timey variety where the pharmacist made your cough syrup while you soothed your sore throat with an ice cream soda. A business profile in their small-town newspaper showed an even younger Delia and her graying-but-fit husband, posing with the mountain bikes they rode every weekend. It said that they had met when she worked as a cashier at one of his stores. Two years later, his death certificate said he had died of kidney failure.

According to Delia's second husband's obituary, they had met when he hired her to research his genealogy, and they had just three years together before he died at sixty-eight of Alzheimer's. She had buried him only a few months before she met Oscar. His obituary said he had recently closed the last location in his chain of video rental stores. Poor Delia. Had she married a wealthy man just in time to see his fortune evaporate when movies went streamable?

As Faye thought about it, she realized that she had known a lot of men who developed near-obsessive interests in things like genealogy and their family's history as they got older. Delia's services were expensive, so her clientele would naturally be weighted toward people with money. It was almost like she was running a one-woman dating service for golddiggers. Make that one golddigger. Faye guessed she'd never given much thought to how someone would go about looking for a meal ticket.

A text came in from Joe, directed to both her and Gerry:

How cd Delia do this stuff? Is she snkng out after he goes 2 sleep? Did she fake gttng atakd? Cn u send smbdy ovr there 2 see if she's home?

Gerry answered immediately. He was as persnickety with his texting grammar as Faye was.

We don't know that Delia's our killer. There's no law against having rich husbands who die conveniently. Don't forget Oscar's awkward history with women. And Tommy's awkward history with the world. I'm sending somebody to check their houses. If they're at home, they're not out here stalking us.

This left Faye with a smartphone in her hands but no good ideas to chase. Joe said that the shoeprint could have been left by a tall woman or a man of small-to-medium height. Delia, Oscar, and Tommy all fit that description.

If Delia had been on Joyeuse Island, uninvited, what, exactly, would her motive be? Faye thought back to the time she had spent with Oscar and Delia. She remembered Delia's hand patting Oscar's shoulder and the times she'd let him touch her. Delia had walked into the room just as Oscar was groping Faye's arm. Faye had caught the younger woman in one unguarded moment, studying Faye and Oscar through narrowed eyes. If Delia was trying to get her hands on Oscar's money and if she really was a murderer, Faye had become a target in the instant that Delia first perceived her as a threat to her attempts to land yet another sugar daddy.

By the same logic, Emma had become a threat when Delia saw that Oscar was attracted to her, probably on the very day of Emma's break-in. Faye had heard Joe tell Gerry that he'd seen them all together that day—Oscar, Delia, and Emma.

Faye wouldn't have had to overhear this, if she and Joe had been talking. She would have known it days before.

If Delia had seen the emotional spark that had prompted Oscar to ask Emma to dinner later in the day, she would have had any number of opportunities to swipe the security fob. All she would have needed was a quick distraction for Oscar. Joe's arrival might even have been that distraction, but Oscar was such a lecher that Delia could probably divert his attention any time she liked just by showing a little skin.

What about Liz? Oscar had certainly visited her marina. Faye had seen a picture of him leaving the parking lot with Delia. Gerry had underlined that point this evening by telling her that Oscar had enjoyed a nightly drink at Liz's bar. It wouldn't have been hard for a jealous Delia to go back to the bar after closing time and put a bullet in her back.

Jealousy. Sexual jealousy made all the puzzle pieces fit, but so did avarice. Whether Delia was worried that another woman would take her potential lover, or whether she was concerned about losing the man she wanted for her next meal ticket, the stakes had been high for her. Had they been high enough to prompt her to fake an attempted rape?

She shot off a text to Gerry:

> Could Delia's wounds have been self-inflicted? Do you have any evidence beyond her word that anybody came in her window that night? Or do you think it's possible that Oscar was the attacker and Delia didn't know because she was blindfolded? I think I'm afraid of both of them.

She had hardly pressed "Send" when she got a response, but the text wasn't from Gerry. It was from Magda, another spelling champion who refused to compromise just because she was on her phone.

> Sorry to be so slow getting back to you. Rachel has had strep throat for a solid week. Ear infection, too. I looked up the last yellow fever epidemic in this part of Florida for you. It was in 1888. "Jowl mooker" took me a while. If you hadn't said it was from India, I'd never have found chaulmoogra. It was an oil used to treat skin infections. Hope you're surviving the visit with Joe's dad.

The chaulmoogra oil of Cally's friend Elias should have been Faye's last concern, but she was antsy and Gerry wasn't answering her. She had found that resting her phone on the windowsill allowed her to work while she kept an eye out for intruders, so she did a web search for chaulmoogra, just to pass the time and just because she was curious.

One of the snippets offered her by the search engine jumped off the computer screen:

> "...extracted from the nuts of the chaulmoogra tree was used until the advent of modern treatments in the 1940s. It largely replaced earlier treatments, which included mercury, arsenic..."

Faye wanted to read anything that connected something she knew to have been on her island—chaulmoogra oil—with the unexplained presence of arsenic. She clicked on the snippet and found a brief entry in an encyclopedia of medical history.

> "In the days before modern treatments were developed, chaulmoogra oil was applied to the skin and injected as a treatment for leprosy. Oil extracted from the nuts of the chaulmoogra tree was used until the advent of modern treatments in the 1940s. It largely replaced earlier treatments, which included mercury, arsenic, and elephant's teeth."

These two sentences took Faye straight to a theory about Elias Croft that fit all the facts. She knew that a man named Elias had lived on Joyeuse for years and that he'd ordered a steady supply of chaulmoogra. She knew that Cally had scared her daughter away from a cabin on the west end of the island with stories of a Monster Man and threats of being switched. She also knew that Cally thought Elias had taken a big risk by coming to meet the supply boat during the yellow fever epidemic, and that he'd disguised himself with a hat and scarf to do it.

Thanks to Gerry and Nadia and their testing, she knew that traces of arsenic still remained on that end of the island. Could it have seeped, over time, out of the buried body of a man treated for leprosy over years and years? The arsenic-tainted chunk of wood came to mind, and she thought that this was exactly what a lab would find if it tested a sample from a wooden tub used by a sick man to soak regularly in a medicinal bath of arsenic. If these arsenic baths had been emptied onto the ground over a period of years, they could explain the pattern of arsenic contamination in the soil in a way that Gerry and Nadia hadn't been able to do.

Faye tried to put herself in the shoes of a man using Joyeuse Island as his own private leper colony in the late 1800s. He would have needed help. He would have needed someone to bring him food and order his medicine, while he treated himself with arsenic and chaulmoogra oil until his body finished failing. He would have needed to lock himself up in a cabin far from anybody, and his helper would have absolutely beaten her daughter's legs with a switch before she let the child's curiosity expose her to leprosy.

What if, in the middle of that long decline, yellow fever had come to Joyeuse Island? Wouldn't that man have risked being exposed as a leper? Wouldn't he have covered his skin lesions and rushed to the dock to get help for the woman who had sheltered him?

As time passed, he would have needed someone to help him through the last stages of leprosy. And he would have asked that person to write his beloved wife when he died. Faye thought he probably would have asked the person to leave his illness out of the letter, just as he had left it out of his last letter home, because an honorable Victorian man wouldn't have wanted his family to carry the stigma of leprosy. He would have told them good-bye, then asked a trusted friend to help him drop off the face of the earth, sending his sword home as a remembrance when he was gone.

Was Cally that friend? Faye was sure that she was. To a man desperate for a place to hide, a gracious and resourceful woman who owned an island had probably looked like a gift from God. Captain Croft would have seen that grace and resourcefulness in Cally when he visited Joyeuse and she helped him feed his troops. Perhaps he had sensed he was in the presence of a woman who would someday say, *"Sometimes there is only one gift a body can give another person. Sometimes that gift is silence."*

She texted Magda back to say

Thank you! You are not going to believe how helpful a simple definition of chaulmoogra oil has been. Can't wait to tell you about it.

A moment later, her phone rang. It wasn't Magda, hoping to get the scoop on why chaulmoogra oil was suddenly so impor-tant. It was Gerry.

"I heard from the officers I sent to check on our suspects. The lights are on at Delia and Oscar's house. The TV is on. The boats are both out back. The car's out front."

"They didn't knock on the door and see who was home? Delia could be watching TV while Oscar sits out there in the woods, waiting for a chance to shoot us. Or maybe Oscar's watching TV and Delia's out here. Or maybe they're both out here and they left the TV playing."

"I don't want to tip my hand yet. I've got someone watching the house. If anybody comes or goes, we'll know."

"But if they've already come or gone?"

"We won't know. This is the best I can do right now. But I didn't call to talk about Oscar and Delia. I called to tell you about Tommy. He's gone."

"Gone where?"

"All I know is that his house is dark and Lolita's been seen walking the street in Tallahassee, so he's not with her. His car's at the marina. His boat's in its slip there."

"Maybe he's in the house asleep?"

"We've been watching him for a while now. He's a carouser. He doesn't go to bed at sunset. And there's a boat missing."

"Whose boat?"

"Don't know. The guy I've got doing surveillance took a picture this afternoon of the slips Tommy uses for his customers' boats. One of the boats in his picture is gone now. Not the biggest one—he left a few behind that I'd call yachts—but it looks expensive and fast."

"You think he ran? He was afraid of facing charges for polluting the Gulf?"

"Maybe. Or maybe he needed a way to get out here. I've got people out patrolling the water between Joyeuse Island and the shore. Sheriff Rainey knows I'm worried enough about you people to be out here tonight, so he agrees that some extra eyes on the water around this island would be a good idea. The officers who are out looking for Tommy and his boat will also be cruising past the island off and on through the night."

Faye said good-bye and hung up. Then she looked out the window and, finally, she accepted the truth. She was wrong when she told herself that she could magically know whenever somebody came and went from her island. Her haven. It was true that her ears were good and she was attuned to the sound of a boat motor. But there were ways. Someone willing to go far out into the Gulf, giving the area around the dock and her house a wide berth, could swing back landward on the uninhabited and heavily wooded east side of her island. It could be happening right now. She had been fooling herself.

Tommy. Oscar. Delia. Any of them could have gotten out to Joyeuse Island without her knowing about it.

Even Wilma could have done it. Maybe she was spreading lies about seeing a big man lurking near the murder site, hoping to distract people from the fact that she did as much business with Liz as Tommy ever did. Wilma could handle a boat. There was nothing to keep her from sneaking out to Faye's island.

Anybody with a boat could have done it, if they wanted it bad enough. And this realization went both ways. Her presumption that Sly couldn't have left the island at any time that week without her knowledge rested on logic that was just as shaky. He would have had to get to the dock without being seen or heard, and Faye judged that this would have been hard to do in daylight, but at night? Even on those sleepless nights, her lids must have dropped over her eyes from time to time.

She had likely crossed the border between sleep and wakefulness several times a night, and Sly might have been lucky enough to make his move during one of those drowsy moments. He would have had to have been lucky again when he came back, but logic dictated that it wasn't impossible.

Faye had spent too much time in grief, too much time in the blurry illogic of a woman wishing to turn back time. She felt her mind slip back into its customary groove of logic and clarity. She knew now that she didn't have enough information to exclude anyone as a suspect. Anybody could be stalking Emma or Delia or Faye herself. Even her husband's father. Even the armed lawman who had volunteered to stay all night to protect Faye and Joe and their family. Anybody.

Chapter Thirty-one

Joe knew that Faye, Sly, Emma, and Gerry were at their posts below him, facing the four directions. He stood above them, constantly turning so that he could keep all the water around Joyeuse Island in his sights. On the island itself, he could see only treetops and he could barely see those without moonlight to help him. The other four watchers could see the open yard around the house, lit by the light streaming from the windows, but they could only see a few feet into the woods that surrounded the house and blanketed the island. There were huge gaps in their ability to monitor their surroundings.

Any of them would be able to see a flashlight or campfire burning nearby, but Joyeuse Island was a big place. Joe could probably track a boat using its running lights. When the moon rose, he would be able to make out motion in the areas cleared of trees and the others would gain a little more clarity in their view of the woods, but the truth was that they were almost blind. Keeping watch defended them from utter surprise, but that was about all.

What Joe didn't know—what none of them knew—was that someone had traveled by rowboat while the sun shone, before the five of them ever thought to watch for an intruder. That person had come by a path that none of them had anticipated, rowing east and hugging the swampy coast of the mainland so closely that, even if anybody had been looking, the boat would have been hidden in the shadows of overhanging trees. But no one had been looking.

The small and shallow-drafted boat had skirted the eastern tip of the island, far from the house, the dock, the everyday lives of Faye and her family, finally beaching on a spot of sand just wide and firm enough to support it and the footsteps of a single human being. That stretch of Joyeuse Island's coast had the usual fringe of needlerush and cordgrass, so the vegetation hid the boat from anyone passing by water or land.

The intruder had been there before, sneaking ashore in the dim evening light and waiting until moonrise made it possible to move around.

It had been easy for that intruder to step into the trees, though not so easy to fight through the undergrowth to the path that circled this end of Joyeuse Island. By daylight, it had been possible to find and follow the paths that criss-crossed the island. By moonlight, it would be possible to retrace those steps. But in the moonless time just after dark? Not possible, not with a reasonable chance of success. Those hours must be passed by finding a place to sit and wait.

An odd quirk in the human psyche meant that nobody in the house was expecting danger to come from the east end of the island. It was too overgrown to navigate in the dark. It didn't occur to them as they planned their defense that, just maybe, the intruder had already arrived. Perhaps someone had been out there for hours, waiting for dark to come.

Even in Florida, the air gets raw in November. A person sitting on a stump near the open water can go numb in the sea breeze. This is not optimal when those hands will be needed to aim a firearm and pull a trigger.

Out of eyeshot of the world—out of earshot, too, but a tiny fire doesn't make much noise, anyway—there is no reason not to clear some dry grass and set a few broken branches afire. A very few dry branches will do it, when the fire only needs to be big enough to warm two hands.

Darkness was dripping out of the cold sky and it would hide any faint breath of smoke. The house was so far away. It was impossible that anyone would see the red flicker of a handful of burning branches.

And if they did? If Faye and her husband and her husband's father saw the flames and were drawn to them, so much the better. They would be easier to shoot as they streamed through the woods, separate and undefended, with one of them carrying a toddler.

Let them come. Whether they did or whether they didn't, there would only be one person left standing, and that person would not be one of the ones cowering behind the walls of the big white house on Joyeuse Island. The person left standing would be the one lurking in the trees with bullets enough for all the others.

When Faye's web search uncovered the photograph, she almost called to Joe out of instinct. Then, she remembered that she didn't trust anybody in the world but Joe, not fully, so she didn't want anyone to hear her news but him. Instead, she made sure that her phone was totally silenced, even the keyclicks, and she typed out a text.

The return text from Joe was instantaneous, and it went out to all four of his fellow watchers.

Get away from the windows.

Faye unlaced her boots and slipped them off her feet. She wanted to move freely through her house, and she wanted to do it without being heard.

She moved along the walls, peering out of each window as she reached it, then dropping to her belly to get past. Walking in front of a window with the never-before-used electric lights blazing behind her would have been suicidal. The photo she had just seen on the cover of *Stock and Barrel* magazine had been innocent enough, just two people dressed for a weekend hunting trip, but an experienced hunter could pick her off in a heartbeat and there was more than one experienced hunter on Faye's long suspect list. Two of them were with her in the house. Sly had taught her woodcraft-obsessed husband how to handle a bow. He was holding an ax, right that minute. And just because Gerry had learned his shooting skills as part of law enforcement training, did that mean that he could be trusted?

She crawled over Joyeuse's slick heart-pine floors and descended the sneak staircase. Standing in the basement hall, she clutched the grip of her weapon, acutely aware of her own inexperience in marksmanship. The door to Michael's room was cracked open and she could see her son's form beneath his soft and downy comforter.

The door at the end of the hall led outside, into the space underneath the house's front porch. Even that area had been wired for lights, so a bright rectangle extended into the hall through the open door. A shadow appeared into that rectangle, blocking the light that had been washing across her body. She felt the shadow's coolness on her skin and turned her head in its direction.

Sly stood in the door, ax in hand. He turned to look outside, then faced her again. "Something ain't right."

Faye said, "No, it's not and somebody could shoot you through that door. Close it and get in here."

Sly lingered some more.

Hearing their whispers, Emma appeared in the doorway of Michael's room. "You okay?"

Faye nodded and said, "For the moment." Sly adjusted his grip on the ax, then gave a short nod.

Emma reached into a pocket sewn into the seam of her voluminous skirt and pulled out a dainty pistol fashioned of gleaming metal and inlaid with mother-of-pearl. Showing it to Sly and Faye, she said, "Douglass worried about me, and he liked to buy me jewels, so I got this for Christmas one year. I'm good with it. Your grandson will be safe with me." Then she disappeared into Michael's room.

Sly took a step closer to Faye. "Where's Joe?"

"I guess he's still upstairs, despite the fact that I just texted him a picture of two people holding high-powered rifles fitted out with telescopic sights. Somebody with a gun like that could pick him off in that cupola, easy. He probably decided we needed him to keep watch, regardless of what kind of firepower might be pointed this way."

Joe leaned into the corner of the cupola. He stood in a single room with four walls of glass, but each of those windows was framed with wood and set into a wood-frame wall. Even when he stood in the corner, he wasn't completely invisible to someone looking through a scope, but he wasn't a six-and-a-half-foot silhouette, either. A shooter who was looking for him would see him, but he wasn't an easy target.

As soon as he had stepped off the ladder and into this room, he had raised the windows. He couldn't hunt when he was closed off from the world. With the windows open, he was like an eagle surveying his world for motion, sound, light, and scent. The cold wind on his face was the same wind that blew on the face of his prey.

It was dark now, and Joe saw nothing but a dark blur of treetops, but he sensed something indefinable. He leaned into the corner and slid to the floor, crawling from window to window, looking for the one thing that wasn't right. Kneeling at the window that faced east, he realized what it was.

He smelled smoke.

It was a faint scent, more like the memory of a fire than the actual smell of smoke, but it was there. It was real.

Joe lunged for the trapdoor in the cupola floor, dropping through it feet first. He took the spiral staircase three steps at a time, lofting himself over the banister and dropping the last eight feet to the floor of the entry hall. Sprinting down the front staircase, he leapt over its banister, too, saving precious seconds in the trip from porch to ground.

His father must have been standing inside the basement, watching out the door, and he must have been there since Joe forwarded him Faye's text. Of course he was. That's where Joe would have been if he thought someone was coming for his family, telescopic sight be damned.

Sly was at his son's side before Joe had straightened up from the impact of another eight-foot drop and started running again. Faye, Emma, and Gerry were right behind him.

Sly grabbed his son by the shoulders and started saying, "What's wrong? Why—" but he interrupted himself. "I smell smoke. I think I been smelling it for a while, but it's faint. Barely there. What's burning?"

It wasn't easy for Joe to shake himself free of those powerful hands, the only hands that might have stood a chance of holding him back, but he managed it and he was running again. Sly was following him, ax in hand. Joe turned to face him, but he kept moving backward, hands stretched palm out, as if to hold his father back.

"No, Dad. No. I need you to stay and take care of my family."

Sly stopped cold in his tracks. His son sprinted into darkness.

Joe was trusting him with his whole world. Sly had gotten on the plane from Oklahoma to Florida, determined to find a way to make things right between him and his son. Here was his chance.

A black-haired blur passed him, tracking Joe into the trees.

"You can't do that. You can't go out there," he called after Faye, but she kept moving. "*Daughter.* Listen to me. He wants you to stay here."

Faye paused, still leaning in the direction she intended to run.

"Joe told me to take care of his family. You have to stay here and let me do it."

"He needs me. And as much as he hates guns, he needs this tonight." Faye inclined her head in the direction of the heavy revolver in her hand. "I'll take care of Joe. You help Emma take care of Michael."

And she was gone.

Chapter Thirty-two

It was too dark to see. It was certainly too dark to be careening headlong through the darkness. Faye pictured disastrous possibilities ranging from the ridiculous—running full tilt into the trunk of a stout tree—to the mundane—putting a foot down into a hole and breaking an ankle. Ridiculous, mundane accidents like those could put her on the ground with a fractured skull or a broken tibia protruding from her skin.

If Faye did something stupid that took her out of the action, Joe would be running into danger alone. She had an urgent need to be careful, but she was always careful. The only extra safety measure she could take would be to pray. So she prayed. And she kept dodging trees and trusting that no holes would open up under her feet.

She couldn't have kept going if she hadn't trusted Joe with everything she had. He, too, was plunging into impenetrable blackness, but he had a hawk's eyes and she didn't. He walked these paths every day, even the ones that led nowhere interesting. He knew them. The soles of his feet knew them. Faye trusted Joe, all the way to the soles of his feet, so she listened for his footfalls so that she could run in his footsteps. Joe's ability to move noiselessly through the forest had put many a rabbit on their table, so she had to listen with her whole being. Only Joe's wife could have tracked him by sound.

Faye's eyes might not have been as good as Joe's, but her nose was doing its job. She knew why Joe had burst out of the house and run headlong into danger. She smelled smoke. She hadn't smelled it at first, but now it was unmistakable.

Faye had no idea how far she was from the house, but she had run long enough to be gasping for air. Any minute, she would follow Joe around the broad curve in the trail that skirted the water's edge before turning back to the west. Surely, he didn't plan to run off the end of the island, nor would he have run all this way if he only intended to turn around and run back. They must be near their destination.

The smell of smoke grew with each step.

Sly left Emma and Michael in the basement, scaling the staircases and the tall ladder between him and the cupola with the speed of a man half his age. If danger was coming, whether it be in the form of a gun or a human or a raging fire, there was no better vantage point than the cupola to get a look at it.

The ladder took him up through the cupola's wooden floor. He saw nothing.

There was nothing outside the windows but blackness. Now and then, the wind brought a breath of air that made Sly think, ever so slightly, of smoke, but he couldn't pinpoint its direction. Where was the fire?

He stood in the middle of the cupola, facing the four directions one at a time—south, west, north, east. Nothing.

He imagined that he saw the occasional glint of water to the south, west, and north, but it was only because he knew the Gulf was out there. Starlight alone wasn't bright enough to show him those waves. To the east, the long axis of Joyeuse Island stretched out. He knew this, but he couldn't see it. Sly felt in his heart that the danger lurked in that direction. He stood silhouetted in the east window and peered into the darkness, looking for his son and praying that he would be able to make sure that Joe found his family safe when he came walking home.

Gerry had been waiting too long for a response to his last text to Faye.

How long had he been waiting? Five minutes. A woman sitting at a window with nothing to do but web-surf and watch for criminals had plenty of time to answer a text. Five minutes was too much time.

He checked his phone for the time and compared it to the time of his text. No, not five minutes. Eight minutes. That was way too long.

He dialed her number. No answer.

The feeling that something wasn't right took him off the back porch and into the house, where Faye wasn't waiting at the parlor window. His heart sank when he saw her cell phone on the windowsill. There was no way to find out where she'd gone.

The cold, sick feeling at his core took him onto the front porch, where Sly wasn't sitting in the rocking chair with his ax in hand.

Thumbing the button that dialed Joe's phone and clamping his own phone to his ear, he sprinted down the front entry stairs to the front yard. Joe didn't answer.

As Gerry turned and ran through the basement door beneath the front porch, he prayed that he would find Emma and Michael safely where they were supposed to be. He found nothing but Joe's cell phone lying beside the banister of the front staircase, face-down in the dirt.

◇◇◇

Joe only paused for an instant, because that's all the time it took to do the mathematics of projectile flight in his head. If he launched himself silently, traveling at the proper angle and the proper speed, he would hit an unaware target.

Delia sat staring into a small campfire. If he launched himself now, she wouldn't see him coming before his dense body, curled into a compact crouch, struck her like a cannonball. Conjuring the scene in his mind's eye, he could see the angle at which the rifle would fly out of her hands and he knew how far it would fly before it landed. When he had calculated that the rifle would fly far enough to render her unarmed, he jumped.

◇◇◇

Faye couldn't believe that Delia hadn't heard them coming. Joe's footfalls made no more sound in the forest than they ever did, so he might have been able to sneak up on her, but he wasn't alone and Faye didn't have Joe's knack for silence.

Faye hadn't been making as much noise as she might have, since her boots were still lying unlaced on the parlor floor, but she knew how many sticks had snapped beneath her feet because she had felt all their splinters cut into her soles. She had made plenty of noise breaking those sticks, enough to catch the attention of someone listening for trouble, but Delia had been staring abstractedly into the fire ever since Faye came into sight. Maybe the hiss and crackle of its flames had masked the sound of her footsteps and her breathing.

By the time Joe paused for the leap onto Delia's back, Faye was fully winded. Crouched on her hands and knees, she fought for breath. Her wheezing had to have been audible, but still Delia sat there, clothed head-to-toe in camouflage clothing in the exact dappled-green needed to hide in woodlands like the ones on Joyeuse Island. Delia warmed her well-manicured hands over the small fire and its flickering light played on her glossy pink fingernails. Faye could see those hands trembling in the orange light. What was the woman planning to do that made her so nervous?

Delia's weapon said that her plans involved death. That weapon, a long and sleek rifle that looked capable of taking out a deer from three hundred yards, lay across her lap. Perhaps the rifle was the answer to the question of why Delia didn't hear Joe until he was upon her. Perhaps long hours of target practice had dulled her hearing.

Faye was frightened by the mental image of Delia spending hour after hour pumping bullets into paper targets, growing ever more accurate and precise in her ability to put them into living people. This was the kind of practice that would render a person capable of putting a bullet into Liz's back. It would also render that person capable of putting a bullet into someone standing watch on the porch of Faye's home or sitting at the window of her child's bedroom or even standing silhouetted in the window of a cupola three stories above the ground.

Delia could do it. It was possible.

Faye had seen the photo, the one she had texted to Joe. It had been part of an article about Delia and her second husband that had been published in *Stock and Barrel*. Her husband had been one of those hunters who liked to shoot really big things. Moose, bears, elk. The article had detailed the intensive marksmanship training he'd given his young wife, and it had featured a photo of the happy couple clad in camo and holding rifles... scary-looking rifles with scopes.

She and Joe must not let Delia leave this spot, not with a rifle that would give her the capacity to take out Sly, Gerry, Emma and—oh God— little Michael in four quick shots.

And for what? If Delia had killed Liz because she'd attracted the attention of the rich old man she'd targeted to be her third dead husband, and if she had been stalking Faye and Emma for the same reason, then Faye guessed the woman was willing to kill all her rivals. Why shouldn't she also be willing to kill Sly, Gerry, Joe, and Michael, too? Why leave witnesses?

Lovely young Delia didn't fit the profile for a mass murderer, so she might have been able to pull it off. Faye imagined Delia, beautiful and impassive, watching the endless national news coverage that would ensue if six people were found shot to death on a lonely island. She would watch calmly, secure in the knowledge that no one had any reason to suspect her.

The events after that were predictable. Delia would try to get Oscar to put a wedding ring on the finger that still bore the marks of her last dead husband's rings. She would probably succeed. And Oscar would soon succumb to a lingering illness.

In the last second before Joe jumped, Delia raised her head slightly and Faye got a good look into her face. Her unfocused eyes looked drugged. Together with the rifle and her trembling hands, those dazed eyes helped Faye shove the last clue into place. They showed her how Delia had managed to kill Liz, terrorize Emma, leave a butt-print on the bluff above Emma's house, and come out to Joyeuse Island long enough to leave a footprint, all without Oscar ever noticing she was gone.

Delia's second husband had been the hunter who taught her to shoot that rifle, but her first husband had owned a chain of pharmacies. Delia had worked at his store. She'd had years to pilfer a stash of amphetamines to keep her awake when she needed to be up all night. She probably also had a stash of tranquilizers to help her sleep when she needed to sleep or to slip into Oscar's drinks when she needed him unconscious. And Delia's second husband had died from Alzheimer's, an ailment that, like her first husband's kidney failure, would be pretty damn easy to fake for a woman who had once had access to a drugstore full of pharmaceuticals.

Before Joe's body struck Delia's, he passed between her body and the fire, and his shadow fell on her face. She jerked backward, showing the twitchy reaction time of a woman on speed, but there was nothing she could do to stop him. They went down in the dirt and the rifle landed four feet away.

Faye knew instantly that it was her job to get it.

Joe had the upper hand. He was larger and he had struck first. He had Delia's shoulders pinned to the ground, and Faye could see him working to immobilize her flailing arms. Delia wasn't a heavy woman, but she was tall and long-limbed. Joe needed some leverage to get her under control, so he raised himself on his knees and shifted his body weight forward.

As he focused on her right arm, her left arm shot out to the side, groping for the rifle. It was out of reach but she found the next best thing, a long branch that she'd been using to poke the coals of her fire.

The branch was stout and Delia swung it through the air like a bullwhip. Faye heard the crack when it broke against Joe's temple. He shook his head, ponytail slinging through the air, and she caught sight of his eyes. For a moment, they looked as dazed as Delia's. He quickly gathered his wits and pinned her right shoulder with his knee, grappling with her left hand for control of the branch.

Faye saw that she could end this, if she could just get to the rifle. She stepped into the open, revealing herself. Delia struggled harder, knowing that the odds of her getting the upper hand over Joe had just dropped even further. As she arched her back to get a look at Faye, she also got a look at the piece of tree branch clutched in her own hand. Its end glowed where it had been resting in the burning fire.

Delia knew a weapon when she saw it. She raked the branch across Joe's throat and the red coals broke off and scattered.

Faye heard her husband gasp. A streak of soot and an angry white-and-red mark slashed diagonally across his neck, and the sight gave her an electric shock of sympathetic pain. She covered the ground between her and the rifle in a heartbeat.

Delia used that heartbeat to drive the burning end of the branch into the hollow at the base of Joe's throat. He jerked back, hard, and Delia used that off-balance moment to shift her weight beneath him, throwing him onto the ground beside her. She straddled him, pinning his arms under her knees and holding the branch high. It was still tipped with glowing coals that lit her smiling face. Searching for her other adversary, she looked over the shoulder and saw that the rifle was aimed at her and Faye was staring down its barrel.

Faye had once stood on the other end of a rifle barrel while the woman who held it pulled the trigger. If it hadn't misfired, she would have been dead. She had watched Joe pull the trigger of another rifle on the same woman. Together, they had watched her die. Faye herself, however, had never held a rifle in her hands. Her entire experience with the real-world use of firearms consisted of firing a revolver once at a woman and hitting her boat's gas tank instead. The shot had been effective, because the exploding gas tank had absolutely taken the woman out, but Faye couldn't take credit for good aim. After that day, she had spent many afternoons practicing with the same gun, so that she'd know how to use it the next time the real world required her to do so.

Where was that gun now? Glancing down, she saw that she had carefully laid it on the ground behind her right foot so that she could use both hands to grip the more dangerous weapon. If Delia wanted that handgun, she was going to have to come through Faye to get it.

Delia put a hand on Joe's throat and pressed down hard, fighting off his big hands as she bore down. He couldn't breathe.

Faye had only an instant to decide what to do. She could almost have reached out and touched Delia and Joe with the tip of the rifle in her hands, so she suspected that its scope would be useless. It had been designed to be effective over long distance, not at point-blank range. She was too close to worry about the bullet dropping in flight, so she shouldn't have to worry about hitting Joe, not if she aimed passably well. If she intended to shoot Delia, she could almost certainly do it. (And, to be honest with herself, she had to acknowledge that shooting Delia with such a behemoth from this distance probably meant killing her.)

Faye knew that she was not meant to be a killer, because she wasn't capable of pulling a trigger without first taking the time to think through the consequences. Sometimes a critical moment didn't leave time for thought.

Delia saw Faye hesitate and she let a silvery laugh pass from her perfect lips. "Put the gun down or I'll grind this thing into his eyes. First one, then the other." She waved the burning stick around. Bits of ash fell in Joe's face and he closed his eyes tight to protect them. "I'll probably mess up his pretty face while I'm doing it, and you don't want that. But if burning the skin off his face isn't enough to make you put that weapon down, I will do this."

She lifted her hand and let Joe gasp for breath while she again held the branch perpendicular like a spear over the soft spot at the base of his throat. "I will open up his throat with this thing. Poking, burning, tearing...whatever it takes, I will kill this man with nothing but a stick...a burning hot little stick."

Maybe it was just the drugs talking. Maybe Delia really did think that she still had the upper hand, even though Faye possessed all the firepower. Maybe she had a death wish, but Faye thought that the woman had no inkling that a mild-mannered archaeologist might really kill her. Maybe she was thinking, "Nice girls don't shoot."

If so, then Delia was thinking wrong. It took nothing more than a glance at her suffering husband to make up Faye's mind. She pulled the trigger.

The bullet struck Delia in the chest and traveled out her back, poetically taking the opposite path of the bullet she'd pumped into Liz. Its momentum took Delia's body backward and left her sprawled against a tree. Bits of bone and flesh surrounded her, and the ground was splashed with blood. Faye would have stood staring, stunned at what she'd done, but Joe needed her.

She threw the rifle aside in her thoughtless hurry to get to her husband's side. Then she straddled him, just as Delia had done. Unlike Delia, she was careful to keep her weight on her knees so that she wouldn't impede his breathing. And he was breathing, thank God. The wound on his neck didn't pierce his trachea, and Faye counted herself lucky that she hadn't given Delia the extra seconds she'd needed to do just that.

His eyes were closed and she was so afraid of hurting him, but she gently kissed his lips and his jaw and, finally, the eyelids that Delia had threatened to gouge away. Then she pulled away to let him breathe. As she stood, she felt his big hand close on her ankle, as if he were making sure she was still there. Leaning down, she took that hand and helped him to his feet. He moved like a man who was going to be okay.

Only after she saw that Joe was back to himself did she look around her. A dozen small fires licked across the forest floor. The coals from Delia's branch had landed among the dry leaf litter and pine straw that lay thick over all of Joyeuse Island. The fires were moving as fast as a human being could run, maybe faster.

They needed to be at home, and it was time to run. Once again, Joe was leading the way through the night and, once again, Faye was sprinting barefoot over uneven ground. The moon had still not shown its face, but the fires behind them and on either side lent enough light to put Faye in terror.

In the flickering firelight, Faye and Joe ran for home.

Chapter Thirty-three

Sly stood in the cupola, practically hanging out the open window. The smell of smoke had grown steadily since he heard the gunshot. He wanted to find his son and help him. He had learned the island's paths pretty well, so he thought he probably could get to Joe in the dark, but first he had to have some inkling of where he was.

The smoke seemed to be coming from the east, and his half-century-old eyes were not telling him what he wanted to know.

How bad was it?

When a warm glow lit the eastern horizon, many hours before dawn would light those same skies, he knew the answer. It was bad.

◇◇◇

Joe extended a hand back to help Faye and she slapped it away.

"Don't wait for me," she said. "Get back to the house and save our…"

She swallowed, and he knew she was unable to spit out all the things she wanted him to save. Son. Father. Friends. Home.

When Faye found her voice, she flapped her hand in the direction of their big old house, still running. "We have to save it all. Go. I'll be right behind you."

He stretched out his stride and ran for home.

◇◇◇

Gerry had wandered the house, finding Emma and Michael

in the basement but no one in the rest of the house or on the porches. There was only one more place to look, the cupola, and he was heading there when the sound of a single gunshot drew him away from the staircase, toward an east-facing window.

Unless Faye, Joe, and Sly were all crowded into the cupola, some or all of them were out there in the dark. He wanted to help them and he wanted to know the answers to the questions that were holding him at the window. He was a scientist, so he lived for questions, but he was finding that unanswerable life-and-death questions left him paralyzed.

Where were Faye, Joe, and Sly?

Who pulled that trigger and what was the target? *Who* was the target?

Why was the air heavy with smoke?

Gerry stood indecisive, wishing desperately that he knew what his duty was, so that he could do it.

A tremendous clatter sounded behind him, and he turned to see Sly descending the spiral staircase at top speed, still carrying the ax. Halfway down, he put both big hands on the banister and lofted over the side, hitting the ground at a run. It was the action of a foolhardy and headstrong youth, not a man running on aging knees. Sly Mantooth would feel those knees tomorrow—and his hips and his neck and his lower back—but tonight he was moving like a young man running into battle.

More important in Gerry's mind, was this: Sly was moving like a man who knew where his duty lay and Gerry intended to help him do it.

Sly was still running, out the front door and down the stairs. He bellowed "Fire!" Seeing the question on Gerry's face, he wasted precious breath telling him how he could help. "Shovel's under the porch."

Before Gerry could voice his question—"Where?"—Sly had answered it without wasting any more breath. He had pointed the big ax eastward toward the fire, while running as hard as he could in that direction.

◇◇◇

Emma heard the shot and snatched a sleeping Michael out of his bed. She'd checked the back porch for Joe and the parlor for Faye, and she'd just reached the front door when Sly barreled past her.

She heard Sly cry out "Fire!" to Gerry, who was standing on the front porch, and she called after them. "I'll wet some towels down. We can use them to beat back the fire."

This announcement stopped Sly cold. It actually made him turn around and walk a few steps in her direction, away from the emergency. "No, you will not be going near that fire."

She was preparing to tell him that nobody, not even Douglass Everett in his prime, had ever told her what to do, but his next words stopped her. "It's too dark for you to even set that child down. He could wander two steps away and none of us would see him. When the fire is on us, and I'm here to tell you that it's coming fast, we can't be running around looking for that baby."

He was right.

Sly took one more step in her direction. "I told my son I'd keep his family safe. You're family to him, too. You take that baby down to the beach. You walk out in the water with him in your arms and you stay there until the fire's done. That's the most important job of the night. Will you do it?"

She nodded.

Gerry came out from beneath the porch, carrying an armload of wet towels and a bucket of water. "I'll help here. You get the little boy someplace safe, ma'am."

Without a word, she turned away and found the path that would get her to the water the quickest. It wasn't hard to follow, even in the dark, because so many feet had beaten it down over so many years. Emma herself had walked this path many times when she came out to visit Faye and Joe.

The wind brought a sudden gust of smoke. Michael coughed and so did she. She looked back over her shoulder at the house her friend Faye loved so much. Tall windows, shady porches, walls that were always as clean and white as Faye's paintbrush could keep them. Those walls were a dull red now, reflecting the coming flames.

Faye was going to lose it.

She was going to lose this heap of old wood that her ancestors had hewn with hand tools. Its roof was going to fall when the burning timbers could no longer support its weight. She was going to be left with nothing but memories of her mother and grandmother and the stories they'd told her about the people who had gone before. Photographs, clothes, furniture, books. It was all going to go up in flames.

Michael cuddled his sleepy face into Emma's neck, spurring her to walk faster. She couldn't save Faye's house, no more than she'd been able to stop the miscarriage that had wounded her friend's heart so deeply, but she could save this boy.

She had meant to linger, waiting until the fire got close before she took Michael into the water, but she didn't. The fire had grown close enough for her to see it in the short time it had taken her to walk to the shore. She was scared.

The sand made soft noises under her feet as she walked across the beach. When she reached the water's edge, she kept walking, shoes and clothes and all. The water was November-cold and it made Michael cry, but a little cold wasn't going to kill either of them. When it reached her waist, she turned around and saw that all the coastline to her right was alight. Straight ahead, where Gerry and Sly were defending the house with an ax and some towels, she saw only darkness. She had no idea where Faye and Joe were.

As the wet cold seeped into her bones, it occurred to her that she should have called the sheriff, 911, Sheriff Mike, somebody, but the phone and gun she'd tucked into her pocket were both drenched. It hadn't occurred to her to call the law, because Gerry was the law, but he was in as much trouble as the rest of them right now. They all needed help.

Sacrilegious though it might be, she always turned to Douglass for help in trying times, even before she asked God. She asked him to watch over Sly and Gerry and Joe and Michael and her and, especially, she asked him to watch over Faye. She didn't know how much more pain her friend could take.

◇◇◇

Faye staggered on, falling further behind Joe but always moving forward.

The trees in front of her still seemed draped in black velvet. Where was the moon? It had to rise sometime. No disaster could stop the proper progression of the seasons and the tides.

Behind her, the fire forced a sighing wind through the trees. It blew hot on her back. Trees were crashing to the ground. The fire's roar grew louder with every breath she took.

A spot of white ahead of her said that she'd reached the opening in the trees where her house stood. It was too small. The clearing was too small for her to hope that the fire would miss her house as it leapt from tree to tree.

She saw Gerry standing at the edge of the clearing. A ditch stretched behind him, and he was making steady progress at lengthening it. A fire break was an excellent idea. In the absence of fire hydrants and a fire department, it was probably the best weapon they had, but it wasn't going to be enough. Gerry was smart enough to see that there was not going to be enough time for one man to separate her house from the blaze. The fact that he was out here digging anyway, instead of heading for the safety of the water, made him her friend for life. If Gerry ever needed help, his friend Faye would be there.

He kept digging as he said, "Emma took Michael to the beach. They'll be safe there."

"Joe and his dad?"

He jerked his head in the direction of the house. "I don't know where they went. I lost them in the dark. I figure you've got other shovels and they're over there doing the same thing I am."

A spark set off a small fire just a few feet away from where she stood. Gerry nodded at a bucket of wet towels. "I've been fighting hot spots with those. If you'll do that, I can dig faster."

She picked up a towel and slapped at the flames until they went out. If she had a big enough towel, she could drop it over the whole island and snuff out all the danger. She could put the whole island out. Since she didn't, she just attacked the flames that were in her reach and tried not to think about the ones that weren't.

"I called the sheriff when I heard the shot," Gerry said. "Several officers should be here any minute."

Faye couldn't believe she hadn't already thought of calling for help. Her phone was on the windowsill where she left it, and that should have been the first place she went when she came out of the woods. Where was her mind?

It was stuck in the mode of fighting only the crisis directly in front of her, and it had been stuck there since she followed Joe out of the house to the place where she killed a woman.

With two words, "Delia's dead," she told Gerry who had killed Liz and stalked Emma and Faye. Those two words told him who had been on the wrong end of the gunshot he'd heard. Later, she could explain to him how and why Delia did what she did, and she could take responsibility for shooting Delia dead. Right now, the important thing was this battle against a wildfire that was bound to beat them.

Joe saw his father and he saw the ax. He saw Sly running faster than any man his age had a right to run, and he knew where Sly was going.

His father went first to the biggest cistern, nearly as tall as the house itself. It collected all the rainwater that ran in gutters off the east side of the house, as if its long-ago designer had known where danger would someday arise. Its wood was just as old as the house's timbers, and Faye kept it painted just as white. Sly readied his ax and chose his spot. Drawing the ax back and turning his body hard to maximize its power, he swung hard and the ax hit the cistern in exactly the spot he had chosen. Wood chips and sawdust flew, and he drew back the ax again. He struck the cistern again and he struck it a third time.

Joe heard a loud crack, and water began to spray out of a hole opened up by his father's ax. It spewed hard, driven by the weight of twenty feet of water, and both men were instantly wet to the skin.

Sly swung his ax again, opening up the hole. The gush of water grew bigger and it began to flow down the sides of the cistern, rather than shooting out of its side in a single stream. He struck again and the power of this blow destroyed the old tank's structural integrity. It failed spectacularly, collapsing in a heap of wooden beams and loosing a gush of water that reached far enough into the woods to quench a large swath of flames.

Sly was fast, but he wasn't fast enough. Joe saw Sly collapse under the weight of the falling timbers, and he knew that he couldn't bear to lose his father when he'd just gotten him back.

Chapter Thirty-four

Joe's voice cut through the wind and fire. Faye heard him say, "Dad!" and she heard fear.

He was behind her, somewhere between where she stood and the house. Still holding a wet towel, on the off-chance that it was the secret weapon that would save everybody and everything, she ran for Joe's voice.

She found him bending over a pile of broken wood. The biggest cistern on Joyeuse Island had stood since 1857, at least, but it wasn't standing anymore. Faye knew that Joe's father and his ax must lie somewhere beneath the wreckage.

Joe lifted a timber heavy enough to bow his back. He shoved it aside and reached a hand down into the pile. He had found his father.

Faye, who had never known a father before now, rushed to help Joe pull the debris off Sly. She could see him pushing up against the boards piled on top of him. Was the fire lighting Sly's face as it peeked through the wreckage or was the moon finally starting to rise?

"I'm fine, Son," he said, lifting a beam that lay across his legs and handing it to Joe. "Daughter, I'm fine."

When Joe had set that beam aside and turned back to finish uncovering his father, he found a big arm extending out of the debris, an ax in its hand. "You got four other cisterns, Son. You know what to do. I can get myself out of this mess."

Joe started to help his father anyway, but Faye stayed his arm. "I can do this," she said. "I can help him. Take the ax and go."

She draped her wet towel around her husband's shoulders, knowing that he would shed it when he needed to swing the ax, but maybe that little bit of wetness would help him. Maybe a damp shirt would hold up better against the sparks that were starting to fly.

Red light reflected on her husband's face as he ran to the first of the four cisterns that stood near the house's four corners. The ax swung and swung again. In just a few blows, Joe brought the smaller cistern down, leaping free of the water that first shot out of its side and then gushed across the ground. He dodged the falling frame of the cistern, too, and ran for the second one.

The water was helping, at least a little. In two broad swathes of the woods surrounding her home, the flames on the ground were quenched. Faye could see that Sly and Joe had chosen their points of attack so that the water wouldn't spew straight out into the woods. It had flowed laterally, parallel to the nearest wall of the house. They were doing their best to make a watery buffer that circled the house.

Faye gave Sly a hand as he lifted himself out of the rubble of the cistern. "We need to find Gerry. If the three of us get out there with shovels and some towels, we may be able to finish digging that firebreak. Let's go."

A cracking, splitting sound told them that Joe had finished wrecking the second cistern. As Faye ran for the last place she'd seen Gerry, she realized that she could see better, a lot better, but that there was still no moon. She needed to face the fact that the fire was bringing all the light. It was closing in, and they would soon need to run for the shore and let the Gulf of Mexico protect them as all of Joyeuse Island went up in flames.

But not yet. Faye wasn't ready to run yet.

They found Gerry and showed him where the water from the cisterns had opened up big holes in the encroaching fire. Starting from those openings, they worked with shovel and wet towels to complete the ring of protection around Faye's house. Around her home.

Faye wasn't stupid. She could look deeper into the woods and see that flames were working their way toward them through the tree canopy. They couldn't fight a fire that was twenty feet above their heads. Failing to run from a fire like that could kill them all, but Faye wasn't running yet.

She slung her towel so hard at a chunk of burning bark that she knocked it right off the tree. It lay there on the ground, still burning, so she had to flap her towel at it again. This wasted time she didn't have. She swatted the burning bark until it went black, like charcoal, then she moved on to the next burning thing.

The sound of an ax splitting wood told her that Joe had reached the third cistern. That left two more. When the cisterns were gone, there would be nothing left to fight the fire but four people, a shovel, and a bucket of wet towels. If something hadn't changed by then, it would be time to run.

Faye started trying to make her peace with the loss. Joe and Sly and Gerry shouldn't risk their lives for her house. It was a symbol of her hard work in preserving it and it was a symbol of all the people who had lived in it before her, all the way back to Cally and beyond, but it was just a symbol, just an object.

It was time to let her home go.

A percussive noise near the house told her that Joe was slinging the ax at the last cistern, unleashing its water to fight the fire that would never stop coming. She gestured to Gerry and Sly that it was time to leave. They drew back from the fire's edge, into the front yard of Joyeuse's big house.

Faye knew every square inch of it. She had patched the tabby walls of its basement. She had run wiring and ductwork to bring it up to twenty-first-century standards of comfort. She had painted its walls, restored its murals, hung vintage wallpaper to replace the antique paper destroyed by the hurricane. She and Joe, working together, had rebuilt the spiral staircase and both exterior staircases. They had made a new cupola to replace the one that had blown away. They had installed up-to-date roofing.

Long ago, and this memory threatened to take her to her knees, her grandmother had taken a teenaged Faye up on that roof and taught her to patch the ancient tin that had covered it in those days.

She was losing it. She hadn't been sure she could walk away and let the fire come, but it was just a house. She had survived the loss of her baby daughter. She would survive this.

She heard Joe's ax strike again. Collected rainwater rushed out of the last cistern with such power that she could hear it, even over the roar of a fire that had nearly come. He had done everything in his power to save their home, and she loved him for it, but the fight was done. She went to him, held out her hand, and said, "It's time to go to the water."

Joe's face was wet, and it wasn't cistern water shining on his cheeks. "Faye, I tried."

"I know you did. We all did. Let's go."

The fire had crept way too close to the path to the beach. They should have fled long ago. Gerry handed wet towels all around. They wrapped their heads and upper bodies in them. When a burning branch crashed to the ground ten feet away from the entrance to the path, they ran. By the time they had pushed down the path far enough to feel branches brush their arms on either side, the opening behind them was alight.

As they ran, more branches fell all around them, and some of them dropped coals onto the path ahead. Faye had only enough of her wits about her to think, "I'm barefoot," as she ran across them.

Joe had an arm curled around her back. He wasn't pushing her and he wasn't carrying her, but she saw that he was prepared to do either. If she staggered, he would throw her over his shoulder, but that wasn't what she wanted. She wanted to leave her home for the last time under her own power.

The beach and its sand looked so soft and so cool. Her feet wanted her to get there, where the sand would soothe them and they could rest. They took her there but the dry grains of sand did no good at all. They did nothing but stick to her burned and bleeding feet.

Emma and Michael were waiting in the water. Her son was already wailing, but when he saw Faye and Joe, he held out both arms and shrieked.

They went to him. Their family was all together, almost. When Amande got home, everything would be right. Even if she came home to a family that was camping out on an island that had been burned black, everything would be right. Or close enough to right.

She heard another crack, much louder, as if Joe, Gerry, Sly, and Emma had all sunk axes into a wooden tank of water while Faye waited inside. Sly's ax had been left behind and no one but the dead Delia was left on the island to wield it, so she had to be hearing something else

Faye and all the others stood in the water, like penitents waiting for baptism, and looked ashore to see what was making all that noise.

A flash of light broke open the black sky. Less than a second passed before they heard another loud crack. Faye looked up and saw a great cloud gathering itself overhead. She saw pinpricks of stars on the sliver of sky just above the water to the south. Those stars hadn't been there a moment before. They had been covered by the cloud that had rolled off the water and spread itself over Joyeuse Island. Among those stars was a brightness that grayed the black night. The gray light looked like hope.

Sure enough, the clouds pulled further away from the horizon, revealing a moon that had been shining behind them for quite some time. Those clouds rushed in front of a strong wind that piled them up over Faye's head. Thunder pealed again, signaling the clouds to release the rain.

And it fell.

Water fell on them like a blessing. The water rinsed the smoke from Faye's hair. It ran off Joe's face in black streams of soot. It pattered on Michael's cheeks and Emma's curls and Sly's broad shoulders and Gerry's upturned face. It washed them all clean.

Chapter Thirty-five

Sheriff Rainey had been in his car within two minutes of answering Detective Steinberg's call. Steinberg had said he'd heard gunfire from somewhere near the Longchamp-Mantooth house, and that couldn't be a good thing. The sheriff hadn't been sure yet where he was going, to his office or to one of the department's boats, so he had used the drive time to call the dispatcher and try to get the whereabouts of all the officers out on the Gulf. While the dispatcher did his work, Rainey's phone had rung again. One of the officers out on the water looking for Tommy Barnes had called to give him the news that Joyeuse Island was burning.

Rainey had started barking questions. "Did you call Detective Steinberg? Is he still out there? And what about the people who live there?"

"Steinberg's not answering his phone. I can't tell you anything except I see a really big fire." The young woman's voice was cracking under the strain of shouting over a boat motor, but she sounded calm and ready to do what needed doing.

"Tell me you already called the Coast Guard."

"I'm not stupid." There was a moment of dead air while she reconsidered her tone of voice. She amended her error by adding a belated "Sir."

"No, you're not stupid. You're a good officer. Go help Steinberg. I'm on my way and, thanks to you, so is the Coast Guard."

He had hardly hung up the phone when it rang again. Mike McKenzie's name was on the screen.

"You got the situation on Joyeuse Island under control?"

The former sheriff's spies knew all, so he knew all, but he usually pretended he didn't. McKenzie's power in Micco County would linger for the rest of his life, but he had never rubbed it in Rainey's face before tonight. Rainey had known why McKenzie was being suddenly upfront about the scope of his web of insider informants. Faye Longchamp-Mantooth and Joe Wolf Mantooth were among his closest friends.

"I've got people on the way. The Coast Guard has been called. I'm in my car now."

"I knew you'd be doing things right. It's just that my wife is about to lose her damn mind. I may have to sit on her to keep her from going out to that island and fetching those people home herself. And we don't own a boat."

"I've got boats, and I've got good people to pilot them. We'll get your friends home."

"See that you do. And Sheriff?"

"Yes?"

"You have our gratitude. Nobody knows more than me and Magda how hard your job is."

Shortly after ending his call with Mike McKenzie, Sheriff Rainey had seen fat drops of water spatter across his windshield. He had never been so glad to see an ordinary rainstorm in his life.

Faye lay sprawled on a gurney being pushed into the emergency room of Micco County General Hospital. Joe was in the gurney next to hers. Emma, Sly, and Gerry had been wheeled in right behind them. Even Michael had a special little-boy gurney to get him into the hospital. Part of Faye thought it was dumb for the sheriff to insist that they all be thoroughly checked out, since they were all just fine, but the other part of her knew that their bodies were pumped so full of adrenaline that they had no idea whether they were fine or not.

For example, she could see that her burned feet were all shades of red, black, and white. Some of the cuts on her soles looked pretty deep, but they were only now starting to hurt. Joe didn't look like he was feeling the awful burn that slashed across his throat yet, but he would soon.

Now somebody was spraying something wonderful on her feet, but she still didn't want to be here. She wanted to go home. She wanted to see if she had a home left.

Joe knew what she thinking. He always knew what she was thinking. The person who had just sprayed something wonderful on her feet was spraying it on his throat now, and she knew he had to be glad about that.

Instead of enjoying the wonderfulness, he turned his green eyes on hers and said something so reasonable that she wanted to hate him for it. "There's no point in going back out there tonight. It's too dark. We need to make sure the fire's really out before we go traipsing across the island, trying to see if the house is still standing."

Faye had found things to occupy her during that long night. Michael had needed tending. She and Joe had needed to get Amande on the phone and tell her they were okay, before somebody on the Internet sent her a picture of Joyeuse Island aflame. She had needed to keep an eye on the Internet herself, hoping that some enterprising reporter had flown a helicopter out there and taken some kind of fancy night-vision video that would tell her whether her home was still there.

No luck. She was going to have to wait for sunup.

The hour was early and the department boat was full. Sheriff Rainey had not argued when Sheriff Mike and his wife showed up, presuming there was room on the boat for them. It wasn't strictly necessary for Emma and Gerry to be part of the expedition, but they had survived the inferno. They deserved to see what it had left behind. Sly was family, so there was no question that he was where he needed to be.

When they left shore, Faye was seated between Joe and Magda, holding tight to both their hands. Emma sat with Sly, facing them. Rainey noticed that the man left a deferential inch of space between them, because that's how gentlemen of his generation treated ladies, but Emma looked glad to have him next to her.

No one said a word until they reached the dock. Even then, they were quiet, speaking only as they went about the business of moving from boat to dock. Faye took the lead. She walked perhaps three steps before breaking into a run. Long-legged Joe was able to keep up with her, but the rest of them held back. There was a sense that the couple might need some privacy when they saw what was at the other end of the path.

Faye knew Joe was behind her, so she didn't look back. She got the information she needed in little dribs and drabs. Even from the dock, she could see the white painted walls of the house, so she knew that it hadn't burned to the ground. Running along the fire-blackened path, she could see green lawn in the front yard, so she knew that the fire hadn't roared through and destroyed everything. But that didn't mean that she wouldn't get to the clearing and see a white painted shell surrounding a burnt-out heart. It didn't mean that a burning tree hadn't fallen onto the roof and taken it down to the ground.

In one heartstopping moment, the line-of-sight between Faye and her home opened up before it should have. The undergrowth that should have blocked her view was burned away and the forest floor was littered with fallen trees. The remaining trees around Faye were sooty twenty, thirty, maybe forty feet in the air, but the house was unchanged.

She stepped across a hard line that divided blackened grass from green grass. The fire, quenched by water from a cistern and from the sky, had been stopped here. The line ran roughly from north to south. Almost everything east of it was torched, but everything west of it was spared.

This is where they had held the line with towels and shovels and an ax. This was where the fire had been when the rain came.

Disbelieving, she turned to Joe. This time, he was the one running, urging her on.

She ran headlong up the grand staircase to the front porch, her feet clad in boots borrowed from Magda. Papery ashes of tree leaves littered the old boards under her feet. When she crushed them, they didn't so much crackle as whisper.

The rocking chairs and porch swing were dusted in soot, but they were still there. The cavernous rooms of the main floor were empty of everything but smoke. The vintage wallpaper was darkened by it, but this was nothing that couldn't be fixed with a bucket of soapy water and some time.

She clattered down the sneak staircase into the basement that she and Joe had made into a comfortable home. This was her nest, and it was unchanged. She might have expected at least a little water damage on the floor, left behind when the Mantooth men and their ax loosed thousands of gallons of water. Nope. The people who had contoured the ground around the house all those years before Faye was born had known what they were doing. The water had all flowed outward, toward the fire it was fighting.

The crib Michael had outgrown, the bed where Joe kept the sheet untucked so he could hang his big feet off the end, the family room and its groaning bookshelves—everything was where it was supposed to be. She had imagined everything charred and dead, and she had been wrong.

"Let's go look," Joe said.

Faye was confused, because she *was* looking. She was looking at everything she owned as if she'd never seen it before. She wanted to go into the kitchen and fondle her grandmother's cast iron skillets. In the night, when she'd lived with the idea that her home was gone, she had hung on to the fact that no fire was going to destroy those skillets.

"Let's go up top and look at everything." Joe gestured over his head, in the general direction of the cupola.

So they did. They walked together up the reconstructed spiral staircase. It was still standing! They stood together on the landing while Joe fetched the tool that opened the cupola's trap door and lowered the ladder. Here was a reminder of how close they had come to disaster.

Joe had left the cupola's windows open when he rushed out to meet Delia, so the fire had been able to leave its mark here. Every visible surface—floor, walls, and ceiling—was dotted with burnt spots where cinders had blown in and tried to set their lives on fire.

The rain had blown through the same windows, drowning those fires before they took hold. Only the scars, black and star-like, remained. Faye thought she would resist the urge to sand and stain and paint them away. She would never be the same after losing her baby girl, but she would find a way to be whole again. Maybe if she let her house keep its scars, they would remind her that it was possible to heal.

Joe pulled her to him and she leaned against his side. Together, they looked out at their island.

To the east, blackened ground, dotted with tenacious green trees, stretched out to the horizon. The burnt acreage covered way more than half the island. To the west, nothing had changed. Greenness covered everything. She could see the old tree shading Gerry's environmental cleanup site, and she was glad it still stood. Surrounding it all, the Gulf of Mexico moved under the early morning sun as it always had and always would.

"Fire's good for the trees," Joe said. "Longleaf pines like it. Cleans out the competition. Gives 'em space and sunlight. They'll grow better now. They'll take their time about it—we won't live to see everything this fire does for 'em—but they'll grow."

Faye wanted to bury her face in his chest, but she wanted to look at her reconfigured island more.

"The fire uncovered a lot of new places for you to dig, Faye. You'll probably be spending all the day out there, looking for stuff. I might never see you."

"You're not really worried about that? You'll see me. You'll always see me."

When he didn't answer her, she said what she knew he'd been waiting a month to hear. "Joe, I'm going to be okay. We're going to be okay."

"When you talked to Amande last night, did you tell her about the baby?"

She nodded.

"What did she say?"

"She cried. She wants to come home, so I bought a ticket and e-mailed it to her. Her plane lands late tomorrow. We need to be together. And I want her to have as much time as possible with her grandfather."

Faye felt a tightness in Joe's back ease. He laughed and said, "The old man was pretty awesome last night, wasn't he?"

"Like father, like son."

Wrapping both arms around her husband, but keeping her face pointed at the miracle spread below them, Faye said, "He saved it. He saved the house. Without your dad and his ax, this house would have been gone before the rain came."

"We would've been okay. We would've had each other and the kids. Not the baby. Not Jessica. But the rest of us would have been together. I love this place, but it's just a house."

Faye felt the tightness in her own neck ease. It had happened. She had heard the name they'd planned to give their daughter, and she hadn't broken. She would never stop wishing that there was a Jessica Eagle Longchamp-Mantooth in the world, but she was going to be herself again.

"Aren't we enough to make you happy, Faye? Michael, Amande, me? Am I enough?"

She pulled on his shoulders in the way she always did when she wanted him to lean way down and kiss her. "Always. You're everything, Joe."

Chapter Thirty-six

From her vantage point under the old oak tree on the far west end of Joyeuse Island, Faye could see no evidence of the fire. If she had looked up, she would have seen waves lapping at a weedy narrow beach, but she was too excited to look up. She was busy with her camera, because there was no such thing as taking too many pictures of an exciting find.

Amande's plane was landing in seven hours. Faye hadn't been sure she would make it through those hours until she saw her daughter, so she had grabbed a trowel and set out to do the thing she did best—look for the past and the stories it tells.

Faye had imagined herself in Cally's shoes and, armed with all she'd learned, she had walked straight to the answer to so many questions. What was the source of the arsenic contamination? What was the story behind Courtney's Monster Man? Most importantly, what had happened to Elias Croft?

She had uncovered the Army-issue button first, nestled within a few shreds of a Union-blue uniform and of the sheet that had served the soldier as a shroud. This Yankee soldier had been buried with care, very near the tree that must have shaded the cabin of The Monster Man. She had a pretty good idea that the foundations of that cabin waited for her nearby.

Soon after finding the button and the bits of fabric, Faye had uncovered a skull. She'd stopped digging then, and not just out of respect for the dead and the laws that protected them. She was digging in arsenic-tainted soil, so she had augmented her usual protective gloves with a dust mask to keep out contaminated dust, but this skull spoke of another danger. The misshapen bones around its nasal opening looked like a textbook example of the ravages of leprosy. She didn't think bacteria could linger in the soil after all these years, but it wouldn't hurt to speak to an expert before she excavated further.

She had laid her trowel aside and snapped some photos to document the find, then she had stepped back to a distance that seemed both safe and respectful. Now she lingered, delaying the inevitable paperwork that came with uncovering human remains by taking just a few moments to commune with the body of Captain Elias Croft of the United States Army.

Oscar Croft looked okay. Faye knew that Delia's death had been a shock, but he didn't look like a man who had suffered an emotional gut punch. Not that he looked especially happy, either. His lips were pressed together tightly, like a man determined to squelch any passing emotion that might show on his face, but he seemed to be holding up.

When Faye told Sheriff Rainey that she suspected Delia of drugging Oscar, he had immediately sent paramedics to check on him. They had found the older man deeply sedated and brought him in to the hospital for observation. He'd been released that morning, and Sheriff Rainey had told her that the first thing he'd wanted to do was to talk to Faye and Joe.

Oscar had given Faye a funny look when he first saw her and she wondered whether he remembered fondling her arm.

As if reading her thoughts, he walked straight to her, stopping an appropriate distance away and saying, "I owe you an apology. I probably owe you a lot of apologies. Part of me wants to tell you that I haven't been myself since Delia started drugging me. Another part of me isn't so sure you'd like the man I was before she started drugging me, either. Maybe I don't have to be that man anymore. In any case, I hope you can forgive me."

Perhaps the drugs Delia had fed Oscar had lowered the inhibitions of a man who was already known for appalling behavior.

Faye couldn't say, and it didn't matter to her any longer, because Oscar was going home to Ohio. He'd come to say good-bye. Amande's plane was landing soon, so the good-byes would have to be brief.

Gerry Steinberg had come out to Joyeuse Island with Oscar for no reason Faye could discern, but she needed to thank him some more for helping save her home, so she was glad he was there. As Oscar settled himself, setting a tissue-wrapped package on the couch beside him, Gerry caught Faye's eye.

"We found Tommy. He got as far as Louisiana in that big boat he stole from his customer. These charges are going to stick, and I still have hopes of getting some money out of him for environmental fines, too."

Faye was pampering her newfound emotional balance by pretending that there was no chance that she, too, was going to be saddled with an environmental bill, so she just smiled and nodded.

"You found my great-great-grandfather," Oscar said. "I don't know how to thank you."

Faye handed him a photo, taken close enough to its subjects to show every worn letter on their metallic surfaces.

Oscar held the photo close to his face. "A button from my great-great-grandfather's uniform." He looked up with tears in his eyes. "You found him."

He put on a pair of reading glasses and pulled a folded sheet of paper out of his pocket. "I printed out your e-mail. This kind of story belongs on paper. I'll keep it with this picture of Elias' buttons and buckle that you found for me."

"You can have them," she said. "If I find any more of his personal effects, I'll send them to you. As his nearest relative, you're also entitled to choose his bones' final resting place."

"Here," he said without stopping to think. "Elias' bones belong here, right where Cally Stanton laid them to rest." Squinting at the message Faye had e-mailed him, he said, "It all fits together. Your explanation of our families' stories. Everything fits. The timing of your great-great-grandmother's story about Captain Croft visiting her home fits, because it happened just before Elias disappeared. The lesions on the skull you found confirm your theory that he had leprosy. The later story about him covering himself before going out in public during the yellow fever epidemic works, too, when you think about how a man with leprosy might have looked by that time. If he knew he had leprosy before the Civil War was over, he would have been pretty sick by 1888. And Cally even mentioned chaulmoogra oil…that's the most convincing evidence of all."

"Well, there's the kerosene tank and the arsenic contamination," said Gerry.

"You're right, Detective," Oscar said. "The kerosene tank and the arsenic contamination are important clues. If Cally Stanton helped Elias while he battled leprosy, putting a roof over his head and making sure he had food and medicine, he would have needed kerosene for fuel. And if he bathed in arsenic-based medicines for the rest of his life, the arsenic would have had years to soak into the ground. You're the scientist, Detective. You're telling me that your lab would still be able to see that arsenic after all this time?"

Gerry nodded.

"May I see your great-great-grandmother's memoirs, Faye?" Oscar asked.

Joe fetched copies of the mimeographed sheets from their bedroom. Faye paged through them, showing him Cally's memories of the yellow fever epidemic and the day Elias Croft tipped his hat to her.

Oscar's eyes filled with tears again. He picked up the package sitting next to him on the couch and handed it to Faye. "This is only a piece of cloth, but it belongs in your family."

She unwrapped layers of tissue paper and found the old bedsheet with its leafy green garland. Looking at the mottled fabric made her dizzy. The sheet had been made for the long-gone Turkey Foot Hotel. It had probably been used for years on the beds in the big house on Joyeuse Island. It had traveled to Ohio with Elias Croft's sword and stayed there for more than a century. And it had come home. Now there were tears in her eyes.

"Detective Steinberg says that you and Joe may have to pay a lot of money for cleaning up the kerosene and arsenic that my great-great-grandfather left behind."

Faye was still trying to pretend that this wasn't going to happen, so she was starting to say something like, "Oh, it's nothing. We're made out of money. Really," when he interrupted her.

"I've talked to Detective Steinberg about this. I'm assuming financial responsibility for the problem."

Faye couldn't think of a thing to say. This didn't happen often.

Oscar kept talking, so it didn't matter that Faye was speechless. "I can't let you carry the burden of my great-great-grandfather's illness, not when your great-great-grandmother did so much to make his last years comfortable. I have more money than I need. Let me do this."

She had been clenching the finely woven linen of Cally's bedsheet in both hands. When she let herself hear what Oscar was saying, she felt her fingers relax. Everything was going to be okay.

Joe was grinning like a man ready to go out and drop some money on Christmas presents for his kids. There was nothing left for Faye to do, beyond saying "Thank you, Oscar."

It was going to be a tight squeeze, fitting Faye, Joe, Sly, Michael, Amande, and Amande's luggage into Faye's car, but Faye knew they could deal with it. Nobody wanted to be left out of the trip to pick up Amande at the airport, so nobody was going to complain about tight seating arrangements. The boat ashore had been full of happy, laughing people. Surely they could keep those smiles while they were crowded into a car going to the Tallahassee airport and back.

Faye stood on the dock while Joe tended the boat. She jostled a fussy Michael on her hip and watched Sly operate. For the first time since Liz's death, there were signs of life inside the bar and grill. Sly had walked over to check out the open door, and he'd gotten there just in time to see three people come out. Two of them had been men in predictable business suits, but one had been a revelation. Wilma cut quite a figure in a cobalt-blue dress and a pair of black pumps. Her hair was twisted into a bun on top of her head, and Faye was pretty sure she detected a swipe of taupe lipstick. She decided that she was interested, too, so she followed Sly as he went to check out Wilma's new look.

"If you're ready to buy," one of the suited men was saying, "I see no reason why we can't push this deal through. The longer this place stands empty, the harder it will be to get the business going again."

"I got some ideas on how to do that," Wilma said, surveying the place like she owned it already. "Don't you worry about a thing."

"Well, that's fine," Sly said.

Maybe he was saying it to Wilma. Maybe he was saying it to the air. Faye couldn't tell.

Sly kept talking. "I been looking for a place to buy me some eggs in the morningtimes. Breakfast always tastes better when a pretty woman cooks it, I always say."

Faye was glad Joe was busy with the boat. Watching his father chat up women made him want to crawl in a hole and die, but he might as well get used to it. Sly Mantooth was going to like the ladies until the day they put him in the ground, but Faye had to admit that he treated them all, bartender to wealthy widow, like great ladies. He talked to them like a man who was interested in what they had to say. He respected their space. He made them laugh. Joe and his dad were not as different as her husband might like to believe.

Sly waved good-bye to Wilma and ambled on. The woman's cheeks had pinked up under her carefully applied makeup, but she was cementing the deal of her life. She stayed focused on the men in suits who wanted to sell her a marina. Faye nodded in Wilma's direction and left the woman alone to seal a business agreement.

"I got some jokes I want to tell you and Joe in the car," Sly said, walking like a man who planned to be fully alive for another fifty years, at least. "I need something to say to Amande till I get to know her. I laid awake all night, thinking up jokes I learned on the road, but I need to check 'em out with you and Joe first. I want to make sure none of 'em is too dirty, but I can't have her thinking her granddad is old and boring, neither."

Faye thought that this was unlikely. She also thought that she wanted to be out of earshot when Amande started telling Sly the jokes she'd learned while growing up among fishermen and offshore oil workers. In her pocket, wrapped in a napkin, was the wishbone she'd saved from the chicken Joe had fried for her on a night when she wasn't sure she had what it took to keep going. As soon as Amande got off the plane, she was going to give it to the children so that they could make their wishes and pull.

Joe was finished with the boat and it was time to go. Faye was so ready to get to the airport and get her arms around her daughter. She couldn't wait to get Amande in the car, where she could see up-close whether the girl looked healthy and happy. She was even looking forward to an hour spent listening to Sly's not-too-dirty jokes.

She couldn't wait to get them all home.

Guide for the
Incurably Curious

This is the place where I share tidbits from my research, answering the kinds of questions I usually get about Faye's adventures. People always want to know how much of the story is historically true, so I'll begin with arsenic and chaulmoogra oil. They were both used to treat leprosy in the 1800s, but no effective treatment was available until well into the twentieth century, so Elias' slow decline would have been the likely outcome of contracting the disease when he did.

According to the Center for Disease Control, Hansen's disease (the more modern term for the disease long known as leprosy) is a long-lasting infection caused by bacteria. Though once feared as a devastating contagious disease, it is now rare and treatable. With early diagnosis and treatment, patients can avoid its disabling effects. In Elias' time, patients were isolated in leprosariums. Faced with losing his freedom in this way, it is not inconceivable that he would have grabbed the chance to live out his life in isolation on Joyeuse Island, sparing his family from the stigma attached to the word "leper."

As I considered a plot that would ask Cally to endanger herself to help a man preserve his dignity and freedom, I asked myself, "Would she take that risk?" Cally has been in residence inside my head for nearly fifteen years now, so I have a very clear image of her, and I decided that she would. As a former slave, she would have recoiled from the thought of a man entering a leprosarium, never to emerge into freedom again.

Another quality that I imagine a former slave would have is a certain disdain for the law and for social conventions, a quality that Faye sometimes shares. Cally lived for seventy years after she was emancipated, but she would not have been lulled into believing that her society could be trusted to treat her justly. She would have been past eighty before women were allowed to vote, and she did not live to see the end of Jim Crow. I think she would have felt a certain pride in helping a man keep his freedom. I also think that it is quite reasonable that Faye idolizes her.

This is the third Faye Longchamp mystery, after *Artifacts* and *Findings,* in which Faye learns important things about her family's past by reading Cally's reminiscences. The Works Progress Administration, commonly known as the WPA, really did sponsor a Federal Writers' Project that sent writers out to interview former slaves. Those transcribed interviews still exist today, preserving a part of American history that would otherwise have been lost.

I don't know whether Faye will need to dip into Cally's memoirs again in future books, but I did enjoy revisiting them for *Isolation.* Sharp-eyed readers will notice that one of the passages from *Artifacts* appears again here, tying the two stories together by repeating the story about the Yankee captain who could have left Cally and all the people of Joyeuse Island without food, but didn't. In *Isolation,* we see that he was rewarded for his kindness.

To receive a free catalog of Poisoned Pen Press titles, please provide
your name and address in one of the following ways:

Phone: 1-800-421-3976
Facsimile: 1-480-949-1707
Email: info@poisonedpenpress.com
Website: www.poisonedpenpress.com

Poisoned Pen Press
6962 E. First Ave. Ste 103
Scottsdale, AZ 85251